RISE & FALL

THIRDS BOOK 4

CHARLIE COCHET

Rise & Fall

http://charliecochet.com

http://reesedante.com

Proofing by Susi Selva

RISE & FALL

After an attack by the Coalition leaves THIRDS Team Leader Sloane Brodie critically injured, agent Dexter J. Daley swears to make Beck Hogan pay for what he's done. But Dex's plans for retribution are short-lived. With Ash still on leave with his own injuries, Sloane in the hospital, and Destructive Delta in the Coalition's crosshairs, Lieutenant Sparks isn't taking any chances. Dex's team is pulled from the case, with the investigation handed to Team Leader Sebastian Hobbs. Dex refuses to stand by while another team goes after Hogan, and decides to put his old HPF detective skills to work to find Hogan before Theta Destructive, no matter the cost.

With a lengthy and painful recovery ahead of him, the last thing Sloane needs is his partner out scouring the city, especially when the lies—however well intentioned—begin to spiral out of control. Sloane is all too familiar with the desire to retaliate, but some things are more important, like the man who's pledged to stand beside him. As Dex starts down a dark path, it's up to Sloane to show him what's at stake, and finally put a name to what's in his heart.

ONE

"You're going to get us fucking killed!"

Dex ignored Ash and hit the gas, speeding after the ambulance heading up route 9A toward NY Presbyterian Hospital, its wailing siren and flashing lights an unyielding reminder of what he stood to lose. The ambulance had left before them, but Dex was in his Challenger with its own THIRDS-installed lights flickering and sending out a warning to everyone around him to get the hell out of his way.

When Ash had finally released Dex from his iron grip, Dex had stood on the sidewalk in front of his house, amidst the smoke and burning car parts, unable to believe what had happened. He'd been at a loss, watching the chaos unfold as emergency teams and THIRDS agents flooded the scene. Orders had been shouted, the area evacuated, blue-and-black THIRDS tape marking off his personal disaster zone. And then a bright orange beacon parked near the end of the block gave him clarity.

Dex maneuvered through four lanes of traffic, changing gears and working the pedals. No one knew how to drive his baby like he did, and nothing on God's green earth was going to make him lose that ambulance. Not with Sloane in the back of it fighting for his life.

Sloane...

No matter how hard Dex tried, his head kept replaying the scene like a goddamn looped video: Dex bolting for the front door, not caring what might be on the other side—getting to Sloane had been all that mattered. *He has to be okay. Please God, let him be okay.* Clouds of thick black smoke. The sidewalk in front of his house looking like a war zone, littered with debris and pieces of twisted car parts. The trees on fire. Dex tackled to the ground, the breath stolen from his lungs. Ash on him keeping him safe. Bullets flying. Sloane under a piece of mangled door. Screeching sirens and uniformed bodies rushing in. Blood everywhere. Sloane unmoving. A jagged piece of metal sticking out of his side. Blood, so much blood.

It should have been me.

"Fuck! Mother fucking asshole son of a bitch!" Dex slammed his hand against the steering wheel before swerving around some bastard going the speed limit. He was losing his shit. It was fast approaching much like the yellow—soon to be red—light ahead of him, yet he was helpless to stop it. The Challenger flew past the red, missing an oncoming taxi by inches.

"Enough!" Ash snapped at him. "You're gonna get us fucking killed! Keep your shit together and get us to the fucking hospital in one goddamn piece, or I swear to Christ I will fucking knock your ass out and drive us there myself."

Dex wanted to tell Ash where he could stick his threats, but he didn't. He heard Ash suck in a sharp breath, and Dex eased his foot off the accelerator just enough to keep the ambulance's flashing lights in sight a few cars ahead. Ash held on to the passenger door with one hand, his other pressed against his side to ease the pain along with the slow trickle of blood seeping through his torn stitches. Stitches he'd torn saving Dex.

"Sorry," Dex said through his teeth. They were almost at the hospital, which meant more traffic. "Sorry for being an asshole and for what I'm about to do. Hold on." He hit the gas pedal again, and the engine thundered as he raced forward. After a couple of close calls, they got to the hospital before the ambulance. He skidded into valet parking, put the Challenger in park, jumped out, and tossed his keys to the valet guy. Ignoring his teammate's bitching, Dex called out over his shoulder for Ash to take care of it. The ambulance arrived seconds later, and Dex ran up to it, watching with his heart in his throat as the backdoors swung open and the EMTs rushed out. The gurney swiftly emerged with Sloane strapped down on his uninjured side, an oxygen mask covering his nose and mouth, and the jagged metal piece jutting out from the right side of his torso. Removing it without surgery was clearly out of the question.

Dex followed the EMTs as they rushed Sloane through the huge open glass doorway into the hospital, shouting out codes and medical jargon Dex couldn't make out. One of the EMTs said something about the THIRDS, and a Therian nurse behind the desk snatched up a phone and rambled something off. Within seconds, a handful of Therian doctors and nurses came running, joining the EMTs as they stole Sloane away into a wide, brightly lit corridor. Dex attempted to follow only to have his path blocked by two male Therian nurses.

"He's my partner," Dex pleaded, trying to get around them.

"I'm sorry, sir, but you can't go in there."

"The hell I can't. He's my partner!" Dex grabbed one of the nurses when a pair of beefy arms wrapped around Dex's waist, lifting him off his feet and away. "Fuck off, Ash! Get off!" He couldn't leave Sloane in there all alone. Sloane hated hospitals as it was. What if he woke up and freaked out? What if he didn't know where he was? What if something happened and Dex wasn't there? He couldn't lose Sloane now. It wasn't Sloane's time. They hadn't had enough time!

"You're not the only one who needs him."

Dex stilled. It wasn't so much Ash's words, but the subtle desperation behind them. Ash put him down, and Dex turned, the look on Ash's dirt-smudged face taking the fight out of Dex. He'd never seen the gruff agent looking so helpless, and despite clearly having his own fears, Ash met his gaze.

"He's all the family I've got. Just let them do their jobs. It's the best we can do for him."

Dex swallowed hard and nodded. He had to get a hold of himself. It was only when Ash winced that Dex remembered the guy was slowly bleeding out. "Shit, Ash. Come on. We need to get you fixed up."

"I'm fine," Ash muttered, wiping the sweat from his beaded brow.

"Yeah, you look fine." Dex refused to give in to his teammate's stubbornness. He called over a nurse who took one look at Ash and ran off to get assistance. Ash continued to argue when Dex spotted his dad marching their way. Tony stopped beside them, his gaze dropping to Ash's hand against his bleeding side before he barked out an order.

"Keeler, get your ass in there and get those stitches seen to."

Ash looked like he wanted to argue but knew better. With a resigned sigh, he headed for the anxious looking nurses. As soon as Ash disappeared, Tony put a hand to Dex's shoulder, concern in his deep brown eyes. It was too much for Dex right now.

"Hey. I'm going to take a walk. Call me if anything happens."

Thankfully, his dad knew him well and gave him a nod. He removed his hand from Dex's shoulder and let him go. Right now, Tony had to be his sergeant. Anything else would break Dex's tremulous hold on his emotions. He walked off to gather his strength. He was going to need it.

IT'S NOT FAIR.

How many others had thought the same as they paced these halls? It wasn't fair. But then life rarely was. Dex had learned as much from a young age. Some naïve part of him had believed he'd never find himself in this position again. First his parents, now... He quickly shook the morbid thought away. God, he was such an idiot. His job was as high risk as it was before he ended up falling for his team leader.

For the first time in his life, he was a hot mess over a guy. Then again, Sloane Brodie wasn't just any guy. He was rolling thunder and a sweet summer breeze. Passionate, complex, and intense. Mysterious and brooding. He made Dex laugh, beg, and want to scream. With one look he could crush Dex's heart, with one whisper have him on his knees. It was terrifying and exhilarating. Dex thought he'd been in love before, when he was in high school, then college. Now he knew the difference. Their relationship was hard work, had been from the day they'd met, but every moment with Sloane was worth it. Dex had never met anyone so resolute in tearing through the obstacles the world threw his way than Sloane Brodie. There were moments of hesitation where he faltered in his steps, but he reached deep inside and found the courage to keep going. And no matter how damaged or dirty he ended up, he came out on the other side more determined than ever.

Outside it was a warm September day. The temperature was in the mid-seventies, and the sky was sunny. The street buzzed with its usual activity while the city continued to pulsate with life. Tony, Cael, and the rest of the team sat in the waiting area, had been for hours while Sloane was in surgery. Dex couldn't get himself to sit still long enough to wait with them, not with the way his blood pressure skyrocketed every time someone in a white lab coat or teal-blue scrubs walked out. Plus the TV kept running news reports of the explosion, posting images and video footage of Sloane out in the field. The imposing and larger-than-life images of his lover, the depths of those amber eyes, mesmerized Dex. No one knew what was behind them like Dex did.

THIRDS team leader in critical condition after car bomb explosion... THIRDS agent Sloane Brodie rushed to hospital after Coalition attack on THIRDS teammate goes awry... THIRDS issues Threat Level Red alert after one agent is shot and a team leader is critically injured by Coalition leader Beck Hogan.

The headlines went on and on and on, dredging up anything connected to Sloane. They posted images of Gabe, ran old news footage of his death and his funeral, before they moved on to Sloane's new partner. Once again Dex found his image plastered all over the news, footage of him leaving the courthouse after sending his HPF partner away. It didn't end there. The whole team was dragged into it, most of the footage from before Dex had been recruited.

There was Ash tackling some Therian perp to the ground during a case and restraining him, looking fierce and menacing. Rosa rushing to give medical aid to a wounded citizen. Letty shooting the lock off a warehouse door before the team rushed in. Calvin running toward his partner after setting an explosive device that Hobbs then set off. When Cael's face came on the screen, Dex couldn't take it anymore. He'd wanted to punch something so badly, he'd been forced to leave the waiting area.

For hours he walked up and down the halls, around the hospital grounds, and drank enough coffee from the Garden Café, the staff was on a first-name basis with him. He tried to keep himself busy so he wouldn't drive himself out of his mind with worst-case scenarios. He'd wandered around the Greenberg Pavilion and its wings. Then the Baker, Payson, and Whitney Pavilions before making his way back to Greenberg.

These days, hospitals were trying to look less clinical with art on the walls, bright colors, comfy couches, restaurants, and hotel suites. That was fine with him, but it wouldn't ease his nerves or alter the sick feeling in his stomach. It wouldn't stop him from seeing Sloane unconscious under the battered car door, or the jagged piece of metal sticking out of him. The images had his stomach reeling, and the reality of what had happened, what could still happen, had Dex running to the nearest trashcan. Once he was done losing what little was in his stomach, he wiped his mouth, grateful for the café attendant who ran over to offer him help and some antibacterial wipes. He cleaned himself off and allowed them to lead him to a chair where he sat down and thanked them. The young man brought him a bottle of water and made sure he was okay before going back to his duties. Dex had no idea how long he'd sat there trying to hold on to his composure.

Dex's family and teammates took turns scouring the hospital for him to make sure he was okay. It was usually a quick assessment. No one was ready to utter a word. As if any kind of conversation might influence the outcome. Dex had been staring out the glass doors of the hospital entrance when Cael rushed over. Dex braced himself.

"Dex, the nurse said the doctor's going to come out and speak with us."

"Did they say anything about Sloane?" He hurried after his brother to the waiting area.

Cael shook his head. "Nothing."

When Dex joined the rest of his team inside the tastefully decorated lounge of soothing gray hues, they acknowledged him before returning to their previous fretting. They looked lost. Like they were waiting for Sloane to come out and tell them everything was okay. Dex knew the feeling. The team spent so much time together on the job—and off it—it was hard not falling into their roles no matter the situation, and Sloane's role was as leader. They'd follow him to hell and back. Dex understood how this might be doubly hard for the team what with having lost Gabe. He could imagine what was running through their minds. It was probably somewhere along the same line as his thoughts. Would they be attending another funeral? Dex buried that thought down deep. He couldn't go there. While he waited for the doctor to come out, Dex stood to one side and observed his teammates.

Letty and Rosa were huddled together speaking quietly, their arms linked, while Calvin gave Hobbs a reassuring pat on the shoulder, both glassy-eyed and tense. Dex hadn't seen Hobbs whisper to Calvin once since the two had arrived at the hospital, and Dex feared Hobbs was retreating into himself again like he had after Gabe's death. Ash was sitting in one of the two-seaters, red-eyed and groggy. He sat up and rubbed his eyes. Dex felt for the guy.

The nurses had taken care of Ash's stitches hours ago, and despite whatever they'd given him making him drowsy, Ash refused to close his eyes, even for a moment. Dex had a whole new level of respect for him. The longer he knew the guy, the more layers he discovered. Ash might be a certified prick, but Dex was growing to appreciate the rough agent's underlying qualities. Dex understood Sloane's loyalty now.

Ash bitched and groaned about almost everything. He was tactless and unapproachable, but if you needed someone to go to war for you, Ash Keeler would bring down his wrath like some vengeful Greek god and make it rain blood and pain on whoever made the stupid mistake of crossing him. Despite all that, somewhere deep inside, Ash Keeler still had a heart, because Dex saw evidence of it breaking every time Ash's gaze landed on Cael. Why the guy was so damned determined to be without someone he would die for was beyond Dex.

A Therian doctor who Dex recognized as one of several who'd come out when the EMTs had arrived with Sloane, came barging through the door and into the waiting area, straight to Tony. Dex had learned months ago from his own stay at the hospital after some of Pearce's hired goons ambushed him that the THIRDS had their own appointed medical staff here at the hospital, so he wasn't too surprised to find the doctor royally pissed off. Dealing with the government had that effect on people. Whatever the hell had happened, the doctor was furious. When he spoke, his tone was harsh and clipped.

"Sergeant Maddock, a word please."

Clearly dealing with the THIRDS didn't mandate the same patience required for civilians. The doctor pulled Tony off to one side, and although their voices were quiet, it was clear by the doctor's dilated pupils and his hand movements something wasn't right.

"Screw this." Dex marched over and butted in. "What the hell's going on?"

The doctor eyed him with a frown. "Who are you?"

"I'm Agent Daley, Agent Brodie's partner. If something is going on with him, I have the right to know about it."

"Well, Agent Daley, I hope you care about your partner more than your organization does."

The words hit Dex like a punch to the gut, and he did his best not to panic. "What happened?"

"The THIRDS withheld vital information regarding agent Brodie's medical history, and it nearly cost him his life."

"What?" A series of emotions swept through Dex, everything from shock, to anger, to confusion. The doctor must have picked up on it because he expanded his reply.

"Your partner suffers from malignant hyperthermia, a potentially fatal muscular disorder triggered by general anesthetics. As the anesthesiologist was given no information regarding Agent Brodie's susceptibility to this crisis, he was administered anesthetics along with a paralyzing agent, causing him to suffer an episode. We immediately began emergency procedures, stabilizing his vitals before he could go into cardiac arrest. These complications could have been prevented had the THIRDS been forthcoming."

"Is it possible they didn't know?" Dex asked, hoping

their organization hadn't purposefully withheld such important information. Something told him he already knew the answer.

"It's possible Agent Brodie was unaware of his susceptibility, but malignant hyperthermia is inherited, and the THIRDS refused to release background and medical information on Agent Brodie's family, merely stating there were no concerns."

"Those sons of bitches." Dex's jaw muscles clenched along with his fists. There was no doubt in his mind Sloane's condition stemmed from his time at the research facility. It would explain why those bastards up in Washington were more concerned with keeping their secret safe than saving one of their agents. It had nothing to do with Sloane's parents. The Therian Defense Department withheld information from Sloane's First Gen records in order to prevent the exposing the First Gen Recruitment Program. After all, what was one agent in the grand scheme of things? Tony placed a hand to Dex's shoulder in an attempt to calm him.

"Take it easy, son. Now's not the time."

His dad was right. He'd lose his shit over this later. Dex returned his attention to the doctor whose anger appeared to have subsided. "So what now?"

"He's out of surgery and will remain in ICU under close observation for the next thirty-six hours. Until Agent Brodie regains consciousness, we won't know what—if any —damage may have been caused by the episode. Once I have additional information, I'll determine the next course of action. Hopefully it will simply mean moving him to a general private room before he's well enough to discharge."

"Can I see him?" Dex asked. It wasn't that he didn't believe the doctor, but Jesus, they'd almost lost him. Not that Sloane still wasn't in danger. "Stable" was a word doctors and law-enforcement officers used for the media. It meant a patient's vitals were unchanged. All Dex could do was pray Sloane pulled through this without further complications.

"While he's in ICU, outside visits are restricted to spouses or partners only. We need to minimize the amount of outside contact to prevent any infection."

"But, he's my partner. I swear I'll stay in the room." The last few hours had been excruciating. How the hell was he supposed to get himself through another thirty-six hours without at least having seen Sloane?

The doctor shook his head. "I'm afraid even the THIRDS need to respect the rules. I'm sorry, Agent Daley."

Tony's hand came to rest against Dex's lower back, the Tony Maddock signal for don't kick up a fuss. But if there was ever a time for Dex to stick to his guns, this was it. He had to see Sloane. "Can I speak to you privately, Doctor?"

"Of course."

The doctor walked to one side, and Dex accompanied him, his voice low when he spoke. "When I said I was his partner, I didn't just mean work partner."

"Oh." With a puzzled frown, the doctor removed a tablet from his pocket and scrolled through his information. "I have him listed as 'single' with his emergency contact a Mr. Ash Keeler."

It was risky, but Dex had to chance it. "Yeah, um, it's kind of against the rules. Now I don't want to get transferred from my team. I love my team. But I love him even more. Please. You have to let me stay with him." Dex met the Therian doctor's gaze. The tattoo on his neck marked him as a wolf Therian, and despite his flustered state, Dex got a good vibe off the doc. He couldn't be much older than Sloane, and he had a kind face with sharp golden eyes.

"Agent Daley—"

"If he wakes up or something happens and I'm not there with him..." Dex couldn't bring himself to finish his sentence. He cleared his throat and tried again. "You know what brought him here. You said it yourself, you almost lost him. In our line of work, every moment we have is precious. Please, don't deny me this time with him."

The doctor looked like he was going to politely refuse once again, but instead he let out a resigned sigh. "All right. I'll make the necessary arrangements, but it's important you try and remain in the room. You'll have to wash up first. I'll inform the medical team."

Relief flooded through Dex, and he wanted to throw his arms around the doctor and squeeze, but he restrained himself. "Thank you so much. You don't know how much this means to me. Thank you."

The doctor smiled at him and motioned over to the rest of the team. "Why don't you let them know, and I'll escort you inside."

"I'll be right back." Dex sprinted over to his dad. "Hey, um—"

Tony arched an eyebrow at him. "Let me guess. You convinced him to let you stay."

"Any chance I can have some time off?"

"Sure. I'll take care of it. I'll have Cael bring you your overnight bag and leave it with one of the appointed nurses."

"Thanks, Dad. I'll call the second anything changes. Let the team know, will you?" He hugged his dad.

Ash was watching him, and Dex held a thumb up. He'd send Ash a text message later. Ash gave him a nod in understanding, and Dex was off. He joined the doctor and accompanied him down a long corridor through a door that led to a medium-sized shower room. There were four closed-off stalls in a blue-tiled area with a wall of lockers to the left, and around the corner to the right, he could make out bathroom stalls and sinks. The doctor walked to one of the lockers and pressed his thumb to the small keypad. Inside, toiletry items and stacks of sealed plastic packaging containing gray scrubs filled it. He looked Dex over, shuffled through the packs, and handed Dex a Human size medium, followed by a small toiletry bag.

"We keep supplies for special visitors. There are clean towels on the racks next to the showers." He removed an empty plastic bag from the locker and handed it to Dex. "Place your clothes in here. I'll get one of the housekeeping staff to get them cleaned. You can leave your shoes outside the room. The less we expose your partner to outside elements the better. At least until he's out of danger. I'll return for you in fifteen minutes."

"Thank you." Dex took his supplies and headed for a stall. With everything going on, his clothes and appearance had been the least of his worries. Obviously, he couldn't see Sloane covered in dirt and grime. The doctor would return soon, and Dex didn't want to keep him waiting, so he showered quickly, concentrating on washing off evidence of the explosion. He did his best not to let his thoughts drift off to Sloane and the state he might be in.

As soon as Dex was clean, he dried himself off, changed into the new scrubs and socks, pulled on his sneakers, and shoved his dirty clothes into the plastic bag marked for the housekeeping department. As the doctor had promised, he was there exactly fifteen minutes later. "I really appreciate everything you're doing," Dex said, handing the doctor his clothes.

"To be honest, your organization isn't the easiest to deal with." The doctor headed out and Dex followed. Sounded like this wasn't the first time the guy had issues with the THIRDS.

"Yeah, I'm starting to see that," Dex muttered. He still couldn't believe they'd deny vital information that would impact one of their agent's lives. For all the good the THIRDS did, it was still part of the government, and Dex wasn't so naïve as to have blind faith in any one institution. He'd seen too much in his career, both at the HPF and now at the THIRDS. The THIRDS was a step in the right direction toward uniting Therians and Humans, but it wasn't without its flaws.

"I take it you haven't been with the THIRDS long?" The doctor stopped by one of the nurses' stations and handed Dex's clothes over as he spoke quietly to a young curly haired Therian. She gave the doctor a nod and was off. They were immediately moving again.

Dex shook his head. "A year this month. I was homicide for the HPF."

"Wait." The doctor frowned thoughtfully. "Daley. I've seen you on the news. You testified against your Human partner."

"My claim to fame," Dex replied dryly.

"I apologize. I didn't mean anything by it. I thought I recognized you. Considering the options, I'd rather deal with the THIRDS than the HPF. No offense."

"None taken." He hadn't exactly left on friendly terms. Still, he'd had a good run there. He wasn't about to throw away ten years of good work over a bunch of bureaucratic douchebags. "They're not all bad, but unfortunately the assholes are usually the ones who speak the loudest."

The doctor chuckled. "Preaching to the choir, Agent Daley."

They walked down the ICU corridor and stopped outside one of the rooms where Dex used the hand-sanitizer dispenser on the wall despite having scrubbed himself from head to toe. The glass sliding door was closed, and the white curtain with a blue-and-pink pattern was drawn, preventing him from seeing inside. He toed off his shoes and nudged them to the side so no one would trip over them before he reached for the large button that would open the door. He hesitated. Whatever he expected, it would undoubtedly appear worse. Dex reminded himself about everything his partner had been through in his life. No matter how bad, he'd persevered, and he'd do it again. He held on to that. The doctor placed his hand on his shoulder, his gaze sympathetic.

"Your partner's a fighter, but he's going to need your strength."

Dex nodded, his lips pressed together to keep himself from giving in to the turmoil bubbling up inside him. With a small smile, the doctor gave his shoulder one last squeeze before walking off, leaving him on his own.

Well, he couldn't stand out here all day. Bracing himself, he pressed the button and waited for the door to slide open before he parted the curtain and slipped inside. There was a male nurse with his back to Dex as he checked Sloane's vitals.

"Excuse me," the young Therian said before turning and slipping past him.

Dex thought maybe he recognized the nurse, but it was out of his mind the moment his eyes landed on Sloane.

"Jesus." He wiped a hand over his face in an attempt to compose himself. It was growing more difficult with each breath he took. Stepping up to Sloane's bed, Dex stood, attempting to take it all in. He'd known what to expect, but seeing Sloane lying there in such a state... It was a sucker punch to his heart. The left side of his handsome face was swollen and covered in bruises. The purplish blotches continued down his neck and disappeared under the hospital gown, the blue of which was a stark contrast against his tan skin, skin that was scratched to hell. There were IVs and tubes sticking out all over, while the hum of machines and beeping monitors resounded through the otherwise silent room. Dex had seen worse during his career, but on the job, he found ways to cope. When it was someone he loved fighting for his life, how the hell was he supposed to cope with that?

He dragged a cushioned armchair over to Sloane's bedside and took a seat, refusing to lose his composure. Sloane needed him to be strong. When his partner regained consciousness, who knew what the doctor would find? Dex could only hope for the best. He couldn't afford to think about anything else.

"Hey, beautiful." Dex wanted to touch him but was hesitant to. He'd never seen Sloane like this, and he was finding it difficult to figure out what to do. The bed had been adjusted for Sloane's comfort and raised at a low angle, making it possible for Dex to see the terrible shape he was in. How could a Therian so tough look so fragile?

Many Humans feared and despised Therians, felt threatened by them and their abilities, believed them to be unsusceptible to Human flaws. Therians might be resilient, but they were hardly immune to pain, illness, or death. They weren't perfect, and yes, there were Therians who felt they were superior to Humans, but in Dex's opinion that only went to prove that although the mutation in their DNA made them physically different, on the inside, they were as fallible as Humans.

Dex lifted Sloane's hand to his lips for a kiss and shut his eyes tight against the tears threatening to burst free. *Hold it together, Rookie.* He smiled despite the situation. The word had become a term of endearment when spoken by Sloane. What he wouldn't give to hear that low, gravelly voice or see those soulful amber eyes. He tried not to give too much thought to their future, considering his tendency to move too quickly, but at times silly notions would slip into his head. Like them living together and spending the rest of their lives together. Being a family.

"You have to be okay. I need you to be okay. Hell, I just need you. You promised me an afternoon in bed, remember?" A tear rolled down his cheek, and he swiftly wiped it away. *It's okay. Breathe.* Just this morning he'd stood in Sloane's arms, smiling up at those sparkling eyes. They'd teased each other and laughed before Dex all but melted against Sloane like he always did when Sloane kissed him. He'd been stupidly happy. Everything had started to feel normal again after the last few months. And now... He put Sloane's hand to his lips again and kept it there, his eyes shut tight as another tear escaped. It would be okay. The doctor had said so himself. Sloane was a fighter.

"I need you to be okay, Sloane. Please. I don't know if you can hear me. You probably can't, but I'll say it anyway. I love you. I love you, and you can't leave me."

A tap at the window scared the hell out of him, and he gingerly returned Sloane's hand back to the bed. Damn it, he'd forgotten to close the curtain when he'd come in, and now his father stood outside looking pretty pissed. Shit. He hadn't expected his dad to come back so soon. Cursing himself for being so careless, he grabbed a gown from one of the hooks on the wall and slipped into it, followed by a plastic cap. Sloane's vitals were at normal levels, and Dex didn't want to be the cause of his lover getting an infection. Once he was done, he left the room, closed the door behind him, and faced his father. When he spoke, he tried to sound casual.

"Hey. Everything okay?"

Tony pursed his lips, his stern gaze on Dex. *Oh God. He knows. Of course he knows.* What the hell had made Dex think he could keep his relationship a secret from his dad? He'd never been able to keep anything secret from him. He could count on one hand the number of things he'd gotten away with during his childhood without his father finding out about it at some point. Tony was a sergeant at the THIRDS, for Christ's sake. If his dad didn't know something, he was either being purposefully oblivious or not interested enough to poke around. Dex's best course of action was to remain calm, silent, and still. After an excruciating moment, Tony's expression softened.

"Yeah. Everything's fine. How are you holding up?"

Dex nodded, feeling the sting behind his eyes. Was his dad covering for him? He had to be. It wouldn't be the first time Tony had put his boys before everything else, including the job. Hell, it's what had gotten him recruited to the THIRDS after adopting Cael. The thought of what his dad might be doing for him, plus Sloane lying in the room behind him, had Dex blinking several times in an attempt to keep it together. It wasn't like his dad hadn't seen him cry before, but Dex was afraid if he started, he wouldn't be able to stop.

"Son..."

The soft-spoken word broke Dex. He stepped into his father's open arms and let the tears fall. He couldn't remember the last time he'd cried like this. How long had everything been building up? The last few months had pushed him hard, but he'd put his game face on and did what he had to do to keep on keeping on. He'd always been good at keeping his chin up, finding a reason to smile even if inside he was screaming. Since joining the THIRDS, he'd been kidnapped, beaten up, shot, almost blown up, and now this. If it hadn't been for Sloane taking those keys from him, it would have been Dex caught in the explosion.

"It should have been me..."

Tony pulled back and took hold of Dex's face. "Stop it. I know Sloane. He would have done everything in his power to keep you safe. Forget about what should or could have been and think about how you're going to be there for your partner when he wakes up. He's going to need you to look after him, and we both know, with everything Sloane has been through in his life, he deserves someone good looking after him, even if he's too pigheaded to admit it. Okay?"

"Yeah." Dex sniffed and took the tissue his dad handed him. He blew his nose before chucking it in the bin next to the door. His ears were hot, his throat sore, his eyes stung, and his head hurt. He was forced to breathe through his mouth because his nose was stuffed. God, he was such a mess. He turned and stepped up to the window to observe Sloane. Tony came to stand beside him, put an arm around his shoulders, and pulled him in close.

"He'll be okay, but like I said, he'll need his partner. That's why I came here. With Hogan and his crew still out there, Sloane is in a vulnerable position. I think it would be a good idea for you two to stick together. Maybe have him stay at your place while he recovers. I don't like the idea of him in his apartment alone. There are too many entry points in and around the building. Place is a tactical nightmare. Your street's been cleared, and Hogan's not dumb enough to strike the same place twice. Plus we'll have someone on protective detail close by just in case."

"You really think it's necessary?" Would Hogan really try to come back and finish the job? The bomb hadn't been intended for Sloane. If anything, Ash was the one who needed to watch his back.

"We're not taking any chances." Tony pulled Dex close and gave the top of his head a kiss. "Be good. I've got a shitload of reports to file and a meeting with Sparks. Call if you need anything. Cael's at your house grabbing your overnight bag. He'll be dropping it off in the next hour or so."

"Thanks, Dad. I really appreciate it."

"Any time, son." Tony gave him one last squeeze before walking off, and Dex stood there for a moment watching him go. He wondered if his dad would broach the subject of Dex's relationship with Sloane once everything had settled. The rules against fraternizing with members of your own team were clear, though from what he'd heard, few agents actually adhered to it. They were just good at keeping quiet about their extracurricular activities. Dex doubted he and Sloane were the only ones using the sleeping bays to do more than sleep. With how much time agents spent in the field and on the job, relationships were bound to happen. It was when those relationships interfered with the job that the no fraternizing rule wiped the floor with them.

Dex used the sanitizer dispenser again before going in. This time, he remembered to close the curtain. He returned the cap and gown to their hooks before resuming his previous post beside Sloane's bed. As he made himself comfortable, he thought about how he'd run after Sloane when the explosion went off. He'd been reckless and stupid. If his dad had been there, Dex would have been in deep shit. With a heavy sigh, he sat back and ran a hand through his damp hair. He'd had this conversation with Sloane. How they couldn't allow their personal relationship to interfere with their jobs. What if his relationship with Sloane impaired his judgment? Could he be trusted to make the right call when the bullets were flying? He closed his eyes and tried to clear his thoughts. Maybe he was still a rookie, but he was hardly inexperienced. He could do this. Who the hell wouldn't be caught off guard by an explosion outside their house midmorning? Exhaustion soon claimed him, and he fell asleep.

When he woke up, it took him a moment to remember where he was. He sat up and found someone had draped a blanket over him. He'd have to remember to thank the nurses. Feeling groggy, he pulled the blanket up to his chin and tried to get cozy, his gaze instinctively landing on Sloane to check on him.

Sloane's eyes were open.

"Sloane?" Dex tamped down his urge to jump from his chair and instead gingerly stood, not wanting to startle his partner. Tenderly, he brushed his fingers down Sloane's cheek—the side not covered in bruises and nasty scrapes. "Hey, handsome."

Sloane blinked slowly, his lids heavy and his eyes dazed. He seemed to be staring at nothing in particular. His brows drew together, and Dex waited with bated breath. At one point Sloane closed his eyes, and Dex thought he was out again, but a couple of heartbeats later and Sloane was looking right at him. His lips parted, and a barely there "hi" made it out. It was the most amazing greeting in the history of greetings. Dex's reply was nearly as quiet.

"Hi."

"Thirsty," Sloane rasped.

Dex quickly poured some water into one of the little plastic cups beside the pitcher on the side table along with a small straw. He placed the straw to Sloane's lips with care and Sloane sipped. A few swallows later, and Sloane gave him a small nod. Dex returned the cup to the side table before gently running a hand over Sloane's head, making sure to be careful. Who knew how much bruising there was.

"How do you feel?"

"Like shit," Sloane murmured. He looked like he was trying to fight through the haziness. He'd most likely be falling back asleep any moment. Dex pulled his chair up close and leaned in to put his hand to Sloane's cheek.

"You'll be okay," Dex said, smiling when Sloane turned his head so he could nuzzle Dex's hand. He closed his eyes and let out a soft sigh.

"Stay."

Dex felt a lump in his throat. "I'm not going anywhere," he promised.

Sloane hummed before nodding again. "Good. Need you." His features softened as he drifted off, but not before he said one more word. "Always."

Dex thought back to the night of the Coalition trade when Ash had been shot.

"You okay?" Dex asked Sloane, knowing this couldn't be easy for him.

"No, but I'll manage. Right now, I think you should take Cael home to your place. He's going to need you. He'll want to go to the hospital once the shock wears off."

"What about you?"

Sloane gave him a small smile. "I always need you."

Dex leaned over to kiss Sloane's brow. "Always."

Twice now Sloane had told Dex he always needed him, and both times the admission had knocked Dex for a loop. Not that he didn't believe Sloane, but both instances had been under strenuous circumstances—the possibility of his best friend bleeding to death and now his semiconscious state. Sloane cared about him a lot, Dex was certain, but Sloane was reserved when it came to expressing how he felt about their relationship. Dex was always the more vocal one, the one putting his heart in Sloane's hands and wishing for the best. He understood the whys, but it didn't make it any easier, and the deeper Dex fell, the more he wished he knew. Would Sloane ever be able to love him? Or had that part of him died with Gabe?

Jesus, what the hell was wrong with him? He needed to cut this shit out. Maybe it was time for another nap. Drawing the blanket over himself once more, Dex dozed in and out of dreamless sleep, checking on Sloane constantly before allowing himself to drift off again. Sometime the next morning, someone running their fingers through his hair roused him. Opening his eyes, he turned his head to find Sloane smiling warmly at him. It was the most amazing smile he'd ever woken up to.

"Morning, trouble."

Dex smiled widely before letting out a fierce yawn. "Morning." He sat up, and the blanket someone had wrapped around his shoulders slipped down. "I really need to thank the nurse. He or she keeps tucking me in."

"He," Sloane said before motioning to the end of the bed. "He also brought you your clothes and an overnight bag Cael dropped off a few hours ago. He apologized for not bringing it in sooner, but you were asleep, and he thought you needed the rest. You were out for the count."

"That was nice of him." With another yawn, Dex stood

and stretched his aching muscles when the door opened, and the doctor came in.

"Good morning, Agent Daley."

Dex gave him a nod and watched the doctor stop beside Sloane.

"Hello, Agent Brodie. I'm Dr. Ward, I'm glad to see you're awake. Your nurse should have been in to check your sutures and change the dressing."

"He has. Thank you."

"Good. Did he discuss the incident with you?"

Sloane's amber eyes clouded over as he replied with a solemn, "Yes."

Did that include the THIRDS withholding information? Dex would have to ask his partner. He wondered how Sloane would feel about it. Sloane had been with the THIRDS for over twenty years. He loved his job, but he wasn't blind to their darker side. Hell, he'd been an unwilling participant in it for years. The THIRDS used youth centers to recruit. They were willing to sacrifice an agent to keep their questionable past a secret. And recently their team had discovered someone had been working out of the supposedly decommissioned research facility creating a control drug using scopolamine. Neither he nor Sloane were convinced it was the end of it. The doctor seemed to sense Sloane's change in mood but didn't pursue the matter. Instead he continued with the purpose of his visit.

"Your vitals are good. I'm going to do a few standard checks. You'll feel some pain and discomfort during your recovery, but we'll provide medication."

Dex sat on the edge of his seat as the doctor did some preliminary tests, checking Sloane's breathing, showing him how to support his wound if he had to cough or move. So far everything seemed normal. A little slow, but the doctor said it was to be expected.

"We're going to do a few circulatory tests." The doctor carefully removed the blanket from Sloane's legs and feet. "Point your toes."

Sloane winced but slowly did as he was asked.

"Good. Now make circles with your feet. First the left, then the right. Good. Now slowly, I want you to raise your knees one at a time, pulling your toes toward you."

With his jaw clenched, Sloane gingerly bent his left knee and slid his foot toward him before lowering it again.

"Good. Now your right."

A startled look came onto Sloane's face. "There's something wrong with my leg."

Before Dex could give it another thought, he was at Sloane's side, gripping his hand. He could hear the tremor in Sloane's voice and knew his partner was trying to tamp down his panic. Sloane met the doctor's gaze as he discreetly tucked Dex's hand against his side, but the doctor was sharp. And he already knew about them. He gave Sloane a warm smile that reached his golden eyes.

"Don't worry, Mr. Brodie. While you're under my care, your relationship will remain confidential."

It seemed to take a moment for Sloane to grasp what the doctor was saying. Once he did, he visibly relaxed. He still looked uncertain, but he focused on what was most important.

The doctor came around to the other side of the bed and gently touched Sloane's right knee. "Tell me about your leg. What do you feel?"

"I'm having trouble bending it. I can't lift it either." Sloane squeezed Dex's hand, and Dex returned the gesture. They both waited and watched as the doctor applied small amounts of pressure to different areas of Sloane's leg.

"Can you feel this?" Dr. Ward asked.

"Yes."

"How about now?"

Sloane nodded. "I can feel it fine. I'm just having trouble moving it. Like it's too heavy."

"During your episode, we were able to treat you before your muscles could suffer severe rigidity. There was no nerve damage, but it appears the reaction you experienced has caused muscle weakness in your leg. The fact you've retained some movement is good, but we'll need to increase your mobility to prevent further weakness."

"Is it permanent?" Sloane asked hesitantly.

"With muscle rehabilitation, you're likely to regain strength in your leg within a few weeks, but it could take up to two to three months, depending on recovery and how well your body responds to the therapy. As a Therian in your shape, I would say a month. We'll put you on a mobility plan. I'm approving your transfer to a private recovery room this afternoon. Therian nursing staff will be in to help you up and out of bed. It's also important that while you're resting in bed, you move positions, taking care with your injured side, of course. Once I think it's safe for you to be discharged, I'll give you an information packet for your recovery at home. With the medication you'll be given, and due to your injuries, I highly recommend you refrain from shifting into your Therian form for at least three weeks. I know it's tempting since we heal quicker in our Therian forms, but there's a chance it may do more harm than good, so I'd rather not risk it."

"Thank you, doctor. When do you think I'll be okay to go home?"

"I'd like to keep you another thirty-six hours to be on the safe side." Dr. Ward gave Sloane a gentle pat on the shoulder before heading for the door. He paused and turned to smile warmly at them. "Your partner's not left your side for a moment. You're a lucky Therian, Agent Brodie."

Sloane turned his smile on Dex, and it took his breath away. "Yeah, I am."

With a nod, the doctor left the room. Dex took a seat. His partner's expression turned pensive, and Dex gave his hand a squeeze.

"I'm sorry I told the doctor about us. It was the only way I could stay with you."

Sloane's smile reassured him he hadn't messed up. "I'm glad you're here. Remind me to change my emergency contact form."

"Okay." Dex couldn't keep his dopey smile off his face. At least until Sloane's smile faded.

"What if my leg doesn't regain its strength? Sparks can't have a Defense agent who can't work out in the field. I'll be transferred to God knows where and put behind a desk. I'm not qualified to work Intel. Algorithms drive your brother crazy, and he loves that shit. Recon still requires a hell of a lot of fieldwork. What's left?" His eyes went wide. "Oh God, what if they try to stick me in Public Relations or Human Resources? I'll have to talk to the public. The media. I can't talk to the media. Just looking at them makes me want to shoot something."

"Easy there." Dex brushed his lips over Sloane's knuckles, watching him relax. "Whatever happens, we'll work through it together. And we both know no one in their right mind would stick you in either of those departments. You're a Defense agent. One of the best. It'll be okay."

"You're right," Sloane said, letting out a shaky breath. "Besides, I've been through worse."

"Why don't you get some rest?"

Sloane was reluctant at first but soon settled back against his pillow. "What would I do without you?"

"Lead a quiet, peaceful existence?" Dex teased.

Sloane frowned. "Sounds boring as hell."

A few months ago, Sloane's answer would have been different. Dex tried not to get too sappy over his partner's reply. "Can I get that in writing and notarized?"

Sloane chuckled before letting out a yawn. "Shut up." He closed his eyes, a smile on his face as he drifted off to sleep, his hand still holding tightly on to Dex's. Whether it was the near-death experience, the meds, or something more, Dex wasn't going to question it, simply enjoy it. He kissed Sloane and settled back into his chair, grateful his partner was on the mend. It could have turned out so much worse. Tomorrow Dex would have to report back to work, but until then, he'd spend the rest of the day offering his partner whatever he needed. Whatever came their way, Dex would face it with Sloane.

TWO

"I'D LIKE to take a moment to thank each and every one of you for your hard work, dedication, and perseverance. This has been a difficult month for Unit Alpha, especially for Destructive Delta. Sloane Brodie and Ash Keeler are two of our most experienced Therian Defense agents, and we wish them a speedy recovery."

Lieutenant Sparks stood behind the sleek black podium at the front of the expansive conference room in her signature white pantsuit and five-inch heels giving a speech on Unit Alpha's performance and how pleased the higher-ups were with the results. Thanks to Destructive Delta's hard work, Reyes was behind bars, though not before handing Sloane a list of the remaining active members of the Order during their intense interrogation session. Because of Ash's undercover work, the Coalition was disbanded, for the most part, and the members who'd been arrested the night of the trade-off were starting to crack under the pressure. So far none of them knew where to find Hogan as the guy never spent more than a couple of nights in the same place, but they were able to provide a list of previous hideouts along with interesting facts Dex hoped would turn into leads.

At the office, everything was business as usual. Not that he'd expected Unit Alpha to come to a standstill after what happened to Sloane and Ash, but it was an odd feeling, witnessing the world go on as if nothing had happened. Then again, that was the job. No matter what was going on around you, you had a duty to perform, and Dex was looking forward to getting on with his duty by catching that son of a bitch Beck Hogan.

"I'm happy to report agent Brodie has been transferred from ICU to a private room where he'll be monitored until the doctor sees fit to discharge him. He has a long recovery ahead of him, and I'm certain he'll appreciate your well wishes. HR will be arranging a party for him upon his return. They'll be sending a memo closer to the time.

"Now, as you all know, this case was issued a Threat Level Red. Beck Hogan is our priority, and we've been given the all clear from the Chief of Therian Defense to bring Hogan in using any means necessary. Hogan and what remains of the Coalition have gone underground, but our SSA on this case has informed us they're still in the city. We believe Hogan won't be going anywhere until he finishes what he started."

Dex's jaw muscles clenched. Well that made two of them. Until Hogan paid for what he'd done, Dex wasn't going anywhere. There was no safe place for Hogan to hide.

A hand landed on his shoulder, and Dex tilted his head back to find his brother giving him a warm, sympathetic smile. Dex returned the gesture with an added wink to ease his little brother's concern. They'd texted while Dex had been at the hospital, but it had been days since they'd really talked, which wasn't like them. He'd have to set some time aside to hang with his bro. The screen above Sparks came to life, catching Dex's attention. It showed eight mug shots, a few of them already familiar to Dex and his team.

"Hogan and his followers have been hunting down these Humans. Former members of the Westward Creed who were responsible for the deaths of several Therians during the Riots of 1985. Among the Therians killed, we've discovered two of them were related to Hogan. His mother and sister. All except for two of the Westward Creed went on to become members of the Order. As it stands, Angel Reyes and Richard Esteban are in prison. Albert Cristo and Craig Martin are deceased, as is Toby Leith." Sparks tapped the podium's interactive surface zooming in on three of the mug shots, one of which was labeled deceased. Wait a minute. When the hell had that happened? As if reading his mind, Sparks answered.

"Leith was found by the HPF late last night over in the Bronx. A large Felid Therian mauled him to death. Evidence suggests it was Hogan himself. We expect Hogan to go after the remaining members, Ox Perry and Brick Jackson. We're attempting to make contact, but it looks like they've caught on to Hogan's plan and have gone underground as well. Since our SSA informs us Hogan and his crew are still somewhere in the city, it's safe to assume the same goes for Perry and Jackson."

Dex held a hand up. "Excuse me, Lieutenant? Why wasn't Destructive Delta called out for Leith's murder?" Even if he was at the hospital, he would have been called in, or at the very least his team, and he knew for a fact Destructive Delta hadn't been out in the field since Ash had been shot. What the hell was going on?

"Because Destructive Delta is no longer working this case."

Dex launched to his feet. "I'm sorry, what?"

"You're to gather whatever intel you have on Perry and Jackson, finish any pending reports from this case, and submit them to Themis. As of this moment, Team Leader Sebastian Hobbs will handle Hogan and his crew. His team, Theta Destructive, will be the lead team on this. Destructive Delta is officially on leave."

Cael gasped behind Dex. "On leave?"

"For how long?" Dex asked. He was having trouble processing the blow they'd been delivered.

"Until I feel the team is no longer under threat from Hogan and his crew. I want you all in secure locations watching your backs. Protective details will be assigned where necessary. You've nearly lost two agents. Let's not go for a third. You and your team are dismissed. I expect those reports by the end of the week."

"But—"

Sparks's piercing blue eyes pinned Dex with a subtle warning, her tone firm. "Dismissed, Agent Daley."

The room was deadly silent with none of the other agents daring to make eye contact with him. This couldn't be happening. Dex left the room with the rest of his team on his heels. He headed for his office, not giving a second thought to the fact everyone was following him. Numbly, he dropped down into his chair. The door to his and Sloane's office swished closed, and the walls went white, sending the room into privacy mode before Letty exploded, startling Dex.

"This is motherfucking bullshit!" Letty fumed, pacing from one end of the office to the other, her sparkling brown eyes ablaze. "How can she pull us off the case? She saw what those assholes did to Ash! They fucking shot him. Son of a bitch ordered his little bitches to kill him, and then they almost killed Sloane! *Mierda. Carajo!*" She let out a frustrated growl, looking like she was about to punch something. Rosa grabbed her by the shoulders and brought her pacing to a halt.

"*Oye, calmate,*" Rosa ordered in Spanish. She said something else to Letty in Spanish Dex couldn't understand, but there were definitely some colorful expletives thrown in there. She subtly nodded toward Dex, but he'd caught on to it. Letty inhaled deeply and let it out slowly before turning to him.

"I'm sorry, Dex. This is fucked up."

All Dex could do was nod. He glanced up to find his team standing behind Sloane's desk, all watching him.

"What?"

"Are you okay?" Calvin asked from beside Hobbs who looked equally worried. "You're quiet. I thought you'd be..."

"Flipping your shit," Letty finished.

"Leave him alone," Rosa huffed and came around the desk to wrap her arms around Dex's neck. She gave him a comforting squeeze before pulling away. "Come on. There's nothing we can do. Sparks gave her orders. You all best watch your backs. I don't trust any of those *putas.*" Rosa turned to Cael, asking him where he was going to stay. Cael mentioned something about hanging out at Tony's, and Dex might have heard his brother say his name, but he was too focused on trying to remain calm and not flipping his shit as Letty had suggested. The rest of his team left the office one by one, each giving Dex a reassuring pat on the shoulder, insisting he call if he or Sloane needed anything. Cael was the only one who stayed behind.

This had to be a mistake. Sparks couldn't take them off the case. They'd been working this thing for months. First they'd gone up against the Order. Then Ash had risked his life to infiltrate the Coalition. The bastards had tried to kill him for it. And what they did to Sloane...

"Sparks." Dex shot to his feet. "I need to talk to Sparks. This has to be a mistake." He turned for the door when Cael stepped in front of him, his hands going to Dex's chest to stop him.

"Don't." His little brother looked up at him, his big silver eyes pleading. "Don't do anything stupid, Dex. Sparks isn't Dad. She'll suspend you if she thinks you're going to be a problem. She's done it before."

"I need to know *why*." Besides, what would be the point of suspending him if he was already on leave and off duty? Surely she wouldn't ask for his badge and gun for a simple question. She might be a hard-ass, but she was fair and reasonable. "I need to know why."

Cael's arms dropped to his sides, his voice quiet. "Sometimes we don't get a why, Dex, no matter how bad we want one."

Dex hated seeing his brother looking so miserable. Cael was referring to more than their current situation. His brother was still hurting over Ash's rejection. Even after admitting there was more than friendship between them. Hell, the guy had taken a bullet for Cael. Ash obviously had his reasons, but why wouldn't he share those reasons with the guy he was so crazy about he would die for?

"Lieutenant Sparks rarely pulls a team from a case," Cael added, seeming to gather himself. "If she does, it's for a good reason."

Dex didn't reply. Mostly because he refused to accept the decision or whatever reason was behind it.

Cael motioned to the door behind him. "I'm heading home to pack. I'm gonna hang at Dad's for a while. You know his place is like a fortress. If the zombie apocalypse ever comes, you know where to find me. Sparks will probably reassign him until we're brought back in. You should stay with us. It'll be fun."

"Thanks, bro, but Sloane's staying with me while he recovers." Dex was really looking forward to spending some time with his partner, just the two of them. Looked like he was going to have a little more free time than he'd expected.

"Right. Sorry. Dad mentioned it. How is Sloane?"

Dex felt his heart squeeze in his chest and his anger flare up, but he tamped it down. He didn't want to end up snapping at his brother. It wasn't Cael's fault, and he had his own worries. He didn't need Dex being an asshat. "He's pretty banged up, and he's got muscle weakness in his right leg, so he's going to be placed on a mobility plan, plus therapy."

"Shit. How long?"

"Doctor said in Sloane's shape it should take a month at most. If not, it could be two to three months before strength in his leg muscles returns. Sloane's really worried about it."

"Of course he is," Cael said, shoving his hands into his pockets, his expression turning somber. "Large Felids don't do well in small enclosures for extended periods of time. They need space." He seemed to drift off into his thoughts again, and Dex had no doubt which Felid Cael was thinking about.

Dex took a seat on the edge of his desk, reminding himself his little brother wasn't so little anymore. Cael didn't need him riding in and fighting his wars for him or making a fuss and coddling him. But nothing was going to stop Dex from being there for his brother like he'd always been. "How are you holding up?"

Cael shrugged. "I don't know. I'm trying to keep myself

busy. I don't want to think about it. It's easier with him not being here."

"You miss him, don't you?" Falling fast and hard was a trait he and his brother shared, and despite Cael's initial reaction to Ash's rejection, his brother had put away his claws—for the time being anyway. Dex had expected Cael to shred Ash to pieces for breaking his heart, but instead, Cael was licking his wounds and regrouping. It would appear his brother knew how to handle Ash better than anyone. Dex had witnessed it himself countless times and been stunned stupid. If Cael could manage before, he'd do it again. It was only a matter of time.

Cael let out a heart-wrenching sigh. "I've wanted to call him so many times, but I keep thinking about that day in the hospital. Whatever it is he's dealing with, it's important to him. I wish he'd confide in me."

"Give him some time."

"Thanks, Dex." Cael gave him a small smile. He walked over and gave Dex a hug. "Be careful."

Dex returned his brother's embrace. "I will," he promised. Cael left, and Dex sat in the silent office on his own, his gaze landing on the empty chair across from him. Right now, Sloane should have been sitting there, telling Dex he hadn't had enough coffee to deal with his shenanigans. Damn it, he needed answers.

Determined, he left the office and made his way through Unit Alpha's bullpen, aware of the concerned gazes following him. The door to Lieutenant Sparks's office was open, and she was typing away at her desk's interface. Before he could knock, she addressed him without having to look up.

"Come in, Agent Daley. Please close the door behind you."

"How...?"

"Your scent." She stopped typing and met his gaze. "You're the only agent in Unit Alpha who uses a Citrus Splash and Berry Fusion body wash."

Damn. His eyes landed on the mark on her neck. Right. Cougar Therian. Smell. He wondered if she recognized every agent by their shower gel or if his was weird enough to stand out. Most likely the latter.

"Can I speak with you a moment?"

"Of course." She motioned to one of the two empty chairs in front of her sleek black desk. "I know you don't agree with my decision."

Dex sat and pretended he wasn't as nervous as he felt. Sparks wasn't just intimidating as a Therian and commanding officer. She had a way about her and a gaze that made him feel like she could uncover his deepest darkest secrets. Sloane was mysterious. Sparks was an enigma. It was like she was made up of the job and nothing else.

"With all due respect, Lieutenant, no I don't. How can you pull us off the case after all the work we've put into it, after everything we've been through?"

"That's precisely why I'm reassigning the case, Agent Daley. You're two agents down, and one of those agents is your team leader. They're also the most experienced members of your team."

Agents were shuffled around where they were needed, when they were needed. When Hobbs and Cael had been in the hospital, Taylor had been called in to back up Destructive Delta. Couldn't she do it now? "Yes, but you can temporarily assign someone."

"I can, but I'm not going to."

"Why?" He tried not to come off as insubordinate, but

he needed to understand. It would seem needing to know ran in the family. Not a great trait to have when working for an organization often insistent that they didn't need to know. To his surprise, Sparks's expression turned sympathetic.

"I've been doing this job a long time, Agent Daley. When a team is hit this close to home, it's difficult to maintain objectivity. I assure you, it has no bearing on your professionalism. Over two years ago, Destructive Delta suffered the loss of one of their own, a loss they found difficult to recover from. They performed their duties admirably, but the strain was beginning to show. Then you came along and inspired them. From the moment Sergeant Maddock suggested you as a possible candidate, I knew I'd found the right fit for Destructive Delta. However, you've also had an intense first year. Not many rookies have endured what you have in such a short period of time. I should have sent you on leave earlier, but you possess a resilience and ability to endure I admire. You have a lot of potential."

"Then why not let me work this case?"

"Because Hogan has issued a threat against your team, two members of which he's successfully put out of commission. I won't put the rest of the team at risk. Destructive Delta needs a break whether you agree or not. Sebastian Hobbs is more than capable. Go home, check on your partner, make sure you're both safe. Maddock informed me Sloane will be staying with you. I'm putting a protective detail one block away from your residence. If at any point you feel you're in danger, call it in. I know this is difficult, but my decision is final. You'll have access to Themis until the end of the week. Finish your reports, and Maddock will notify you the moment anything changes."

There was no point in arguing. Lieutenant Sparks had made up her mind, and nothing Dex could say would change it. Her argument was sound but didn't change the way Dex felt about it. Feeling annoyed and pissed off, he opened his mouth before thinking.

"And the decision to withhold vital medical information that nearly killed Sloane? Whose decision was that?"

Something flashed in Sparks's steel-blue eyes, and Dex realized only too late he'd stuck his foot in it. Again.

"Agent Daley, I highly recommend you use caution when challenging decisions against your superiors. The Chief of Therian Defense is not a patient Therian. I understand your anger and frustration. Agent Brodie is your partner, and I hope you believe me when I say I fight tooth and nail to protect my agents. However, I will remind you there is an order to things. One we may not understand or agree with, but necessary nonetheless. I assure you, the decision did not come lightly."

In other words, Sparks had no say in the matter. It hardly eased his mind or made it any less fucked-up, but the last thing he wanted to do was piss off his lieutenant. With a curt nod, he got up and headed for the door when Sparks called out to him.

"Oh, and you'll be receiving a call from PR. They'd like to set up a meeting to discuss possible campaigns. I approved the request. It'll be good for you and the department in light of recent events. Plus it'll keep your mind off the case."

Are you fucking kidding me? He turned to her and mustered up a smile. "Sure." He excused himself and left before he could explode. They'd taken him off the case, but they wanted him to go out there, smile, put on the charm, and tell everyone how awesome and shiny everything was? This day was getting better and better.

He headed for the locker room in Unit Alpha. It would be a lot less crowded than the one down in Sparta's training bays. At least he wouldn't have to worry about training for a while, though he should probably make use of the free gym membership the THIRDS provided. With Sloane staying with him, Dex had no doubt his partner would attempt to convince him to swap his yummy snacks for something healthy. When had vegetables become a snack? It was bad enough they'd forced their way onto dinner plates, now they wanted to take over snack time too? He was so lost in his thoughts he almost ran right into Seb.

"Shit. Sorry, man."

"No problem, Dex. I was coming to find you. I gave you clearance to access the intel on Leith in case you needed to add any additional information." Seb gave him a sympathetic smile. "If you need anything at all, I'm here to help."

"Thanks."

It was easy to forget Hobbs had older brothers since Dex rarely ever saw Hobbs in their company. Then again, the last time the three brothers had been in the same room, it had been a complete clusterfuck, and Hobbs had been unconscious. There was a lot of bad blood between Rafe—the eldest of the brothers—and Seb. It didn't help that Rafe was an even bigger asshole than Ash. Was it even possible?

The resemblance between Seb and Ethan Hobbs was clear, from their bright green eyes with smile lines at the corners to their jet-black hair—though Seb's was interspersed with some silver here and there—and their chiseled jaws. Both were rugged, friendly, and huge, with Seb somehow being even bigger than his little brother. Tiger Therians were the biggest of the Felid Therians. They weighed a goddamn ton in both Human and Therian forms thanks to all the muscle mass. Dex had learned a hell of a lot about the larger Felid Therians since joining the THIRDS and being partnered with one. Enough to know it was in his best interest to remain alert around them. They could go from sweet and cuddly to tear-your-throat-out pissed off in seconds. Like they had two personalities. One loved you, and the other would make a meal out of you. And not in a good way. Cheetah Therians were different. They reminded Dex more of Canid Therians. They had plenty of Felid qualities, but they were more affectionate, less confrontational, and more laid back.

"I'm really sorry, Dex. You know I wouldn't have asked for this."

Seb's apology took Dex aback. This was a big opportunity for the guy. "I know, man. It's okay. Congrats on the promotion."

"Thank you. I swear we'll get Hogan." Seb's expression turned determined, and Dex appreciated his conviction, but it didn't make him feel any better.

"I know." With a reassuring smile, Dex went on his way.

It wasn't Seb's fault he'd been assigned the Hogan case. Years of obscurity after his fall from grace and a transfer from Destructive Delta, Seb was finally putting that part of his past behind him. He'd been handed his own team and a high-profile case. Good for him. Dex just wished it hadn't been *this* case. Seb was a good agent, and Dex trusted him, but Destructive Delta should be the one bringing Hogan in.

There were few agents in the locker room at this time of morning. Everyone was either out in the field or behind their desk. Dex hung his uniform shirt in his locker and stilled when it finally sank in. His team was off the case. Someone else was going after Beck Hogan. There was no telling what would happen. What if the guy decided to make a run for it? What if Hogan changed his mind and decided to cut his losses and disappear?

Anger and frustration boiled up inside him until he couldn't keep it in anymore. It tore through him with a fierce cry, and he slammed his locker door so hard it rattled the whole wall. It wasn't enough. That son of a bitch was out there. First the THIRDS kept vital information to themselves, nearly killing Sloane, and now this? What if it had been Cael or one of their Human teammates? What if they'd been on leave to attend another funeral?

With an enraged shout, Dex kicked at his locker before repeatedly jerking the door open and slamming it shut, each time with more force in an attempt to smash it to shit. He was vaguely aware of fellow agents hovering around him, but he didn't care. His pulse was through the roof, and his face felt like it was on fire as he continued to beat the ever-living crap out of the inanimate object before him. An iron grip clamped down over his arm, and he spun on his heel, bringing his fist with him. He missed. A pair of tree-trunk arms wrapped around him, crushing him up against a hard body. What the fuck? Dex tried to struggle, his face pressed against someone's chest when he heard soft words whispered by his ear.

"It's okay."

Dex stilled. He knew that voice, yet he was certain he'd never actually heard it so clearly before now. How was that possible? Shifting his head back slightly, he spotted the agent's name embroidered on his uniform.

E. Hobbs.

"Hobbs?" The arms around him gave a squeeze, and something inside Dex burst. He clung on to Hobbs and buried his face against his chest. A large hand came to rest on the back of Dex's head as he was held tight. Dex completely deflated. He allowed himself to be held onto, to be supported by his much larger teammate. He didn't know how long he stood in Hobbs's embrace, but when he pulled back, his face was hot and flushed, both from his little outburst and embarrassment. He took a seat on the bench in front of his locker, his gaze on his boots. Hobbs sat down beside him. Around them, the locker room was eerily silent with everyone having vacated the premises. If they didn't think he was crazy before, they probably did now.

"Sorry. I don't know what came over me," Dex muttered.

Hobbs wrapped his arm around Dex's shoulder. "S'Okay."

Damn. Two sentences—sort of—in a span of five minutes. Dex cast Hobbs a wary glance. "I'm not losing my mind, am I? You spoke to me."

Hobbs nodded, a shy smile coming onto his face. He shrugged his shoulders. "We're friends. I like you."

Dex stared at him. His mouth hung open, and he quickly closed it. The last thing he wanted was to make Hobbs feel even more self-conscious. Instead, he returned Hobbs's smile. "You're right. We are friends. And I like you too, big guy. Thanks for stepping in. Security probably would have come to cart my ass away at any moment."

Hobbs frowned and shook his head. "I wouldn't have let them."

"Thanks." It was amazing how simply sitting next to Hobbs made him feel more at ease. Considering how much silence usually surrounded the guy, Dex was surprised he never felt the need to fill it. Hobbs gave off a strangely peaceful vibe. In no time, Dex felt his pulse steady and his anger subside. He looked around the now empty locker room. "Where's your best bud?" The two were usually inseparable. Calvin never went anywhere without his pal. Man, it was like everyone he knew was having relationship drama. Except for his dad, come to think of it. He couldn't even remember the last time Tony went out on a date. He wasn't one to meddle in his dad's love life, or lack thereof, but he wanted to see Tony happy. If anyone deserved it, it was his dad. Hobbs let out a heavy sigh, drawing Dex's attention.

"He went home."

"What's going on with you two?" Dex made sure the locker room was empty before bringing it up. "Come on. It's just you and me in here." He'd been concerned about his teammates since they met. From the beginning they'd seemed off their game; even Rosa had made a comment to Dex in regards to it. Months later, and they were still tiptoeing around each other.

Hobbs gave him a shrug. "Nothing."

"Don't give me that. I was there in your hospital room, remember? Playing tonsil hockey with your best bud isn't nothing. Pining and pouting and looking absolutely miserable isn't nothing."

Hobbs removed his arm from around Dex to clasp his hands together, his green eyes filled with worry. For such a big scary Therian, Hobbs was terribly sweet at times. These two really needed to get their shit together. "I'm scared."

"Of what?"

A long-suffering sigh escaped Hobbs, and Dex felt for him. "Losing him."

"Have you guys ever fought before? Like really fought?"

Hobbs let out a scoff. "Yeah."

"And he's still here isn't he?"

Hobbs nodded. He seemed to be thinking hard on

something. "But he's my best friend. He's always been my best friend. What if being together messes that up?"

"You can be lovers and best friends." Dex hoped his voice hadn't sounded as sappy as he thought it had.

"Like you and Sloane?"

Dex almost fell off the bench. "*What?*" Oh shit. Shit. Shit. Shit. What? How? *Way to play it cool, Daley.*

Hobbs rolled his eyes before poking Dex in the ribs. "We're not stupid."

"*We?* Who else knows?" And why hadn't he heard anything about it? He was always in everyone's hair, especially his teammates'. He could rattle off what Rosa had for breakfast, or the new outfit Letty had bought for her date with Dimples the Firefighter, or the last comic book movie Calvin had fanboyed over. What the hell?

Hobbs nodded. "Cal, Rosa, and Letty."

"*Shiiiit.*" And here he thought they were being super-awesome secret agents at hiding their relationship. God, this day just went from shitty to all out fucktastic. What if Sparks knew and that was why she'd pulled them from the case? What if she was using it as an excuse to break their team apart? What if she'd been typing up his transfer when he'd walked into her office? "Oh God, I think I'm gonna be sick." He doubled over, and Hobbs gently patted his back.

"No one else knows," Hobbs assured him.

"How do you know? If you guys figured it out, what's to stop anyone else from doing the same? We're surrounded by government agents. They're not stupid either, Hobbs. For all we know, they might have fucking cameras installed in their eyeballs or something."

"They don't know Sloane or you like we do. Besides, everyone's too busy with their own secrets. Nina's sleeping with Rafe."

Dex's jaw nearly became unhinged. "Holy donut holes, Batman! You can't drop shit like that on my lap!" *Holy shit.* "Your brother's sleeping with Nina? No offense, but your brother's a dick. Dare I say it? I think he's a bigger dick than Ash."

Hobbs grimaced. "You're not wrong."

"What the hell does Nina see in him?"

Hobbs shrugged. "He can be nice sometimes. He's nice to her."

"Does Hudson know? Shit, does Seb know?" Rafe never missed an opportunity to condemn Seb for getting kicked off Destructive Delta. And Hudson's reaction to Rafe's name alone, back when he'd come to visit Cael at the hospital after the Youth Center bombing, spoke volumes to the tension between the three of them. And now Hudson's partner was sleeping with the enemy. The guy definitely had a talent for rubbing people the wrong way.

Hobbs shook his head. "Nina feels bad, but she really likes Rafe. It happened during a case."

"How long has this been going on?" Dex had to give the pair credit. He chatted to Nina all the time and never once did he get even the tiniest hint she was involved with someone. Nina was friendly and playful. She teased her fellow agents and laughed with them. And Rafe... well, luckily Dex had little interaction with Rafe, but never in a million years would he have guessed the guy was sleeping with Nina. The guy was like he'd said. A dick.

"Four months."

"Fuck me. And Hudson really has no clue?"

Hobbs shook his head. "They're careful. Nina doesn't want to hurt Hudson."

This whole situation didn't bode well. Since Nina and Rafe were on different squads, there was no risk of one of them being transferred. The risk was to Nina and Hudson's personal and professional relationships, which still complicated matters. How long could she keep it a secret? At least Dex didn't have to worry about how his teammates felt about him and Sloane. They all cared about each other. They were a family. A somewhat incestuous family it would seem. And sure, they bitched, fought, and drove each other bonkers, but in the end, they looked out for one another.

Their loyalty touched Dex. None of them had brought it up or so much as dropped a clue they knew. They carried on as if nothing had changed. He wondered what other surprises the day had in store for him.

"When did you guys figure it out? About us, I mean."

Hobbs thought about it. "The first karaoke night. When you were on stage singing." He dropped his gaze to his fingers, his cheeks flushed. "The way Sloane looked at you. And his smile. He has this special smile just for you. Like you're the only one who matters."

"Really? Sloane looks at me like that?" Dex didn't know how to feel, other than stupidly, ridiculously happy. Like doing cartwheels and punching the air like one of those ridiculous training montages in the movies. He loved the way Sloane looked at him and smiled, but he'd assumed it was his partner's warmth shining through. Oh, he saw the affection, but he never thought it was a look Sloane had just for him.

"Yeah. Like you're the most amazing thing he's ever seen."

Dex gave Hobbs a playful nudge. "You mean like how Cal looks at you?" The blush on Hobbs's cheeks deepened, and Dex found himself chuckling. "Yeah, just what I thought. You've thought about it a lot, haven't you? Of being more than friends."

"Every day."

"Man, what is it with you Felid Therians? You can face down an army of feral Therians and not bat an eyelash, but a cute boy tells you he likes you, and you're running for the hills like someone set your tails on fire."

"I'm not running," Hobbs mumbled.

"Wow. So convincing." He hated seeing the big guy so torn. Standing, he gave Hobbs a hearty pat on the back. "Come on. Let's chat over a bagel and coffee." Maybe he couldn't meddle in his brother's relationship, but he could certainly meddle in his other teammates'.

As they walked through Unit Alpha toward the elevator, Dex considered Calvin and Hobbs's situation. The problem was most certainly on Hobbs's end. Calvin had put himself out there plenty of times. He'd made the first move at the hospital by kissing Hobbs. In usual Felid fashion, Hobbs reacted like a deer caught in headlights each and every time. Though he had returned Calvin's kiss, so there was clearly something strong at work under all the fear and hesitation. Like most large Felids Dex knew, Hobbs was kind of crap at communicating his feelings, which wasn't exactly a surprise considering the guy barely spoke. But he'd never had a problem talking to Calvin, who was the only one capable of confronting Hobbs, purposefully pissing him off, and pushing his buttons. Their deep friendship spoke volumes, so it was understandable the guy would be hesitant.

Stepping into the elevator, Dex gave Hobbs a reassuring pat on the arm. "Don't worry, big guy. We'll figure this out." He only wished he could say the same about his own situation.

Beck Hogan was royally pissed off.

He sat on a dusty, beat-up armchair in the middle of a dimly lit, shitty, derelict schoolhouse listening to what remained of his organization spouting off a bunch of useless intel and piss-poor excuses.

"It's like they have nine lives or something," one of them muttered.

Hogan stood, marched over, snatched a fistful of the guy's shirt, and lifted him off his feet with a snarl. "Are you fucking kidding me? They don't have nine lives, you stupid shit! They have one life. One life you can't seem to put an end to." He shoved the guy away from him and paced in front of the dozen Therians lounging on the dusty floorboards. The more he thought about it, the more pissed off he got. They'd had the bastard right in front of them.

"Yeah, but it's not our fault Keeler survived," someone else added. "The guy was bleeding all over the fucking place."

"Yeah," another member piped up. "And how the hell were we supposed to know Brodie would be the one to go out to Keeler's car?"

"I can't believe Brodie survived," someone else muttered, the others murmuring their agreement.

"Christ." Hogan rounded on them. "Do you all realize what fucking amateurs we look like? First, we let Reyes slip through our fucking fingers, then those THIRDS bastards. Three times!"

Drew Collins—the only one who seemed to have any brains—came to stand beside him. At least he had someone at his side he could count on. It was disgusting and humiliating how his once fierce group of freedom fighters had been reduced to a few reliable Therians and a bunch of brainless thugs. Damn it. He'd told Merritt not to take their best Therians to the exchange with the THIRDS, but Merritt had been confident. Now his friend was dead, the best of his crew were behind bars, and he was left with the rabble.

"Hey, you have to keep in mind Brodie and Keeler have been doing this shit for years. Plus they're Alpha Therians. Felid Therians."

"And traitors to their species," Hogan spat out. "Working with those Human pieces of shit." Hogan shook his head. How could their own brethren turn on them? Working with Humans to cage their own kind in the back of a truck? It was unforgiveable. Humans were beneath them. Therians were the next step in evolution. *Genetic mistake my ass.* It explained why Humans were so damn scared of Therians. Why they forced them to get marked like cattle and passed laws to keep them from shifting when they pleased. It was in their nature to be free. To let loose the wild beasts inside them. Humans were weak, and they knew it. One calculated swipe of his claw, and a Human wouldn't stand a chance.

Hogan resumed his seat. If it weren't for the THIRDS, no one could stop Therians from taking their rightful place as the dominant species. As much as he hated to admit it, the THIRDS were winning. Not only did they have military-grade weaponry, but agents like Brodie and Keeler posed the biggest problems. From what he remembered, there was a tiger Therian on the team as well. Fucking great.

"So what are we going to do?" someone asked.

"We've crippled Destructive Delta," Collins said, coming to take a seat on Hogan's armrest. "Without their two strongest members, they're left with the tiger Therian and three Human agents."

"Four," someone piped up. "The female partnered with the twink cheetah Therian."

Hogan sat up. "What did you say?"

"The uh, the cheetah Therian. The one Keeler insisted wasn't his boyfriend."

Hogan's smile grew wide. "The one he took a bullet for." Hogan looked up at Collins, feeling his resolve strengthening. "Merritt said something about the kid having a brother. Wasn't he the guy Stone knocked out and brought back to the base? Keeler refused to let Merritt even go near him. What was the guy's name?"

"Hold on a sec." Collins reached into his pocket and drew out a small tablet. A few taps later, and he had his information. "Dexter J. Daley. Brodie's Human partner."

"So we have two Alpha members of the team recuperating from injuries and vulnerable, both tied to these brothers." Hogan sat quietly thinking while everyone observed in silence. Attacking Keeler and Brodie head-on would be stupid. Vulnerable didn't mean accessible. The THIRDS were expecting Hogan and his crew to make a move. They were watching the streets and most likely their recovering agents. Keeler would be on alert after the second attempt on his life.

Collins interrupted the silence with his concerns. "With Keeler and Brodie out of commission, we're likely to be facing a new team and I imagine backup. There's no way the THIRDS would send four Human agents after us. The cheetah Therian wouldn't last. Besides, he's Recon. What are you thinking?"

Hogan drummed his fingers on the chair's armrest as he thought. "Have some of the guys keep an eye on the brothers. I want two guys on Brodie and another two on Keeler. Don't approach them, watch them. I need time to come up with a plan. I want everyone else looking for those Westward Creed assholes. And remember, I want them brought to me alive. I'll deal with them personally."

Collins gave him a nod and rounded everyone up, issuing orders and leaving Hogan in blissful silence. They had to find those Westward Creed bastards first, and if any THIRDS agents got in their way, they'd deal with them. Then he'd come up with a way to make that son of a bitch Keeler pay. The guy had pretended to care for their cause only to betray them. His act had been good. They'd all fallen for it. Having an agent like Keeler on their side would have taken them to a whole new level. Now look where they were. Keeler had gotten Merritt killed, their men imprisoned, and then the prick had the audacity not to fucking die when he was supposed to.

Hogan wasn't stupid. Even if they managed to find those Westward Creed assholes and make them pay, they wouldn't make it out of this city alive. There was no way in hell he was going to prison. He'd made peace with his decision. What the hell did he have left to lose anyway? The Humans had taken everything from him. But if he was going down, he was going to take some of those THIRDS bastards with him. He'd do more than make Keeler bleed. He was going to destroy him. And he had an idea how he could do it.

THREE

Sloane had been moved into a private room with simple but modern décor. It had a great panoramic view of the East River and Manhattan skyline from its two huge floor-to-ceiling windows. The room was mostly white with a few wood accents. A dark gray armchair sat in front of the window at the far end, a matching sleeper sofa was positioned in front of the second window, and between them sat a small, round, white table with two gray chairs. The room had free Wi-Fi and a flat-screen TV, a private bathroom with shower, and meal service. They were nice digs, but Dex was glad it wasn't a long-term setup.

His partner still looked banged up, but at least the color had returned to his cheeks. The cuts and scrapes were healing, as were the bruises. Dex closed the door behind him and left his shoes on the mat to one side before walking over to Sloane's bed. He placed the insulated lunch bag on the small bedside table.

"Hey, sexy pants. What have you been up to today?"

Sloane turned his attention away from the TV and smiled at him. It was amazing how one little smile could disarm him. "Watching Indiana Jones and eating chocolate pudding."

"The high life, huh?"

Sloane chuckled. His gaze landed on the lunch bag. "Are those what I think they are?"

"Yep. Rosa made you your favorite empanadas." Dex tried not to laugh at the way his partner's eyes lit up. Like a little kid who'd been told he could order whatever he wanted from the ice cream parlor. Dex hardly blamed the guy. Rosa was an amazing cook, and she loved to feed their team. Between Rosa's Puerto Rican food, Letty's Cuban food, and Lou's Dominican food, it was amazing their team fit in the BearCat.

"Meat?"

"Yep, plus a couple of guavas, some chicken, and beef with sweet plantains."

"Oh God, those are *so* good."

It was amusing how even the most steadfast of health nuts had their vices. Dex leaned over to give Sloane's lips a kiss. "How are you feeling?" Sloane had no idea how much his smile affected Dex. Hobbs had been right. Dex never saw Sloane give that smile to anyone else.

"Better, now that you're here."

Dex was caught off guard by the affectionate admission. "Aw, painkillers be making you sappy," he teased. "I like it." He kissed Sloane again, loving the taste of him.

"Mm, I like that," Sloane murmured against Dex's lips.

"Yeah?"

"Yeah. Come 'ere." Sloane carefully shifted over and patted the bed. Good thing it was Therian-sized. Dex was happy to oblige. He removed his leather jacket and draped it across the side table, followed by the off-duty holster attached to his belt securing his Glock, and his badge clipped beside it. He didn't want to unintentionally hurt Sloane. Soon as he was done, he climbed up with care and huddled close to Sloane, resting his hand on his partner's chest. Sloane's larger hand promptly covered Dex's, making him smile. It also made him think of how close he'd come to losing this.

"God, Sloane, when I saw you lying there... I thought—" Dex closed his eyes. He'd known there were risks, but he hadn't expected his resolve to be put to the test so early on in their relationship. He felt Sloane's hand on his cheek, and Dex leaned into the warmth, not quite ready to open his eyes yet. He inhaled deeply and let it out slowly. Man, he was such a goner.

"Listen to me. I'm glad it was me."

Dex shifted so he could look up at Sloane, and the intensity he saw in his partner's eyes amazed him. "How can you say that? Look at you. You were almost killed."

"If it had been you, Dex, you would have been killed. The only reason I survived is because I'm a Therian. An explosion of that magnitude would have killed any Human who'd been as close to it as I was."

"So because you're a Therian, you should automatically be the one to risk your life every time? *I* had the keys. I was the one who was supposed to have gone out there."

"And for whatever reason, I decided to go instead, and I'm thankful for it." Sloane was serious. There was also something else in his eyes. Something Dex wanted to know more about but knew now was not the time. Seeming to sense this, Sloane cleared his throat and averted his gaze. "How's Ash taking it?"

"Man..." Dex sighed. Where did he even start?

Sloane groaned. "What did he do now?"

"You know, when I think I've got him figured out, he does something that completely screws with my head."

"Dex."

Sloane was going to be so pissed at him. Maybe. Dex gave his sweetest smile, but it only earned him a frown. Yep, definitely gonna get pissed. Might as well get it over with.

"He most likely saved my life," Dex said quietly, watching Sloane's eyebrows draw together.

"I don't understand. What happened?"

Deep breath. "When I heard the explosion, all I could think about was you. I ran outside, not thinking the threat might still be out there. We were shot at."

Sloane let his head fall back onto the pillow. "Jesus, Dex. You could have gotten yourself killed! After all the training we've done? After everything we've talked about, you run right into the line of fire without any regard for your safety whatsoever?" He turned his head to glare at Dex. "You're lucky I'm too damn grateful you're here to beat the shit out of you. Also, I can't right now."

"I know. I fucked up. I'm sorry."

Sloane narrowed his eyes. "You best put that lip away because pouting is not getting you out of this one."

"I wasn't pouting," Dex mumbled.

"Yes, you were. I know when you're pouting even when you don't. Now, tell me everything." Sloane gave him a squeeze, which Dex guessed meant he'd been forgiven, though Sloane wasn't likely to forget it. Jaguar Therians never forget. Dex was pretty sure it would conveniently cross his partner's mind during a training session, and Dex would get his ass kicked for it.

"Ash knocked me to the ground. He tore his stitches to keep me safe from the shooters. I kept trying to get away from him to get to you, but he wouldn't let me."

"What about the shooters?"

"Ash said they were in a black van and long gone before emergency services arrived."

Sloane pressed his lips together, meaning he was trying his best to remain calm.

"I swear it won't happen again."

"Damn right it won't. You..." he trailed off and sighed, his gaze going to the ceiling. Sloane pulled Dex closer against him. "I'm glad you're okay." When Dex didn't reply, Sloane glanced over at him. "You are okay, aren't you?"

"Yeah. I was thinking..."

"You really need to stop doing that thinking thing," Sloane muttered, the corner of his mouth twitching with its desire to smile.

"Dick. Anyway, I was thinking you should stay with me while you recover." He was hardly about to tell Sloane his dad and everyone else had sort of already decided for him. But from everyone else's standpoint, it was a tactical move. From Dex's, it was a personal one. He wanted Sloane with him. If he explained all the logical reasons why it would be a good idea, he had no doubt Sloane would agree, but Dex didn't want those reasons to be why his partner accepted.

Sloane stared at him. "But that'll take weeks. Maybe longer."

"It doesn't matter how long it takes." Dex leaned in and kissed Sloane, his thumb stroking Sloane's jaw. "Let me take care of you. Not because you can't look after yourself but because I want to help."

Sloane closed his eyes, and Dex waited. It wasn't an easy decision for his partner, especially since it would feel like they were living together. Dex was always the one to make the first move, to nudge Sloane in the direction Dex wanted their relationship to go. He didn't want to keep pushing. A part of him feared he'd push Sloane too far, and the guy would turn and run like he'd done before. Each time was more painful than the last, and although Sloane always came home, Dex's heart couldn't take it. He'd told Sloane as much. If Sloane needed space, all he had to do was ask, and Dex would be happy to give it, but there was always the worry their relationship would reach a point Sloane wasn't willing to go beyond. After what seemed like forever, Sloane spoke up.

"I need to know something first."

Dex's pulse quickened. "Okay."

"Are you going to wear one of those sexy male nurse's uniforms, the white latex ones with the assless chaps?"

Dex let out a bark of laughter. "Oh my God, I can't believe you remembered."

"Of course I remember," Sloane said with a wink. "I told you. I remember everything."

"Then you'll also recall you didn't wear one for me."

"True," Sloane admitted, "but white latex wouldn't look good on me. I'm more of a black leather type of guy."

Dex's mouth dropped open. "Dude, we can't have sex for like ages, and you're putting all these naughty images in my head."

"I'm not putting anything in your head. I was commenting. Now on you, I think it would be a different story." He ran his hand from Dex's chest down to his thigh.

That *really* wasn't helping the no-sex situation, but he left Sloane's hand resting on his thigh regardless. "You honestly want me to wear white latex assless chaps?"

Sloane's cheeks flushed and he shrugged. "I'm not saying you should, just that I wouldn't mind if you did."

"Uh-huh." Dex held back a smile. He knew his partner had a bit of a kinky side. Not that he was complaining. He loved it when Sloane got all bossy in the bedroom or talked dirty to him. Now he had sinful images of Sloane dressed in leather in his head. Guess he knew what he'd be thinking about in the shower later. Sloane dressed in nothing but a pair of tight black leather pants with maybe some straps around his beefy biceps. Oh yeah. He needed to get off this train of thought before he ended up poking his partner with a different part of his equipment. "We'll see. So, will you stay with me and let me nurse you back to health?"

Sloane's expression turned serious, and he removed his hand from Dex's leg. "I have some terms and conditions."

"All right. Lay them on me." Dex braced himself. He half expected Sloane to whip out a monocle and unfurl a list of rules long enough to reach the end of the room.

"I control the music."

Dex gasped. He might have whimpered a little too. "Does that mean no *Retro Radio*?"

"I wouldn't dream of it. It means I'll decide when and how often we tune in to *Retro Radio*. I would rather give up my left testicle than sit through another one of their Musicians with Mullets marathons."

Dex let out a snicker. "You were so ready to lose your shit."

Sloane smiled pleasantly and *booped* the end of Dex's nose. "And that's how serial killers are made."

"Okay," Dex said with a laugh. "Okay. No mullet music marathons. Anything else?"

Sloane grinned widely. "You bet your cute little ass. I'll give you my list of demands after I've settled in."

"Hold up. So I have to accept the terms and conditions without knowing what they are first?" So not fair! And pure *genius*. Why the hell hadn't Dex thought of that?

"Yep."

"Are you going to make me regret asking?"

"Quite possibly."

Dex eyed him suspiciously before pretending to think about it. "Fine. It's a deal."

"Good." Sloane let out a yawn, his eyelids growing heavy. "You'll need to pick up some clothes and toiletries for me at my apartment."

"No prob. I'll drop by on the way home."

Sloane let out another yawn. "Can you pick up my mail?"

"Sure thing." Dex gave his cheek a kiss, earning himself a contented smile. It was most likely the meds putting Sloane in such a sappy mood. Dex might as well enjoy it. He ran his fingers through his partner's hair. It was starting to grow long again after he'd been forced to get it cut, thanks to Tony finally carrying through with one of his famous "get it cut before I cut it for you" threats. Poor Sloane. It had been a traumatizing experience for his Felid Therian partner. Sloane hummed and turned his head toward Dex. When he opened his eyes, he looked uncertain.

"You really want me to stay with you? I mean, you'll have enough to deal with at work without having to worry about me."

Shit. Work. For a moment, Dex had forgotten about work and the case. The case he'd been pulled from. He leaned in to kiss Sloane, being gentle while at the same time trying to show Sloane how glad he was they were together. Sloane placed a hand to Dex's cheek, his thumb stroking softly, and a lump formed in Dex's throat. He smiled up at his partner, a guy who was quickly taking over his world. How could Dex tell Sloane their team was no longer out there searching for the bastard who'd done this to him?

Dex kissed Sloane once more before carefully getting

off the bed. "I'm sure. I'd worry if you *weren't* there." He clipped his holster back into place, along with his badge, before he picked up his jacket.

"You're leaving?"

Sloane's pout was adorable, and Dex was tempted to hang around longer, but he wanted to pick up a few things before taking his partner home. "Yeah, I'm going to stop by your apartment and finish a couple of reports. I'll be back tonight. Call me if you need anything, okay?"

Sloane nodded with a yawn. "Okay."

Dex was about to head out when his phone rang. Distracted by Sloane's sweet face as he wrinkled his nose at something he saw on TV, Dex answered without checking the caller ID.

"Daley here."

A PR agent rattled off excitedly about all the possibilities for their upcoming brainstorming session and a host of dates he could come in, plus a load of other words Dex wasn't quick enough to make sense of. The PR department was either on a constant caffeine high or crack. Nothing else could explain the earsplitting grins or unrelenting excitement.

"Yep, okay, sure. Pencil me in whenever. Okay. Send it to my diary. I'm looking forward to it as well," he forced out before hanging up. Sloane gave him a questioning look as Dex returned his phone to his pocket before walking over to the window and knocking on it.

"What are you doing?" Sloane asked.

"I'm wondering if this is bulletproof."

"Why?"

"Because I want to know if I can shoot my way through it before trying to jump out." He turned to the couch and pointed to it. "Do you think if I dramatically throw myself onto this like one of those old Hollywood starlets it'll have the same effect? I feel like I need to have some kind of bitch fit right now."

Sloane's throaty chuckle relieved some of Dex's frustration, but he still wanted to break something.

"Let me guess? PR?"

Dex nodded and headed back to his partner. "Seriously. When did I become the poster boy for the THIRDS?"

"You said it yourself. It's hard to resist all that Daley charm." Sloane's grin grew wicked. "They clearly got swept up in the gravitational pull of your awesome."

"You really need to stop remembering everything I say."

"And miss the opportunity to one up you? Never."

Dex's phone pinged, but he refused to look at it.

"Guess they penciled you in," Sloane teased.

Dex kissed Sloane and *booped* his nose. "And that's how serial killers are made." With one last lingering kiss, Dex reluctantly left his partner to his movies and empanadas. He couldn't keep his dopey smile back. Sloane had agreed to stay with him, and he'd done so without freaking out about it first. Maybe he was finally settling into the idea of them. Dex tried not to get too excited. It wasn't as if they didn't spend a lot of time together. They worked together, and Sloane slept over at Dex's more often than he did at his own place. But this was different. Sloane's injuries would keep him from coming and going as he pleased.

The longer Dex spent with Sloane, the more he came to understand his jaguar Therian partner. Therians were far more complex than Humans, and Humans were difficult enough as it was. Not only did you have to get to know their Human side, but their Therian one. As a jaguar Therian, Sloane's instincts demanded freedom. Dex had learned that the hard way. His partner's need for space wasn't so much because he wanted it, but because he simply needed to know the option was there. He needed to know he was not caged in.

On the drive to Sloane's apartment, Dex listened to his favorite station, *Retro Radio*. He smiled when Journey came on. It was stupid, but he always thought of Sloane now when he heard the band's music. He had a feeling Sloane wasn't as put off by it as he pretended he was. As Dex drove, he sang along and tapped his fingers on the steering wheel, letting the music seep down into his bones. He always felt relaxed after listening to his '80s music.

Luck was on his side. He found a parking spot on Sloane's street not far from the High Line. He climbed out of his Challenger and set the alarm before heading for the large brick-and-steel building. No wonder his dad didn't want Sloane staying here on his own. With all the busy streets surrounding it, the connecting buildings, all the foot traffic, shops, and the High Line running alongside it, there were plenty of places for a perp to hide.

There were also far too many ways in and out of the building and too many glass panels and windows for Dex's liking. It was a new modern-style building. Simple and elegant. Two sets of metal stairs led to a small foyer with one elevator and another outside set of stairs led up to the High Line. If Hogan did decide to strike, Sloane would be a sitting duck. For all of Sloane's Therian strength, his injuries would make him no match for a healthy tiger Therian like Hogan.

Dex took the empty elevator up to the seventh floor, making sure to remain observant every step of the way. The hallway was empty and brightly lit thanks to the daylight coming in through the floor-to-ceiling window at the end. Using the key Sloane had given him for his birthday, Dex let himself into the apartment. He quietly closed the door behind him and stood there for a moment, listening. He was met with nothing but silence. Leaving his Chucks by the door, he headed upstairs to the bedroom. Everything appeared to be where it should be. Once upstairs, his gaze immediately landed on the dresser's top right-hand drawer that contained Dex's clothes. It had been the best birthday present he'd ever received. Well, the My Pet Monster his dad had given him for his sixth birthday came pretty close. He remembered nearly wetting himself in his Ninja Turtle footie pajamas out of sheer excitement. The memory made him chuckle. Poor Cael. He'd been absolutely terrified of the furry blue thing.

Standing in the middle of the elegant black, gray, and white patterned room, Dex decided he should probably find a bag or suitcase or something. Opening Sloane's closet, he let out a shriek and jumped back, his hand flying to his chest. At first, he thought someone had been hiding in there. Good to know his initial reaction to a possible intruder was to scream like a five-year-old. Man, he needed to get his shit together. He would've been annoyed with himself if he hadn't realized what had scared the hell out of him. Reaching in, he pulled out a life-sized cardboard cutout of Han Solo. "Damn." His boyfriend was a bigger nerd than Dex had given him credit for. Sloane was so never going to hear the end of this one. Dex planted Han to one side, snickering as he rummaged through the closet for a bag or something he could carry Sloane's clothes in. He found a medium-sized travel suitcase shoved in one corner.

"Perfect." He dropped it onto the bed and opened it before heading to Sloane's dresser. Dex went for the softest and most comfortable clothing he could find, which consisted of a variety of sweatpants, pajama bottoms, and T-shirts. When he finished there, he grabbed some jeans and cardigans just in case. He'd be dropping by to check on Sloane's apartment anyway, so he could always come back to pick up anything he might have forgotten.

After grabbing Sloane's toiletry bag from the bathroom, along with his toothbrush, Dex stopped again to think. Had he left anything out? Shoes. He went back to the closet and had picked up a pair of Sloane's biker boots when he noticed a shoebox with a furry black tail poking out of it. Inside he found the stuffed toy jaguar with its paws still bandaged. Sloane's little pal from his time at the facility. He couldn't blame Sloane for not being able to get rid of it. As determined as his partner was to leave his past behind, this toy had been the only comfort Sloane had before meeting Ash. A lump formed in Dex's throat at the thought.

Sloane refused to tell Dex what he'd suffered at the facility, believing nothing good would come of it. How the knowledge of what they'd done to him would only hurt Dex. The past couldn't be changed. Sloane was protecting him, and Dex appreciated the thought, but a part of him still wished he knew. It was a piece of Sloane he'd never get to understand.

Dex remembered the research facility all too well. He remembered being strapped to a chair in the cold lab surrounded by strange machines. He'd been scared. Who wouldn't be? He could imagine Sloane there in his place. Except Sloane had been just a little kid at the time. They'd experimented on him. Poked. Prodded. Caused him pain. All in the name of science. They'd discovered life-altering information and saved countless Therians at the cost of Therian children. How many like Sloane hadn't survived? He'd been through so much, yet he continued to push forward. Dex admired his partner's fortitude most of all. And now Sloane needed him.

How could they expect him to sit around and do nothing while Hogan got away with hurting Sloane? While that asshole threatened those he cared about? But if he went after Hogan on his own, he would be in deep shit with Sparks. Sloane might have let him off the hook for disobeying orders back during the Therian Youth Center bombing, but he doubted Sparks would be so forgiving. Since the incident, the only thoughts occupying his mind had been of Sloane. Now that Sloane was recovering, other thoughts started to creep in. The anger he'd felt toward Hogan during the explosion stirred inside him once more, while a darkness he hadn't known he possessed threatened to seep into his every pore.

He sat there holding on to the stuffed toy, its shiny amber eyes rousing emotions inside him. Emotions he shouldn't pursue if he knew what was good for him. After returning the toy back to its shoebox, he placed Han back in the closet and closed the door. He finished packing Sloane's suitcase and went downstairs. Whatever dark thoughts were trying to plow their way into his head, they had to stop. Who knew where that path would lead? Besides, he wasn't a detective anymore. Going off on his own, especially when he was off duty, would be unacceptable. Instead he concentrated on what he could do to make Sloane comfortable at home. As he put his shoes on, he made a mental shopping list. He locked up behind him and headed for his car where he popped the trunk. Something felt... off. He slipped the suitcase in and paused. It was like he was being watched.

Having always trusted his instincts, Dex closed the trunk and removed his cell phone from his pocket. He pretended to send a text, using his phone's adjustable camera to zoom in and discreetly look around. It could be his overactive imagination, but Dex had never ignored his gut before. He wasn't about to start now. A Therian stood on the High Line a few feet from Sloane's apartment. He was leaning against the rail among the potted flowers and plants with a newspaper in his hand. It wasn't typically the sort of behavior to bring up any red flags. At this time of the day, joggers, tourists, students, or folks out for a stroll could be found on the High Line, though Dex doubted this guy was out for a stroll. Not with the way he kept glancing up from his newspaper to Sloane's apartment building right about where Sloane's living room window was.

As Dex looked up, their eyes met, and the guy took off. Shit. Definitely not out for a late-afternoon stroll. Dex shoved his phone into his pocket and raced back to Sloane's apartment, taking the stairs two at a time to get up to the wooden deck of the High Line. He bolted out onto the platform and immediately spotted the guy speeding down the underpass of the building next door. Dex gave chase, running as fast as he could while doing his best to avoid any foot traffic. As he closed some of the distance between them, he passed rows of small round tables lined up along either side of the High Line. Citizens chatting and eating currently occupied a couple of the accompanying chairs. Before Dex reached the last table, the asshole he was chasing grabbed it and tossed it in Dex's direction like he was throwing a discus.

"Shit!" Dex hit the boards as the aluminum table whizzed over him, grazing his hair. It landed with a clattering bounce somewhere behind him. *Son of a bitch.* Assault on an agent. Dickbag was going down. Jumping to his feet, Dex took off after the guy, emerging on the other side of the underpass and heading for the High Line's sundeck. Thank God the guy wasn't a cheetah Therian, though he was still fast as hell, and Dex found his lungs burning as he pushed himself to catch up.

"THIRDS! Stop! I'm ordering you to stop!"

"Fuck you!"

Okay.

The Therian headed for the handrail, and Dex knew he was going to jump it. On the other side, a set of stairs went down to street level. He couldn't let the guy make it to the street. Giving it everything he had, he sped up and launched himself at the guy. Both of them hit the boards hard, the large Therian landing on Dex and knocking the wind out of him. Fuck. Why did these guys have to be so damn heavy? The guy rolled off Dex, hissing as he pulled back a fist, but Dex had already swiped his Glock from its holster. He aimed it at the Therian perp whose fist came to an abrupt halt.

"That's right. Now back the fuck up. Slowly," Dex ordered. He breathed in deeply through his nose, letting it out slowly through his mouth as he tried to steady his breath. He kept his gaze on the Therian as he got to his feet. The mark on his neck stated he was a Leopard Therian. Comfortable with heights, water, agile, and astoundingly strong. Duly noted.

"What were you doing outside Agent Brodie's apartment?" Dex asked, taking a step back, the hold on his gun unwavering.

"I was just out for an evening stroll. Reading the paper. That's not a crime now is it?"

"No, it's not. But trying to blow someone up is." Dex cocked his gun. "Your boss tried to kill my teammate. Twice. Instead, he sent my partner to the hospital."

The bastard grinned at him, fangs bared. "Maybe your

partner should have minded his own business. What's that Human saying? Curiosity killed the cat? Well, nearly."

Dex aimed low and fired.

With a howl, followed by a litany of curses, the Therian dropped to the boards clutching his leg. He gaped up at Dex. "You shot me? What the fuck!"

"It's only a flesh wound. It won't even need surgery." Dex moved his gun to the other leg. "This one might. Now, I asked you a question. What were you doing outside Agent Brodie's apartment?"

A female's shriek pierced the air, and Dex cursed under his breath. He held his gun in both hands as he backed up and circled the Therian on the floor so he could keep an eye on him and see what the hell was going on. In the shadows of the underpass, a cougar in his Therian form was clawing at a Human jogger. The asshole must have been hiding in the thick greenery. The jogger balanced precariously on the small table screaming for help, her pant leg shredded and leg bloodied.

"What'll it be, Agent Daley? Bring me in or preserve civilian life. That's your number one directive isn't it? Preserve civilian life?"

Another scream, and Dex let out a frustrated growl. Fuck. Not only did he not have any zip ties with him —*fucking genius, Dex*—but he didn't have time to come up with an alternative other than shooting the guy. How the hell was he going to explain himself? He took off toward the cougar Therian in time to watch in horror as it swiped at the woman's leg, sank in its claws, and jerked her off the table. She shrieked, bringing the table and chairs clamoring down with her. The cougar Therian hissed and roared as the woman flailed, unable to get away due to the slippery pool of blood beneath her.

"THIRDS! Stop!" Dex shouted as he fired a round, hitting the cougar Therian in the shoulder. It let out an ear-piercing cry before it released the jogger and leapt over the High Line banister. Dex's priority was to neutralize the threat and prevent any loss of life. He ran to the banister and leaned over to find the cougar Therian long gone. Knowing he'd never catch up to it, he rushed back to the jogger, securing his Glock back in his holster as he kneeled beside her.

"Hey, it's okay. Look at me." Dex called out for help over his shoulder, grateful when a couple nearby rushed to their aid. He instructed for them to call emergency services and quickly removed his jacket while reassuring the injured woman. His gaze darted over to where he'd left the first asshole he'd shot, but as Dex expected, the guy was gone. Remembering he was wearing an undershirt, he pulled off his long-sleeved T-shirt, wadded it up, and pressed it to the woman's leg. He held it down tightly, talking to her and distracting her, even managing to make her smile while they waited for the paramedics to arrive. A few minutes later, and the medics were carrying the woman away. He thanked the couple who'd helped and thanked the EMTs for the sterilizing hand wipes. What a damned mess. A large figure headed for him and Dex cursed under his breath.

"Dex? What are you doing here?" Seb frowned as he approached.

"I came to pick up some stuff for Sloane." Dex pointed at Sloane's apartment a few feet away. "Sarge suggested he stay at mine while he recovers."

"Right." Seb seemed to relax some, but he still had on his "on the job" face. "So what happened?"

The wheels in Dex's head spun at Mach speed. If he told Seb he'd come up here suspecting someone was staking out Sloane's apartment or anything having to do with the Coalition, Seb would think Dex was going behind his back. Which he technically sort of was. Then Seb would start keeping tabs on him, and Dex didn't need the grief. He went through the recent events in his head. Had there been any witnesses during the first shooting? He hadn't seen any. Not until the jogger came along and everything went to hell. It was a long shot.

"I'd just put Sloane's suitcase in my trunk when I realized I'd forgotten to pick up his mail." Which he now realized he had. Stick to the truth as much as possible. "I was on my way up when I heard a woman screaming. When I ran out here, a cougar Therian was attacking her. I managed to get a shot off. Hit him in the shoulder. He leapt over the handrail and made it to the street. Lost him after that."

Seb nodded, his expression giving nothing of his thoughts away. "You mind giving your statement?"

"No, of course not." Dex waited as Seb removed his tablet. He repeated everything he'd told Seb, answered questions, keeping his statement as concise as possible. It only took a few minutes, with Seb giving him a smile at the end and telling him it was a good thing he was in the area. As a THIRDS agent, Seb would clearly question every word out of Dex's mouth. The guy was probably wondering if the attack had truly been random or just a coincidence. Whatever Seb's thoughts on the matter, he wasn't sharing them with Dex, and it was probably better that way. They exchanged some pleasantries before Seb told Dex to have a good night and walked off.

Dex headed back toward Sloane's apartment, picked up his mail, and made for his car, his mind going over the encounter. The bastard had called him by his name. There was no doubt in his mind he was one of Hogan's crew. So was the cougar Therian. He'd attacked the jogger so his friend could escape. These assholes had to be stopped. Once he was sitting behind the wheel, he pulled out his smartphone. There was no way in hell he was letting this go. He flipped through his screen until he found the contact he needed.

A tap and two rings later, he heard a familiar voice answer. "Yes?"

Dex had made his decision.

"We need to meet."

FOUR

RECOVERY WAS GOING to be a bitch.

Sloane looked forward to spending time with Dex, but he had some niggling doubts. He'd never had anyone to take care of him. Not since he and Ash were kids back at the research facility. What if they drove each other crazy—more than they already did? Sloane was cranky at the best of times without throwing his current condition into the mix. Not being able to do things for himself would frustrate him after a while. He was certain of it. Part of him worried if they spent too much time together it would expose cracks in their relationship they might not otherwise have noticed.

Why the hell was he even worrying about this? It wasn't like they were moving in together. Jesus, he'd almost died, and he was worrying about spending a few weeks at his partner's house? Besides, he spent more time at Dex's than he did at his own apartment anyway. It was thoughtful of Dex to ask. His house was bigger and more maneuverable than Sloane's apartment. Dex also had a sofa bed in the living room. It would save Sloane from having to sleep on his own couch, which didn't have that option. He'd already read through the home-recovery pack the doctor had given him, and it strictly advised against any active work that might impede his healing. At least for the first couple of weeks. He was limited to how many stairs he could climb, how long he could walk, and what housework he could do. Definitely no driving. He let out a heavy sigh. Maybe this would be good for them.

An image of Dex and his dopey smile came to his mind, and Sloane found himself following suit. His gut clenched when he thought about how close he'd come to losing Dex. He'd tried hard not to think about it. He meant what he'd said about being grateful he'd been the one to go out there. It was bad enough they faced danger on the job, but for some asshole to come at them so close to home? Now Dex was going to be out there without him. Maybe he should contact Maddock. Make sure he assigned Dex a partner they could trust to watch Dex's back. He didn't like the idea of leaving his partner's safety in anyone else's hands. As soon as he was back to his old self, Sloane was going to put his partner through the training of his life. Idiot. He couldn't believe Dex had run out there into the middle of God knew what without assessing the situation.

"Are you decent?" Ash's voice snapped him out of his thoughts.

Sloane smiled broadly at his friend. "Hey." He'd been wondering when Ash would be coming around. It wasn't because his best friend didn't care. No one understood better than Sloane how difficult this was. The guilt was written all over Ash's face.

"You look like shit," Ash grumbled, causing Sloane to chuckle.

"It's good to see you too, bud."

Ash came to linger beside his bed, his hands shoved

into his jacket pockets and his gaze everywhere but on Sloane. "I wanted to come sooner, but..." He swallowed hard, and Sloane reached out to take hold of his wrist, getting his attention. Why did Ash insist on beating himself up for situations out of his control? His shoulders slumped, and he let out a resigned sigh. "I'm sorry, Sloane."

"Don't. That asshole could have targeted anyone of us. Come on." Sloane motioned toward the chair beside the bed. "Talk to me." After some hesitation, Ash took a seat.

"But he didn't target anyone. He targeted me. Son of a bitch tried to kill me twice," Ash growled.

"Because you were doing your job. You risked a hell of a lot to infiltrate the Coalition. Their organization crumbled because of you."

Ash didn't look convinced. "Except for Hogan and his band of merry morons, which are still out there."

"Which reminds me. I need you to do something for me." Sloane had been giving it a lot of thought since Dex had left for Sloane's apartment to pick up his things. In the year they'd been partners, Sloane had learned a lot about Dex. It hadn't been difficult. Dex wore his heart on his sleeve. Most of the time, he was easy to get a read on. Dex didn't play mind games, and Sloane appreciated that. He also knew his partner was headstrong, and when he set his mind to something, nothing was going to deter him. Most of all, Dex was fiercely loyal. Sloane had no doubt what was on his partner's mind.

"Anything."

Sloane braced himself as he answered, "Stay close to Dex."

"Anything but that."

Sloane couldn't help his smile. He knew Ash would do

it anyway. It reminded him of what he'd done for Dex. "Thank you."

"For what?"

"For keeping him safe for me." Sloane sat back, his gaze directed out the huge window across from him overlooking the Manhattan skyline. "When he told me what happened, I was so pissed off at him. All I could think about was what if I'd woken up to find he'd been shot and killed while trying to get to me?" The thought still twisted his insides, and he had to pause and take a deep breath.

Ash gave his arm a pat, and Sloane turned his head to see the concerned look on his friend's face. "You okay?"

Damn it. Maybe it was time for a nap. "Yeah. I think the meds are messing with me," Sloane muttered. Why was he having so much trouble with this? It had to be the meds making him hypersensitive. These drugs always had some kind of side effect, and being a Therian didn't make him immune to them, especially when they were so-called Therian-strength. God only knew what that meant.

"The meds, huh?"

Was that amusement he heard in Ash's voice? Sloane scowled at him. "What?"

Ash sat back with a scoff. "Come on, man. You're crazy about him."

The words caused an unexpected flutter in Sloane's pulse. His face felt hot. Was it getting hot in here? "I'll admit I care about him a lot. But I don't think that's what you're insinuating." He'd always been reserved with his emotions. He wasn't an excitable guy, and yes, he cared about others, and in Dex's case, cared deeply. But he wasn't drawing little hearts around his and Dex's initials or using photos of them together as his phone's wallpaper.

"Poor choice of words," Ash admitted. "Do you love

him?"

"Fuck off."

"I'm serious. Do you love him?"

"Ash, a few weeks ago he confessed he loved me, and I freaked. I hurt him. Again. Do you really think that would have happened if I loved him? Besides, it's too soon." He wasn't like Dex, who could throw himself wholeheartedly into a relationship. He knew exactly what he wanted and why. Dex wasn't afraid to risk his heart if it meant the possibility of a future with someone he loved. Sloane had trouble looking to the future when he was only starting to let go of the past.

"Look, people talk a lot of shit. Who you're supposed to love, when, how. Fuck 'em."

The conviction in Ash's words surprised Sloane. He sat quietly watching his friend. There was a fire in his amber eyes Sloane hadn't seen in a long time. Passionate wasn't a word he would have ever associated with Ash. Brash, bold, and tough as nails. But passionate?

"Sometimes you find that one person, and you just know. And even if you don't love them right away, you know you will. It's just a matter of time. Because no one you've ever known has come close to making you feel the way they do. It keeps you up at night and drives you fucking crazy, but you pray to God the feeling never goes away no matter how much it's killing you."

Sloane stared at him. "Wow."

"Shut up," Ash mumbled, looking embarrassed. Like he hadn't realized what he'd said until then.

"I've never heard you talk like this." He thought he knew everything there was to know about his best friend. Apparently, he was wrong.

Ash shrugged. "Yeah, well, almost dying makes you

think."

"About Cael?" Sloane asked quietly.

Ash let out a weary sigh, his gaze falling to his hands. "Like I don't think about him every other day."

"What are you going to do about him?"

"I don't know. I really thought he'd give me some time, but he's going out for drinks with Seb this Friday."

"And?"

"Seb's a good guy. He's got his own shit to deal with, but at least he's not one of the fucked-up Pre-First Gens. No psych evals. Never saw the inside of the research facility. The Hobbs brothers never had to worry about that kind of shit, what with Daddy Hobbs being a tiger Therian himself. He did what a father's supposed to do. He kept his boys safe. Cael would be a lot happier with Seb. Less baggage. Not to mention Seb's out and proud. I'm not exactly skipping down the yellow brick road."

Sloane arched an eyebrow at him. "Okay, now that you've gotten that bullshit out of your system, how about the truth?"

"Sloane..."

"Nope. Look me in the eye and tell me you really think Cael would be better off with someone else."

Ash opened his mouth, but Sloane's scowl seemed to make him think better of it. He scratched the stubble on his jaw. "Truth?"

"Yes." He might be discovering new sides to his friend, but he was all too familiar with the old parts, and he knew when Ash was bullshitting him.

"No. I don't think Cael would be better off with someone else because no one could possibly love him as much as I do. I've never met anyone like him. When I see him, I don't know what to do with myself." Ash got to his feet and started to pace. Something else Sloane wasn't accustomed to seeing his friend do.

"He's fucking gorgeous. I can't believe I'm saying that about another dude, but fuck me, he's beautiful. His eyes are amazing. These really pale silvery pools—pools, Sloane! I'm calling his eyes fucking pools. Just seeing him makes me smile. He's funny, sweet, damn sexy, and I don't know why the hell he fell in love with me. No clue. I do know when I see him with Seb, I want to seriously punch Seb in the face, and if he wasn't such a fucking nice guy and Hobbs's brother, I would have already done it. God, I want to kick his ass! And I don't give a fuck he's a tiger Therian. I can totally take him down. It's driving me fucking crazy." Ash let out a frustrated growl. He turned to face Sloane. "I know I hurt Cael, but..." He returned to the chair and dropped down into it. "Fuck me sideways. I don't know what to do with all this emotional shit. It's fucking exhausting." He let his head fall back. "Fuck this shit."

"Jesus, Ash. Why don't you talk to Cael?" Damn. Usually he could gauge how upset his friend was over something by the number of times he dropped the "F" bomb.

"And tell him what? I already told him I needed time, and he turns around and accepts an invitation from Seb?" Ash folded his arms over his chest. He looked miserable. Not that Ash ever looked happy, but he was even more miserable than usual.

"You told him you couldn't be with him. What did you expect?"

"I expected him to... I don't know. I don't know what the hell I expected. He said he loved me. Why can't he give me more time? I don't want to mess things up with him. All I wanted was some time to figure out what to do about... you know, what happened."

"You have to forgive yourself, Ash. What happened with Arlo was fucked up, but it wasn't your fault."

Ash's jaw muscles clenched. "I could have protected him."

"Or you could have been killed along with him. You were a kid, Ash. As tough as you were, you were just a kid."

"Arlo had been just a kid. It didn't stop those motherfuckers from bashing his skull in with a fucking crowbar." Ash blinked away fresh tears and sat up. "Even if I'd ended up like Arlo, at least I would have gone down fighting. Instead—"

"Instead you lived to fight another day. You changed my life and became one of the fiercest agents at the THIRDS." Sloane felt his anger rise at Ash's quick dismissal of himself. "I'm not saying forget Arlo. I'm saying figure out what you need to do to forgive yourself and accept there are those in your life now who need you and love you. Talk to Cael. Tell him why. Tell him about the nightmares. Tell him about your regrets, your anger, your heartache. If I had been upfront with Dex about the facility and my past, we could have been spared a lot of drama and heartache."

Ash frowned and gave a noncommittal shrug. The conversation was over.

"Back to your nerd boyfriend. What do you need me to do?"

"If I know Dex, he's not going to rest until he gets his hands on Hogan. I'm worried he'll do something reckless."

Ash's eyebrows shot up. "You think he'd go against Sparks's orders?"

"Hold up." Sloane held on to his side as he sat up. "Orders? What orders? What the hell are you talking about?

"Shit. He didn't tell you?"

"Clearly, he didn't." Sloane didn't like the sound of this, and his best friend's hesitation didn't bode well. "Ash, what's going on?"

"We're off the case. Sparks put us on leave. Seb is lead agent on this now."

Sloane was silent for a moment. He didn't know what he found harder to believe, Sparks pulling his team off the case or Dex conveniently forgetting to mention it. He wanted to think it might have slipped Dex's mind, but his partner wasn't nearly as absentminded as he pretended to be. Which meant one thing. "Shit. Dex is going to go after Hogan on his own."

"How do you know?"

"Why else wouldn't he tell me? I can't believe he lied to me." How could Dex look him in the eye, tell him he loved him, and lie to him, especially about something this dangerous?

"Technically he didn't lie. More like, withheld information."

Sloane gaped at Ash. "Seriously? Not helping."

"Sorry."

"You have to stick by him. He'll get himself killed."

"What? You don't think your boy's got the skills?"

"Biology, Ash. Hogan is as big as Hobbs except he's a killer. He's meaner, angrier, and doesn't care who he has to take down to get what he wants. He tried to kill us and almost succeeded. Had it been Dex, Calvin, Rosa, or Letty, they'd be dead now. Hogan won't stop until he's gotten revenge on the remaining members of the Westward Creed, and if Dex gets in his way..."

"Yeah, all right," Ash groused. "I get it. I'll keep an eye on him. So does this mean you're not going to tell him you know?"

"Not yet."

"Is that really how you want things to go?"

Unbelievable. "Are you giving me relationship advice?" He needed to think about his next move, but he was too exhausted right now.

Ash appeared to be mulling over Sloane's words when he shook his head. "Man, we are both so fucked."

"Yep." Despite the situation, Sloane couldn't help teasing. "You're in love with Dex's brother. Do you know what that means?"

"First of all, *adopted* brother. They don't share the same genes. Second of all, what the hell are you talking about?"

"Those two are attached at the hip. They hang out all the time, borrow each other's stuff, share a lot of the same quirks, get excited over the same things, are both sugar addicts, and are both total geeks. You'll have Dex in your hair. All. The. Time."

Ash's horrified expression had Sloane laughing.

"You are such a dick, you know that? I hadn't even thought of that."

Sloane couldn't stop himself from laughing. "Still interested in being part of the family?"

"Not even Daley can ruin what I feel for Cael."

"Wow. Then it *must* be love," Sloane teased.

Ash jumped to his feet and started fiddling with all the equipment around Sloane's bed. "Where's the morphine? I need to shut you up." Despite the low growl, Sloane knew his friend was teasing. Sloane batted his hand away with a laugh.

"Stop. You're going to break something, and then Maddock's gonna lose it. You know how pissed he gets when we break shit."

"When your partner breaks shit," Ash corrected. "Or drops gummy bears in the grenade launcher."

Sloane let out a snicker at the memory of Dex's stunned, wide-eyed expression after the jelly treat had fallen in. Like a kid who realized only too late he'd put too much Mr. Bubbles in the tub. With no time left to do anything about it, he'd had no choice but to fire the weapon. Sloane found himself laughing harder.

"What's so funny?" Ash asked, his lip twitching. Sloane knew he was trying so hard not to laugh.

"When he fired the grenade launcher and the gummy bear flew out and hit the perp in the face?" Sloane was in tears, and even Ash couldn't keep himself from laughing any longer.

"Your boyfriend is such a fucking dweebus."

After Sloane managed to get a hold of himself, he gave Ash a wicked grin. "Admit it, you kind of like him."

"I'm not going to dignify that outrageous remark with a response."

"Okay, then." Sloane motioned toward the insulated lunch bag on the small table. "Empanadas."

"Rosa's?"

Sloane nodded.

Ash considered this. "Guava?"

"Yep. There's some beef and chicken too."

With a sigh, Ash got up and unzipped the bag. "You twisted my arm."

As Ash set up a makeshift picnic on the table for the both of them, complete with cups of OJ from the pitcher Sloane had asked the nurse for, Sloane couldn't think of a time when he'd felt this at ease, which was odd considering the past few days. After all the shit they'd been through, not only did he have his best friend back, things between Sloane and Dex couldn't be better. Finally, they were starting to settle down. At least until he thought about his partner going rogue. What the hell was Dex thinking?

"Hey." Ash reached out and put his hand on Sloane's shoulder. "Don't worry. I won't let anything happen to him." He handed Sloane a napkin with an empanada.

"Thanks." He hoped Ash knew how grateful he was.

"Are you sure you're okay? You look a little..." Ash motioned to his eyes. "Misty."

"Fuck off," Sloane laughed. "It's the meds." He was sure of it. It had absolutely nothing to do with the possibility of having a family after a lifetime of being alone. Or having someone who loved him and would stick by him despite all his fucked-up baggage. Dex loved him. Which was why Sloane had to figure this mess out. He had to protect Dex, even if it meant protecting him from himself.

DEX STOOD under the terrace near Bethesda Fountain in Central Park and waited. At exactly quarter to eight—as he'd been instructed—a figure emerged from the shadows with a swagger and a cocky grin. *Here we go.*

"Thanks for agreeing to meet with me," Dex said, holding his hand out to Austen who gave it a casual shake. No one would ever mistake the cheetah Therian for a THIRDS agent. Not with his bad-boy looks, from his cuffed 501 jeans to his pompadour haircut. Austen was slim and sinewy, about Cael's height, which made sense considering his Felid classification. The first time they'd met, after Sloane had been forced to literally drag Austen in to get information from him, Austen had used the excuse that cheetah Therians were skittish by nature, but Dex was coming to learn there was more to it. Was it a survival instinct from his days on the street? There was a lot Dex didn't know about Austen, and he was curious. Mostly because he had the feeling Austen knew more about him than he was letting on.

"No sweat, Daley. How's Broodybear?"

"He's got a lot of recovery ahead of him, but it's looking good."

Austen nodded, his sharp amber eyes studying Dex. Like he knew something Dex didn't. What the hell did a THIRDS Squadron Specialist agent do, anyway? Other than mysteriously pop out from the shadows every now and then.

"You didn't call me to talk about Sloane."

"I'm going after Hogan."

"Sparks pulled Destructive Delta off the case." Austen cocked his head to one side in thought when his eyes widened. "Oh no. Listen, I know you want to get Hogan for what he did. I understand feeling pissed off and wanting to kick him in the fuzzy sack, but this isn't just any Therian you're going after. Hogan is fucking huge in his Human form. In his Therian form he's lethal. He's a tiger Therian, man. You've seen them. Look at Hobbs. The dude's like three hundred pounds and you're like what? One sixty?"

"One seventy-five."

"Dude's like two of you put together."

"This guy tried to kill Ash twice. He put Sloane in the hospital. I'm going to do this whether you help me or not." Dex would only have access to Themis for two more days. After that, any searches he performed under his "on leave" status would get flagged and reported to Intel, who would most likely pass it on to Sparks.

"Do you realize what would happen if Lieutenant Sparks found out?"

"That asshole has threatened my family and my team. I'm putting a stop to this before anyone else I care about gets hurt. It's not going to stop until Hogan is behind bars or dead." Dex hesitated, wondering how much he should confide in Austen. Sloane trusted him, which meant Dex would trust him. "There were Felid Therians staking out Sloane's apartment today."

"Shit. I was going to pass by but got held up. Were they Hogan's?"

"Yeah. One of them knew my name. I don't know what the hell they were doing there, but it couldn't be anything good."

"Damn it. Are you going to tell Sloane any of this?"

Dex thought about it for a moment before shaking his head. "Not yet. I don't want him worrying about it. I'll tell him once he's settled in at home."

"Fine. What do you need?"

"Information. I have access to Themis for a couple of days to finish off my reports on the Coalition exchange and the explosion outside my house. I'll get what I can without raising any red flags, but I might need you to follow up on some leads. I need to find Ox Perry and Brick Jackson before Hogan does. If you get any information on either of them, on Hogan, or any of Hogan's guys, I want to know about it first."

Austen gaped at him. Not exactly the reaction Dex had been hoping for. "You want me to keep information from Sebastian Hobbs? I know he looks like a nice guy, and he is, sexy too, but if you fuck with his case, he will bust your shit up. He fucked up once, he's not going to let it happen a second time."

"What did happen?" Dex leaned against the terrace wall, and Austen followed his lead, getting a little closer to him than Dex would have liked, but he let it slide. If anyone came nosing around, they'd think they were a couple of guys sneaking in a little make-out session. It wasn't exactly uncommon. Especially with Austen being a Therian. It was amazing how many Humans got stupid when they saw a Human and Therian kissing in front of their kids. It was okay for them to suck face, but the moment it wasn't two Humans. *Bam.* Bring on the plague of locusts. He turned his attention back to Austen. "I know Seb was on Destructive Delta, and he was transferred, but I don't know much else. Everyone's pretty tight-lipped about it."

"Because it was messed up," Austen replied with a shake of his head. "Seb and Hudson were involved at the time. Seb was crazy about the guy. They were inseparable. Really sweet. Anyway, the team was at a murder scene, and they'd been given the all clear. Except it wasn't clear. The gunman was still there. Hudson was seeing to the body when the shooting started. The guy shot at Hudson, and Seb broke protocol. He should have made sure all the civilians were safe. Instead, he went for Hudson. A bullet missed the doc and killed a kid."

"Shit." Dex had known it was something bad, but he had no idea. No wonder Seb had looked devastated when Dex had brought up the incident at the hospital.

"Yeah. A shitstorm of epic proportions rained down on them. The family pressed charges, the lawyers came out, and it went to court. In the end, the agent who'd reported the all clear took the fall. He's probably working in a pretzel kiosk in a mall somewhere. Seb got demoted and transferred from the team, and the THIRDS introduced the "no fraternizing" rule. The most dangerous cases he dealt with were the ones giving him paper cuts. They stuck him in archives for a while. The world moved on, and Seb was put back in the field. Of course, by then, there was no salvaging his relationship with Hudson. I don't think either of them could face what happened. Guess the THIRDS decided to give Seb another chance by promoting him into Stone's old position. Can't believe the bastard turned traitor on us."

Dex was hardly about to lose any more sleep on Levi Stone. Right now, he had his own problems. Knowing what happened to Seb made him feel worse, because no matter what, he couldn't back out of this. He'd never impede another agent's investigation, but that didn't mean he wasn't going to conduct his own. "Austen. Please."

"I can't withhold information."

Damn it. He'd really thought Austen would help him out, if only for Sloane's sake. The two went way back. Sloane had taken him off the streets, gotten him recruited to the THIRDS, and trusted him like family. Austen gave him a cocky grin, and Dex held his breath.

"*But* I can give you whatever intel I get on this case before I give it to Seb. I'll hold out as long as I can."

Dex couldn't keep his relief from showing. He gave Austen a smile and shook his hand. "Deal. Thank you. I owe you one."

"I'm gonna hold you to that, Daley." Austen winked at him before disappearing into the shadows again. How the hell did he do it? Dex walked off in the opposite direction toward Seventy-Second Street where he'd parked his Challenger.

Tomorrow morning, Sloane would be released from the hospital, and Dex would take care of him like he'd promised he would. He would also try his damn hardest to find Hogan. The tough part—besides finding the guy—would be trying to do so without rousing Sloane's suspicion. The thought of lying to Sloane made him feel like shit, but he had to see this through. If he told Sloane, his partner would most likely try to talk him out of it, and if that didn't work, Dex was sure Sloane would come up with a way to stop him. He couldn't let that happen.

As he headed home, *Retro Radio* played in the background, relaxing him. He thought about his next move, because as good as Austen was, Dex couldn't sit around waiting for intel to fall into his lap. Austen had his work cut out for him. Had Hogan sent those two to finish Sloane off? It didn't make any sense. Hogan was smart. He had to know the THIRDS would be keeping a close watch for him. Damn it. Dex needed more information, but he needed a place to work from first.

Traffic stopped for the red light near Columbus Avenue, and Dex's gaze landed on La Pain Quotidien on his left. An insane idea struck him. Shit. And he was only five minutes away from the place in question as well. Instead of turning on Columbus to head home, he continued toward West Seventy-Seventh Street. He managed to find a parking spot next door to Clove Catering.

Lou's catering business was open twenty-four hours a day. It was fancy but reasonably priced. They catered weddings, corporate events, galas, and fundraisers. Dex didn't know anyone else who worked as hard at their career or loved it as much as Lou. His ex was also a bit of a control freak, which most likely played a part in his success. But his hard work had paid off, and over the last couple of years, Lou had been featured in the media as an up-and-coming talent. He'd been interviewed in *New York Weddings* magazine among a host of other big-name wedding magazines and newspapers. The company had doubled in size. The food was top-notch, the service second to none, and Lou wasn't pretentious like some of the owners of a few other companies Dex had met while accompanying his ex-boyfriend to a couple of conferences. He hadn't even been aware caterers had conferences. It was weird going somewhere to see the latest in food-tray technology. But the eats had been awesome, so Dex never complained.

The little bell above the glass door jingled merrily and announced his presence as he walked in. There was a large greeting area containing several sleek white tables with couples sitting across from event organizers browsing through menus and albums. Event photos lined the walls in elegant, antique-style frames. The circus roses in frosted white vases added a burst of color to the mostly white-and-black décor. At this time of night, Lou would still be in. He always worked late on Wednesdays to catch up on invoices. Dex greeted some of the employees he recognized along the way to the main reception area where he found the twins, Jeremy and Joseph. They were a couple of cute blond twinks who were Lou's assistants. They smiled brightly when they saw him, greeting him in unison.

"Hi, Dex."

"Hey, guys. How's it going? Still saving the world from the fashionably challenged?"

"Oh my God. Seriously, Dex. Some people can't be saved, no matter how much you try," Jeremy said, leaning forward and adjusting his trendy black-framed glasses. "Have you ever been to a vampire wedding?"

"Thankfully, no." The thought alone made him cringe.

Joseph shook his head sadly. "Sweetie, Mauricio spent ten hours gluing tiny white rhinestones to the groom so he would sparkle when he walked down the aisle."

Dex let out a bark of laughter with Jeremy and Joseph

joining in. "Oh shit." He doubled over at the thought of what Lou's face must have looked like when the request had been put in. Dex had always tried his best not to laugh when Lou came home ranting about some of his clients' crazy wedding ideas, but Dex had to admit this one took the proverbial wedding cake.

Jeremy let out a delicate snort and smoothed out his preppy sweater vest. "Lou told the kitchen staff to add a little extra kick to the sangria in the hopes no one would remember it the next day."

"We were just lucky it wasn't an overly sunny day," Joseph added, "or we might have ended up with mass casualties. I can see the headlines now, 'Wedding Guests Spontaneously Combust via Rhinestone Vampire.'"

"Wait, isn't that a country song?" Jeremy asked.

Joseph gave his brother a gentle pat on the head. "It's 'Rhinestone Cowboy,' sweetie."

"Oh."

The three laughed until Dex heard Lou behind him.

"What's going on here?" Dex turned with a wide grin, and Lou rolled his eyes at him. "Should have known. Are you flirting with my staff again? And before you ask, the kitchen's closed."

"Hey, Lou." Darn. He'd hoped to sneak into the kitchen before seeing Lou to charm some tasty treats from Brian the head chef. Despite his arched eyebrow, Lou gave Dex a hug, and Dex returned the embrace.

"It's nice to see you, Dex." Lou motioned toward his office, and Dex followed, waving to the boys who went back to discussing the sparkly vampire wedding debacle. Inside Lou's office, everything was exactly as it had been the last time he was here. Dex took a seat in the flowered wingback chair in front of Lou's white vintage-style desk.

He hadn't realized how worn out he was until he was sitting.

"How are you? You look tired." Lou's gaze was sympathetic as he took a seat behind his desk. "How's Sloane doing?"

"He's getting better. Thanks."

"You haven't been to see me here in a year."

"Yeah, well, technically, you told me not to come see you at work." Lou had been clear about it, though Dex was more than aware Lou hadn't meant never to come near the place.

"When we broke up," Lou said. "I thought you'd try to win me back or something."

"Are you disappointed I didn't?"

Lou had told Sloane he'd had his chance with Dex and blew it, how Sloane shouldn't make the same mistake. Was it possible Lou regretted their breakup? Lou seemed to have moved on with his life. Dex certainly had. Lou was a great guy, and Dex was glad they could stay friends, but as a couple they hadn't been right for each other.

"Why are you here, Dex?"

Was it him, or was Lou being a little touchy today? Ignoring Lou's frustrated tone, Dex came out with it. "I need a favor."

"Okay," Lou replied, his gaze suddenly turning suspicious. "It's not about adding a donut wedding cake to the menu, is it? Because the answer is still no."

"A tower of glazed goodness. Don't know what you're missing," Dex teased.

"I'll learn to live with it. Now what did you need? I'm waiting for someone."

"Oh, sorry. I didn't know you had an appointment."

Lou cleared his throat and averted his gaze. "Not an

appointment. Bradley's meeting me for dinner."

Reeeally. Dex leaned his elbows on Lou's desk and propped his chin on his laced fingers. No wonder Lou was dressed all snazzy. Lou always dressed well, but now he was dressed for a night out on the town. There seemed to be a little more gel in his dark hair, and Dex caught the subtle whiff of Lou's most expensive cologne.

"Bradley as in bartender Bradley?"

"Bradley as in bar *owner* Bradley," Lou corrected with a sniff.

Dex grinned broadly. "Therian Bradley." He tried not to laugh at Lou's huff.

"Yes, Dex. How many Bradleys do we know?"

"Wow." Lou was getting all grumpy. Interesting.

"Sorry," Lou mumbled. "I'm nervous."

Dex nodded but didn't say a word. He didn't have to. He knew Lou. The guy would give himself away. A few weeks ago at Dex's birthday party, they'd seen Lou and Bradley getting cozy by the bar as they chatted.

Lou frowned at him. "What?"

"Nothing."

"You think I like him."

"You seem a little... flustered is all." Dex watched in amusement as Lou closed his appointment book. Straightened it. Nudged it. Unstraightened and restraightened it.

"It's only dinner."

"Uh-huh." Anything Lou labeled as "only" something meant it was usually anything but.

"I'm trying not to think about anything else."

"Why not? Bradley's a really nice guy." He'd liked Bradley from the first day he'd stepped foot in Dekatria, and not just because Bradley had been secretly cheering for Dex and Sloane to get together, but because he was a genuinely nice guy who always seemed to care about people. He was friendly, always smiling, laid back, and ready with a wink.

"So, what kind of favor did you need?"

Dex held back a laugh. "Not even gonna try and be subtle about it? Okay. I'll butt out. I came to ask you about the empty office you have next door. Is it still empty?"

Lou observed him. "Yes. Why?"

"Can I use it? I have some undercover work and need somewhere kind of off the grid to work from."

"And your ex's catering company is off the grid?"

"How many exes do you still keep in contact with?" If it hadn't been for Sloane, Dex probably would have been another ex-boyfriend Lou never spoke to again. Dex wasn't in the habit of keeping in contact with any of his other ex-boyfriends, but he was glad Lou decided he wanted to remain a part of Dex's life. Four years they'd spent together, sharing a lot of ups as well as downs. He liked having Lou as a friend.

"Point made," Lou said. "Yes, it's empty. Why can't you work from your house?" The question was more out of curiosity than frustration.

"Sloane's staying there while he recovers."

Lou blinked in surprise. "He's staying with you?"

"Yes. I asked him to. He has a lot of recovery to do and a list a mile long from the doctor about what he can't do if he's going to heal quickly. Luckily, he's in great shape, and his Therian body has already started the healing process. Why are you looking at me like that?"

"Are you sure you're not moving too quickly, Dex? Sloane's kind of... restless."

How the hell did Lou know? "We're working on it. And it's not like I asked him to move in. I'm just taking care of him while he's getting better. He could have said no."

"He could have." Lou got up and walked over to a framed painting of cloves, the sweet yet spicy aromatic flower buds the company was named after. Behind it was the small wall safe where Lou kept some cash, important paperwork, and spare keys, including the keys to the office Dex was asking to borrow, though right now he was more interested in whatever point Lou was trying to get at. "Maybe you haven't noticed, Dex, but Sloane has a really hard time saying no to you." He removed a set of keys from a key box and tossed them at Dex who caught them in midair. "Granted, you have a knack for getting your way, but Sloane in particular has trouble putting his foot down around you."

"What are you talking about? Sloane says no to me all the time."

Lou put his hands up before closing up the wall safe and returning the frame to its original spot. "Never mind. It's your relationship and none of my business."

"You can't start something like that and not follow through. You've obviously got something you want to say. Come on, Lou."

"When you and I were together, you did and agreed to a lot of things to make me happy, even if you weren't ready."

Dex frowned. "Like what?"

"Like moving in together."

They'd already been over this. He'd even been over this with his dad. It was all in the past. Yes, Dex had gone through the motions with a lot to make Lou happy at the time, believing it was also what he wanted, but his relationship with Sloane was different. "I don't see what this has to do with my current situation."

"Are you sure Sloane's not doing the same? Moving at your pace to make you happy? He obviously cares about you a lot, but he doesn't strike me as a relationship kind of guy, so if he really is trying for a future with you, maybe you need to go at his pace for a while." Lou sat down again, and Dex tried not to sound annoyed, even if he was.

"No one makes Sloane do anything he doesn't want to do."

"This is different, Dex, and you know it."

Dex opened his mouth when he heard a familiar voice calling down the hall.

"Lou?"

Lou sat up straight and smoothed down his shirt. "In here, Bradley."

Bradley peeked into the room, a broad smile on his face. "Hey, guys." He walked in dressed in trendy faded jeans and boots. The charcoal V-neck shirt and leather jacket covered up his arms' tattoo sleeves, though part of a tattoo could be seen poking out from under his collar. The tall jaguar Therian extended his hand to Dex.

"Hey, Dex. How are you?"

"Good." Dex returned Bradley's smile and shook his hand.

Bradley's smile faded, concern coming into his amber eyes. "How's Sloane? I'm sorry about what happened. I've been really worried about him."

"Shit, you called that day. Sorry, man. I meant to call you back."

"Don't worry about it. You had your hands full. I completely understand."

Dex stood and backed up toward the door. "You could say that. Sloane's doing better. Thank you. Listen, I don't want to keep you guys."

"If you need anything, you have my number." Bradley turned to Lou with a wide smile. "You look amazing."

"Thank you," Lou replied, his cheeks turning pink. He stood and fidgeted with his hair.

"We should go. Reservation's for nine."

"Right." Lou came around his desk to Bradley who gave his cheek a kiss, and Lou went red to the tips of his ears. As Bradley ushered Lou to the door, Dex whispered over at Lou.

"You're blushing."

Lou jabbed a finger in his direction. "Shut it, mister."

The three of them walked out, saying good night to the staff on the late shift. Outside it was breezy, the scaffolding against the building's façade making the sidewalk a little darker than usual. It would give Dex a little more cover for when he came and went, which was helpful. Bradley waved at Dex, his free hand going to the small of Lou's back as they headed for his car.

With a chuckle, Dex waved the pair off. "You crazy kids have fun."

Dinner reservations, blushing, telling Dex to shut it. Lou was definitely crushing on Bradley. Dex was glad. The pair looked sweet together. Soon as he saw Bradley's slick Grand Cherokee drive off, Dex headed for the black metal door next to Clove Catering to check out the state of the office. Making sure no one was watching him, he unlocked the door and slipped inside, locking it behind him. He flipped the light switch in the narrow hall, noting how it had been recently given a fresh coat of cream-colored paint. At the end, a wooden door led downstairs to an office and supply closet.

Downstairs, Dex couldn't have found a better setup. "Thank you, Lou." There wasn't much to it, but it was more than Dex could have hoped for. The rectangular room had a large metal table against the far wall, some electrical outlets, a drab but clean gray carpet, some cabinets, a small fridge, and a long couch Dex remembered had been upstairs when Lou had first rented the place. Lou had gasped in horror at its seventies-green velour and demanded Dex get it out of his sight immediately. This would be perfect. His phone rang, and Dex fished it out. It was Sloane. Fuck. He'd told Sloane he'd be back tonight. He closed his eyes as he answered.

"Hey, handsome."

"Hey, you okay to talk?"

"Yeah, what's up?"

There was some hesitation before Sloane answered. "I was wondering if you were going to stop by tonight. I understand if you're in the middle of something."

"Actually, just finished wrapping up a long-ass conference call with PR." Dex winced at the lie. "I've still got my bag there with you, so I'll shower there and crash on the couch."

"Yeah?"

"Of course." Dex smiled at Sloane's hopeful tone. Was Sloane missing him?

"Okay. See you soon, then."

The smile in Sloane's voice wasn't lost on Dex, and he found himself smiling too. "See you soon." He hung up and stood there staring at his phone. Was he really going to do this? He wouldn't be able to keep the fact their team had been pulled from the case from Sloane, not when his partner could easily find out from Ash or any of the others. Which meant he'd have to have an excuse for being out. His phone pinged, and he let out a frustrated groan. Another meeting with PR. On second thought...

Looked like he'd found his excuse.

FIVE

"THIS SUCKS."

Sloane was pouting. The hospital had given him crutches to use, along with a list of exercises he was supposed to do each day before the therapy sessions for his leg started. The crutches annoyed him. His leg not cooperating annoyed him. The asshole pulling out of his parking space with his head up his ass annoyed him.

"That guy's pulling out," Sloane grumbled.

"I see him."

Sloane chose to ignore the amusement in his partner's voice. "Well, I don't think he sees you." Sloane reached over Dex and slammed his fist against the horn before pressing the window button and bellowing, "Hey, watch it!" The car stopped, and the guy glared at Sloane. Wait a second. "Did he just flip me off?"

"Um..."

"I think he flipped me off. Stop the car. I'm going to get out and beat him with my crutch. Asshole. Thinks he owns the whole fucking road."

"Easy there, grumpy pants." Dex reached over and took

hold of Sloane's hand. He gave it a squeeze and smiled. Sloane wanted to be annoyed at Dex's lopsided grin, but he couldn't. He sat back with a heavy sigh and hit the window's button to raise it.

"Sorry," he muttered. "This just... It sucks."

Dex chuckled. "You sound like me."

"No. If I wanted to sound like you, I'd have said 'this sucks aaaaass,' followed by the chewing of gummy bears or crunching of Cheesy Doodles."

"You are as wise as you are grumpy."

"I *am* a grumpy pants," Sloane admitted. "You sure you want me around like this?"

Dex stopped at the red light and leaned over to give his lips a quick kiss. "Absolutely."

It felt like hours before they reached Dex's house, but in reality, it hadn't been long. He was pretty sure he'd dozed off once or twice. Damned meds. Getting out of the car was the first challenge. Sloane had been forced to lean on his crutches. It was going to take getting used to. He already wanted to chuck them into the middle of the street so they could get run over by a truck. Dex took hold of one of the crutches and wrapped his free arm around Sloane's waist. His smile kept Sloane from bitching and cursing every step of the way. Though he did a fair amount of it anyway. Each step had been excruciating, and the few steps leading to the front door might as well have been the goddamn Andes Mountains. His body ached all over, his side was killing him, his head hurt, and he was already out of breath. Fucking awesome.

"It's okay. We have lots of time," Dex said, his voice soothing in Sloane's ear. By the time Sloane was at the top, his brow was beaded with sweat.

"I'm fucking heavy."

Dex chuckled and gave his bicep a squeeze. "It's all that sexy muscle."

His partner was crafty. Sloane knew what Dex was doing. What he'd been doing since Sloane had been released from the hospital. He was distracting him. From the frustration, the pain, the urge to throw a punch at something. Sloane appreciated it to no end. Somehow he wasn't surprised Dex was the only one who could drive him to distraction. Even now as Dex unlocked the front door and bent over to pick up the mail on the floor, Sloane found himself distracted. It was the first time he'd thought about anything sexual. Now he couldn't stop thinking about it. About Dex lying under him gasping and moaning, begging for Sloane to fuck him. God, he missed that.

"Fuck!"

Dex spun around, his eyes wide. "What is it? What's wrong?"

"We can't have sex," Sloane whined.

Dex stared at him before bursting into laughter. "Is that what you're worried about? Not having sex?"

Sloane glared at Dex as his partner helped him inside and closed the door behind them. "I don't see what's so funny. This is a serious situation." The sinful look on Dex's face was enough to have Sloane swallowing hard. It was followed by Dex slipping his arms around Sloane, his hand migrating south to Sloane's ass where he gave it a squeeze. When Dex spoke, his voice was low and husky.

"Do you really think not being able to have sex is going to stop me from finding ways to make you purr? To drive you absolutely fucking crazy? You think I don't know how to get creative?"

Sloane licked his bottom lip. "Well, when you put it like that..." The thought of all the new ways they could get off together had Sloane's pulse quickening. Challenge accepted. He kissed Dex, relishing in the low moan Dex let out and the way his partner pressed his hard body up against him while simultaneously being gentle. Being around Dex made Sloane want to hold on to him and not let go. Dex pulled back, giving his bottom lip a tug with his teeth before releasing him. Sloane was reluctant to let go, but he was already feeling tired. Dex removed his own jacket and hung it up on the hooks behind the door before carefully helping Sloane out of his and doing the same. Then Dex helped him into the living room where Sloane turned in the direction of the couch only to get led toward the stairs. "Where are we going?"

"Upstairs."

"But the TV is down here." Even if the meds made him groggy, he had no intention of spending all day sleeping. Plus there was the little problem where he needed to limit the number of stairs he used in a day.

"The TV is also upstairs. It'll be much easier for you to get to the bathroom."

Sloane paused at the bottom of the stairs to look at Dex. "You got a TV for the bedroom?"

"Yep."

"Because of me?"

Dex's smile warmed Sloane all over. "I don't want you to get bored when I'm not here."

"I don't know what to say." He was touched Dex would install a TV in the bedroom just for him.

"Don't worry about it."

The trip upstairs was another trek up the Andes. This one taking much longer. Damn houses with damn stairs. Along the way he'd been in danger of losing his temper, but Dex would step in with a kiss, a tease, or a flirt, and Sloane would forget what he was pissed off about. He'd get lost in those amazing blue eyes, cheeky smile, and infectious laugh. Before he knew it, they were inside the bedroom. Sloane stood inside the doorway, stunned.

Dex had mounted the large flat screen on the wall across from the bed, and to the right of what had become Sloane's side of the bed, was a sleek black minifridge with a basket on top. A small trash bin sat on the floor beside it, and next to the bed was a trendy adjustable rolling tray table.

With exceptional care, Dex walked Sloane to his side of the bed and helped ease him down. The bed was outfitted with a garrison of soft pillows and warm, fuzzy blankets. Sloane watched with a belly full of butterflies as Dex got down on his knees and removed Sloane's boots and socks before gently lifting his legs onto the bed. Once Sloane was settled back against the pillows, Dex walked over to the minifridge and opened it. Sweet Jesus. It was filled with snacks. *Healthy* snacks.

"Water, juice, and your favorite snacks: hummus, guacamole, peanut butter, and fat free Ranch dressing to go with all your raw veggies. There's also fruit, yogurt, cheese, and sliced chicken." He closed the fridge door and motioned to the basket on top. "Mixed nuts, beef jerky, protein bars, blue corn tortilla chips, pretzels, napkins, plastic cutlery, small paper plates, and paper cups." Dex turned to him and stilled. "What's wrong?"

Sloane realized his staring probably made him look like a crazy person. "Sorry. I'm just... amazed you would go through all this trouble for me."

Dex kicked off his shoes and climbed on the bed to settle in beside Sloane. "First of all, it wasn't any trouble.

Second of all, I said I wanted to take care of you, and I meant it."

"Thank you." Sloane held him close, still trying to take it all in. No one had ever been so attentive to his needs, even when he wasn't aware himself of what his needs were. He supposed a lot of it had to do with him never allowing anyone to see him in any kind of vulnerable position. With Dex, it was different. Either Dex had worn him down, which was a possibility, or something in Sloane was changing. Somehow, he didn't feel as nervous about the idea.

As Dex lay against his good side, his hand on Sloane's chest, Sloane wondered if he should bring up the fact he knew Sparks had pulled Destructive Delta off the case. Why wouldn't Dex tell him? Probably because he knew Sloane would get pissed off. It was stupid. How could Dex possibly believe he stood a chance against Hogan on his own? Dex was a capable agent, but he was up against a murderous Therian nearly twice his size. Dex was smarter than that.

"Sloane?"

"Hm?"

"I've got something to tell you."

"Okay." Sloane held his breath as Dex looked up at him.

"I didn't tell you earlier because you were in the hospital, and drama was the last thing you needed, but Sparks pulled us off the case and put Destructive Delta on leave."

A huge wave of relief washed over Sloane, followed by a pang of guilt for having doubted Dex. He squeezed Dex against him and kissed him until they had to come up for breath. When he pulled back, Dex let out a soft laugh and licked his bottom lip.

"Wow. What was that for?"

"Thank you for being so considerate." Something

flashed through Dex's blue eyes, and Sloane's smile fell away. He didn't like what he saw. "Dex, promise me you're not going to go after Hogan. Sparks gave her orders. Leave Seb and Theta Destructive to do their jobs."

Dex pulled away and sat up. "Wait, you knew?"

Pissbunnies. Nice going. "Yeah, Ash came to visit me at the hospital. It came up." Damn it. Dex had been considerate in waiting to tell him while Sloane had been what? Distrusting of his partner? Dex frowned at him.

"Were you going to tell me?"

There were a million excuses Sloane could give, all which would placate his partner. But Sloane didn't want to give an excuse. He wanted honesty between them. "I'm sorry. I understand if you're pissed. I thought you were trying to keep it from me because you were planning on going after Hogan yourself, and it upset me. I hadn't figured out much else."

Dex swallowed hard and didn't reply. Goddamn it. Sloane realized his initial reaction had been correct.

"No." He shook his head. "Dex, you can't."

"Sloane, the guy almost killed you. We should be the ones bringing him in. What if he leaves the city? How can we live with ourselves knowing he'd still be out there somewhere, waiting to regroup and strike again? We've been working this case for months. We know him better than Seb and his team. They'll be working on Hogan's profile from Themis, whereas we've had experience with that asshole and his crew firsthand."

Sloane let out a heavy sigh. He should have known it wouldn't be easy. "You have to learn to walk away, Dex, no matter how much you don't want to. Sometimes there are more important things at stake than the job. You said so yourself." It had been the reason behind their first real fight

—Dex had put his personal emotions before the job. Under those circumstances, his partner had been right to go against orders. One of their own had been in trouble, but this was different.

Dex went pensive before meeting Sloane's gaze. "Would you walk away? If the roles were reversed?"

"At one point, maybe I wouldn't have." He laced his fingers with Dex's and brought him in close once again before kissing Dex's hand. "But I'd like to think I've found something worth walking away for. Something worth walking toward." Sloane watched Dex intently, watched the uncertainty and conflict in his eyes. It was hard as hell for any good officer to stand down in the face of a threat, but he needed Dex to understand what was at stake. "Promise me you won't go after Hogan." He could almost see the little wheels in Dex's head spinning furiously. Finally, Dex looked up and gave him a nod.

"I'm sorry. You're right. Some things are too important to walk away from." He lay back down and snuggled close to Sloane. "I'm glad you're here."

Dex's soft admission squeezed at Sloane's heart.

"I'm glad I'm here too." Sloane let out a yawn and silently cursed himself. Damn it. Now was not the time for sleep. Something was nagging at him, but he was too groggy to figure out what it was. His head was fuzzy, and his body wanted to give in to the drowsiness. He prayed Dex wasn't about to do anything stupid. No one was as stubborn as his partner. As much as he wanted to believe Dex would walk away, something told him this wasn't the end of it.

Sloane forced himself to stay awake a little bit longer so he could watch Dex sleep. He wondered if his partner had managed to get any rest at all over the last few days. Dex would run himself into the ground if Sloane let him. Feeling

Dex against him, watching his chest rise and fall, his lips slightly parted, and a peaceful expression on his handsome face brought on a sudden wave of fierce protectiveness, one akin to the kind he experienced when in his Therian form. It startled him.

This wasn't the first time one of his feral traits managed to make an appearance on his Human side. It was disconcerting. Maybe when he was well enough he'd visit with Dr. Shultzon. There was still so much he didn't know about himself as a First Gen Therian. Was this sort of thing normal? Had any other First Gens experienced something similar? He'd have to ask Ash the next time he spoke to him. Except for the purring part. If he told Ash he'd literally purred while in his Human form, Ash would laugh his ass off, and Sloane would never hear the end of it.

Feeling his eyelids growing heavy, he held on to his wounded side with his right hand and carefully rolled himself onto his left side, trying his best not to jostle Dex too much. He failed, moving the bed and rousing his partner who opened his sleepy eyes with a smile before he closed them, nuzzled his face against Sloane's neck, and fell asleep again. Sloane wasn't far behind. His last hazy thoughts were about how happy he was right here right now and how he hoped nothing would change.

SLOANE WAS DISTURBED from his deep sleep by something vibrating against his thigh. What the hell? He opened his eyes at the same moment Dex rolled onto his back with a groan. He reached into his pocket, letting out a yawn as he looked at his phone. "Shit."

"What is it?" Sloane asked, feeling groggy. Damn, he

hated meds that made him drowsy. His eyelids felt heavy, and if he closed his eyes, he'd be asleep in seconds.

"I gotta go. I completely forgot I promised to check in with PR about the next meeting." Dex quickly got off the bed and almost tripped over himself. Regaining his equilibrium, he swiftly came around to Sloane's side of the bed with an apologetic smile.

"Oh." Sloane wanted to say something, but he held his tongue. He wanted to believe Dex, but he'd been a THIRDS agent too long not to be suspicious. Plus, Dex was a shitty liar. Sloane also knew his partner. When he'd asked Dex to promise him, Dex hadn't actually said the words. King of evasive tactics.

"Yeah. I'm sorry. How about on the way home I pick up some dinner for us?"

Sloane nodded. "Call me?" Did he sound needy? Fuck it, he was injured. He *was* needy. His partner—who had promised to take care of him—should be here with him, especially since he was supposed to be on leave. God, he *did* sound needy. Screw it. He'd almost been killed. He reserved the right to be a big baby and want his partner to coddle him, goddamn it. Wasn't that what boyfriends did? If they didn't, they should. His should. It was seriously time for another nap.

"Of course." Dex gave his lips a kiss and pulled away, but Sloane caught his arm before he could leave.

"Take care."

"I promise." Another tender kiss to Sloane's lips, and Dex was out of the room.

Seconds later, the front door closed downstairs, and Sloane sat on the bed surrounded by silence. His gaze went to the flat screen mounted on the wall and then the fridge. He wanted to be pissed off at Dex, but his partner made it so damn hard. With Dex, there was no questioning motive. His partner needed to protect those closest to him. He needed justice. The question was, at what cost? Would Sloane really have walked away had he been in Dex's shoes? He wouldn't have once, no doubt about it, but then he thought of Dex, and now he wasn't so certain.

Looking around the room, seeing all the evidence of his constant presence, he should have felt restless. Besides Sloane's unopened suitcase by the armchair, there were plenty more of Sloane's belongings lying around. A gym bag sat on the carpet by the door. One of his leather jackets was draped across the back of the armchair. In the bathroom was a bag of Sloane's toiletries and an extra toothbrush. A pair of his pajama bottoms hung from the hook on the back of the bathroom door. Hell, he even had an extra uniform hanging inside Dex's closet, along with an extra pair of steel-toed boots, a cardigan, and some shirts.

The whole thing should have freaked him out, but sitting here on the large bed, he felt... comfortable. Dex's bedroom no longer felt like someone else's bedroom. He wasn't quite sure what to make of all this, and he wondered if any moment the meds would wear off and he'd feel completely different. Fuck this. This was too much thinking for him to be doing right now. He grabbed the remote from his nightstand and turned on the TV, flipping through the cable channels to find a movie or something to distract him and get his mind off his idiot boyfriend. Somewhere between some weird buddy cop movie where one of the detectives was going on about being a peacock or something, Sloane fell asleep. He had no idea how long he was out for or why he'd woken up.

He let out a fierce yawn when he heard something. It was faint, but he heard it clearly. It was coming from the kitchen. Had Dex come back already? What time was it? He checked the time on the TV. A little over an hour since Dex left.

There was another faint *thump*. Sloane pulled out his phone and speed-dialed Dex's number. After a couple of rings, it went to voice mail. If Dex had been downstairs, Sloane would have heard the Journey ringtone Dex had set as Sloane's personal ringtone. Man, his partner was such a nut.

Holding on to his bandaged wound, he used his right hand to open the nightstand drawer. Inside was a small, slim black case with a thumbprint pad. He placed it on his lap and stuck his thumb to the pad. A *click* later, and the case opened to reveal his Glock. He'd picked it up when he sensed someone outside the door. He brought the gun up and aimed it at the intruder stepping right into the line of fire.

"Did I wake you?"

"Jesus, Austen." Sloane let out a heavy sigh and lowered his arm in relief. He returned the Glock to its padding and closed the case. "What the hell's wrong with you?"

"What?" Austen strolled in with a bag of Cheesy Doodles in his hand. He popped one in his mouth and dropped down on the armchair. With a grunt, Sloane stuck the secured gun case back in the drawer.

"Never mind. Took you long enough."

Austen munched on another Cheesy Doodle. If Dex were here, he would have made a stupid joke about Chester the Cheetah Therian eating his Cheesy Doodles. Wonderful, now he was starting to think like Dex.

"I had to wait," Austen said around a mouthful of cheese snacks. "Your boy sat in his car for like ten minutes."

"Doing what? And don't talk with your mouth full."

Austen swallowed. "I don't know. Staring up at the bedroom window. He looked worried."

"You sure it wasn't guilt?" Sloane grumbled. Damn it, his partner was going to ignore him and go after Hogan. He just knew it.

"Maybe. You should have seen his face. Looked like a sad puppy." He looked around the room before wriggling his eyebrows at Sloane. "So, almost a year now."

"Yeah," Sloane murmured. "Thanks for checking up on us at the hospital. He didn't make you."

"Told you. I am the master. Besides, when he wasn't fighting sleep, he was lost in his own little world. I thought he might have recognized me the first time he walked in, but then he saw you, and well..." Austen sighed. "He's got it bad, huh?"

Sloane nodded but couldn't bring himself to comment. Sometimes he still found it hard to believe Dex loved him.

"Damn. Is it serious?"

Sloane ran a hand over his stubbly jaw. He really needed a shave, and to not have this conversation. But if there was anyone he trusted to keep a secret for him, it was Austen. "Yeah."

Sloane's relationship with Dex had been a challenge from the beginning, but if he really thought about it, the signs had been there from the start. From the moment they'd met, Sloane couldn't fight how badly he'd wanted Dex. The more he got to know Dex, the more he wanted to know. With every conversation, every joke, smile, tease, outburst from Dex, Sloane got in deeper. It was fast, but Dex had put himself out there, risking his heart, and although it took Sloane some time to catch up, he was glad he did. Otherwise he'd be missing out on something amazing. He'd tried to be sensible, but lately his heart had started speaking louder than his head.

"He's in love with you, isn't he?" Austen asked.

Sloane nodded.

"You love him?"

Why was everyone asking him that? "It's... complicated." Man, was it complicated.

Austen gave him a knowing smile. "Love is only as complicated as you make it, Sloane."

Why was everyone giving him relationship advice? Or presuming to know what he felt or would feel? They sat in silence until Sloane couldn't keep himself from asking the question swirling around in his head. "Does anyone else know? And don't get any crumbs on there. It's where we put our clothes."

"Among other things." Austen wriggled his brows and Sloane groaned.

"Have you been spying on us?"

Austen rolled up the cheese snacks and put them to one side before getting up and heading for Dex's nightstand. He pulled it open, reached in, and plucked out a wet wipe from the packet inside. How the hell did Austen know they were in there?

"I like to know what goes on with my team. The other guys are fun," Austen closed the drawer and dropped onto the bed next to Sloane, a wicked smile on his face, "but you two? Best free porn *ever*."

"You've watched us have sex?" Sloane gaped at him. Austen didn't seem the least bit bothered.

"Like I said. Free porn. Your boy has a mighty fine ass. And he's so energetic. Seriously. Do his batteries ever wear out?"

"No more spying on us. Now answer the question."

"Everyone around the office thinks you're bosom buddies. A budding bromance. Like Tango and Cash."

"An eighties movie reference? Really? You are spending way too much time around Dex, whether he knows it or not."

"What can I say? The dude is entertaining as fuck." Austen kicked off his shoes and swung his legs onto the bed. He put his hands behind his head as he moved his feet from side to side. Sometimes he reminded Sloane of the scrawny little kid who'd stolen his wallet all those years ago. Austen let out a laugh. "Have you noticed how he picks out all the red gummy bears and eats them first? Or the way he eats around the peanuts of his M&M's before eating the peanuts?"

Sloane scowled at him. "Seriously. No more spying on Dex."

"Got it."

Why did Sloane get the feeling Austen was going to completely ignore him? "So no one suspects anything?"

"Just keep doing what you're doing," Austen assured him. "Everyone assumes that's just what your boy's like. He's always teasing and joking with everyone. He hangs off the rest of the team, so it's not like he's just hands on with you. Some of the other agents in your department, not so subtle. Gerry? He practically has 'I'm fucking my partner' stamped on his forehead. The guy all but jizzes his pants every time he sees her." There was a pause, and Austen's feet went still before he spoke up again. "You guys are good together."

"Thanks. So...?"

"Right. Intel. Work. Wayward boyfriend." Austen rolled onto his side and propped himself on his elbow so he could look at Sloane, his expression serious. "Your boy's not letting this go. He's got me giving him intel before I pass it on to Seb. I sent him some information on one of the old Westward Creed guys. An Ox Perry who's been spotted in Queens. There's no word on Hogan yet, but he's bound to go after one of these guys, so your boy's got a fifty-fifty chance of running into him. I'm not a hundred percent sure yet, but Brick Jackson might have hauled ass to Cali. I'm waiting on confirmation. It's looking like he might have used a fake passport. Of course, we're still left with Perry. Luckily Hogan's only got about a dozen or so crew members left." His gaze dropped to the mattress, and he ran his hand absently over the cream-colored sheets.

"What aren't you telling me?" Sloane knew Austen's little signs. The kid was too clever for his own good. He obviously wanted to tell Sloane something but didn't want to rat out whoever had given him the information. So he purposefully gave little gestures prompting Sloane to ask. If it was Sloane demanding information from him, Austen could get whatever was bothering him off his chest without turning stool pigeon.

Austen met Sloane's gaze. "He's going to tell you. He wants you to get settled in first."

"Now *you're* making excuses for him? What's he keeping from me this time?"

"He had a run-in with two of Hogan's goons over at your apartment." Austen cringed, and rightfully so.

"What the ever-living fuck?" Sloane took a deep breath and let it out slowly. His head was pounding already. "First he lies to me about not going after Hogan, and now he lies to me about this?"

Austen pursed his lips thoughtfully before opening his mouth. Sloane knew exactly what he was going to say, and it pissed him off even more. He held a hand up to stop him.

"I swear if you say technically he's not lying, he's just withholding information, I will beat you with my crutch."

"Wow. Those meds make you grumpy... er."

"What happened?" Sloane demanded.

"I don't know. Considering they ended up getting plugged, and your boy came out of it in one piece, I'm going to say it went well."

Sloane shot Austen a warning look. "Now is not the time."

"He said they were casing your apartment."

Could they have been there waiting for him to come home? Had they been ordered to finish the job? Whatever happened, the bastards must have gotten away. At least Dex had managed to walk away unharmed. The lies were piling up.

"Hey, Broodybear?"

"Don't call me that," Sloane snapped. His partner probably hadn't even called in backup. For all Sloane knew he'd kept the incident from the THIRDS. He'd have to if he didn't want to bring unwanted attention to himself. "That little..." How was it possible to want to protect yet strangle someone at the same time?

"At least give him a chance to tell you."

"Like he told me about Destructive Delta getting pulled only to go out and keep working the case after I asked him not to?" Sloane couldn't deal with this right now. "And Ash?"

"He's keeping an eye on your boy. I called him to let him know Dex was on the move. Those baby blues gotta be going somewhere right? I didn't have an exact location to give him, just a general area. Flushing, Queens. Your boy's going to have to do some digging first. He's got a rough area to work with, along with some previous sightings, but nothing specific. Between Seb, Sparks, and your boy, I've got a pretty tight schedule, but if you need me, let me know."

"Okay. Thanks."

Austen looked like he was going to say something else but instead gave Sloane a nod and walked off, the room once again falling to silence. He knew Dex would have called for backup if he'd thought he was in over his head with those assholes outside Sloane's apartment, but the fact he hadn't told Sloane when he'd brought up their team being pulled off the case, confirmed Dex planned to go after Hogan. Question was, what was Sloane going to do about it?

DEX SAT at the large steel table in his makeshift base of operation with his laptop and a host of other equipment spread across the table's surface. He'd finished the last of his reports for Sparks but hadn't submitted them. On his laptop he was logged into his desk's interface at work with several windows open containing all the information he had access to on the Westward Creed and the Coalition.

Dealing with the THIRDS meant he had to be extra careful. If he transferred, downloaded, or cross-referenced any information, Intel would know. He also couldn't have any algorithms set up, which meant he'd have to hunt down information the old-fashioned way. Every piece of technical equipment was monitored by the THIRDS, and he couldn't ask his brother for help because then Cael would know what he was up to. That didn't mean he couldn't get the job done. He'd been a detective long before joining the THIRDS, and he'd managed to solve cases without all the fancy gadgets and Themis. Thanks to his techno-geek brother, Dex had invested in a pocket-sized, high-end, high-resolution digital information camera. During his time with the HPF, Dex never left home without it. The habit hadn't left him. He kept the camera locked up and hidden in a secret compartment in the trunk of his car under the spare tire.

The DIC captured the information on his Themis screen perfectly, and the wireless signal transferred it to his tablet. Sort of the way spies used to take pictures of secret documents on their tiny cameras. Man, technology was awesome. Though he really wished he'd paid more attention in his computer science classes rather than surfing the internet for porn. He was the only one who'd never gotten caught, thanks to his little brother showing him how to properly dispose of the browser's history.

The DIC beeped, letting him know the transfer was complete. All the images of every file he'd taken screenshots of were on his tablet, clear as day. He submitted his reports and logged off his interface. It went black with glowing blue letters scrolling across the screen reading, *Thank you, Agent Daley. Enjoy your time off.* God, sometimes he hated Themis. He was pretty sure the feeling was mutual.

Thanks to Austen, Dex finally had a lead. Ox Perry had been spotted in several locations around Flushing, Queens. Dex rummaged through his backpack and removed the map he'd bought at the convenience store down the street. He stood, unfolded it across the table, and grabbed a highlighter. It was time to get to work. At least now he could concentrate. He'd left the house and sat in his car for what seemed like ages. He couldn't leave Sloane on his own. What if something happened to him while Dex was gone? Dex would never forgive himself. So he'd called Austen and asked him to use his super-agent skills to watch over Sloane and keep him safe until Dex returned. Austen hadn't been happy about it, but Dex was quickly coming to learn there was little Austen wouldn't do for Sloane. He felt pretty shitty exploiting Austen's feelings for Sloane, but if it meant keeping Sloane safe, he'd do whatever he needed to.

Scrolling through the information on his tablet containing both intel from Themis and Austen, Dex started to highlight streets where Perry had been spotted. Once he was done, Dex went over Perry's record. He'd been the youngest member of the Westward Creed back in the 1980s during the riots and arrested for assault, along with a host of other charges due to the deaths of several Therian citizens. However, the charges against the eight youths had been dropped, the Human judge claiming missing evidence. Considering the time, it was mostly the result of corruption. The new branch of Therian government had still been in the process of passing its laws. According to Tony, with the chaos and violence sweeping through the streets, cases like this were tragically not uncommon.

After Perry was released, he seemed to have kept his nose clean. Human, single, no longer living at the address listed in Themis for obvious reasons. He worked for a construction firm but hadn't reported in for days, or so the guy's boss said. Considering Perry had been working there for over twenty years without a change in management, it was possible the guy was covering up for him. Dex leaned his arms on the table and studied the map.

There had to be a pattern. Reasons for Perry to be visiting these locations. Dex brought up the same map of Queens on his tablet and zoomed in. He began going into Street View one by one, making lists and notes of all the shops, buildings, houses, cars, everything. The more he jotted down, the more he felt he was onto something.

Hours passed until Dex's eyes started to sting. What time was it? He checked his watch. Holy fuck! It was almost midnight. Where the hell had the time gone? Looking up, he found a plate with a sandwich, a glazed donut, and next to it a can of Coke. Beside the plate was a note scribbled in Lou's handwriting.

Tried to say hi, but you were in your weird cop-zone. Don't forget to eat. xo Lou

Damn. Lou had been down here, talked to him, and Dex couldn't remember. He'd been so absorbed in his work that he'd completely blocked everything else out. It was nice of Lou to bring him something to eat. *Eat.*

"Oh my God!" Dex scrambled to remove his smartphone from his pocket. Shit. Shit. Shit. Three missed calls from Sloane and two texts asking him if he was going to make it to dinner and hoping he was okay. "I am the shittiest boyfriend ever!" He tapped Sloane's picture and listened to the phone ring, pacing around the office until Sloane's groggy voice answered.

"Hello?"

"Forgotten me already," Dex teased. He felt so shitty.

"Hey. Sorry, I took some painkillers after dinner, and I guess they knocked me out."

Dex dropped down onto the couch, his gaze landing on the desk scattered with all his work. "I'm so sorry I didn't make it to dinner."

"It's okay. I called Ash, and he picked up some food. We hung out. Meeting ran late?"

"Yeah, you know these PR nerds. Then I went and had too much sugar and totally crashed. I went for a nap in one of the bays and just woke up." He closed his eyes, hating himself for telling more lies. But it was to get Hogan off the streets. To keep Sloane safe. He wasn't a terrible person for wanting to keep his family safe, was he?

"I told you not to binge on sugar after eight o'clock."

"You are wise."

"You okay? You sound... off."

I don't deserve you. "Just tired."

"When are you coming home?"

Dex swallowed hard. Did Sloane realize what he'd said? Sloane couldn't have meant it how Dex thought he did. It was just a turn of phrase. He didn't mean *their* home. It didn't matter. Sloane was waiting for him, in *his* bed, under the covers, and warm. Home. Why did that keep popping up in his head? His gaze went back to the table. Home. What if those locations were connected to someone close to Perry? Why else would he keep going back there?

"Dex?"

"Sorry, um, it's late, I stink, and you're all cozy. Would you think I'm a dick if I crashed here?"

"At work?"

"Yeah. By the time I get in it'll be really late, and I don't want to disturb you. Doc said you need lots of rest."

There was a pause at the other end of the line, and Dex's heart broke at Sloane's soft words. "You do what you gotta do. Just stay safe for me."

"PR's dangerous work, but it's not that dangerous. Unless they ask me to read at the children's library again. Then it can get pretty hairy."

Sloane chuckled. "Better you than me."

"Thanks, partner," Dex said dryly. "You sure you'll be okay?"

Sloane's voice was sincere when he answered. "Yeah, I'll be fine."

"Okay. I love you, you know that?"

"I know."

Dex could hear the smile in Sloane's voice. How could something make him feel both wonderful and horrible at the same time? "Good night."

"Good night, Dex."

Sloane hung up, and Dex sat there for a moment wondering what the hell he was doing. He had an amazing guy waiting for him at home, and he was about to sleep on some pimp's reject couch in a makeshift base in the basement of his ex-boyfriend's catering company. Scrolling through his phone, he found a text from Austen.

No updates.

Dex had to move quickly. If Seb started feeding algorithms into Themis on Ox Perry, something was bound to pop up. Dex was onto something, he just had to figure out what it was. He went back to the table and went over his notes, going over every detail until he was all but falling asleep and drooling on his map, but he shook himself off and continued. He made a mental note to bring a coffee machine. Checking his list for the hundredth time, something suddenly jumped out at him. It might be nothing, but then again it could be everything. Two of the streets had ice cream shops. One street had a pizzeria. Another had a bakery. Then a confectionary store. A children's clothing store. A kid's book shop.

"The guy's got a kid." No wonder Perry kept getting sighted in the area. He had a child somewhere around there. Finally, Dex had something. A Google search later, and Dex was grinning. There was an elementary school in the area. He picked up the sandwich and took it back to the couch. Damn, this couch was fugly. Not even tacky, just really fucking ugly. Even Cael wouldn't go near the monstrosity in his Therian form to scratch it, and his brother loved clawing furniture. Tony had replaced three couches, two armchairs, six sets of curtains, and countless other furnishings while they'd been growing up. Cheetah Therians were incredibly curious. They also liked climbing, touching, clawing, and chewing.

Tomorrow he'd get up early to stake out the school in case Perry showed up. Sloane would most likely be sleeping in because of the meds, so it gave Dex some time. He'd also have to stop by the office and visit with PR for a while. He never thought he'd be glad they called. As Dex ate his sandwich, he checked his watch. If he went to sleep now, he'd get about four hours of sleep. Once he was done eating, Dex lay down, stared at the exposed ceiling, listened to the whir of the boiler in the small room next door and told himself he was doing the right thing. The thought of Hogan getting his claws in Sloane was enough to have Dex digging his nails into the couch cushion until his fingers hurt. There was no way Dex would let that son of a bitch get near Sloane. He fell into a restless, dreamless sleep.

Early the next morning, Dex headed for Queens and Maspeth Elementary. He parked in front of a residence the next block over and turned off the ignition. From here he watched the yellow school buses drive past as they dropped kids off, as well as parents walking their children to the school. Parents were scattered in small groups, chatting to each other while their kids ran around, jumping handrails and climbing fences before their parents could notice and drag them away. It reminded him of when Tony used to hold on to the handle of Dex's backpack while trying his damn hardest to keep Cael from climbing anything and everything he could get his chubby little fingers on. More often than not Tony would end up with one of them under each arm, carrying them inside to their classrooms and dropping their little butts on their chairs before greeting their teachers and wishing them luck.

One lone figure stood on the sidewalk looking down into the basketball court filled with kids screeching and playing as they waited for the bell to signal the start of another school day. Maspeth was a good school, and it accepted both Human and Therian children. Dex's research had informed him it was more concerned with the education of its students and not their species. It was hard to believe segregated schools still existed. They were private schools and fell under the same laws as religious schools, so not much could be done about it.

Today was Dex's lucky day. Ox Perry was wearing a baseball cap and sporting a beard, but Dex recognized him. Was the guy being inconspicuous because he knew he was being hunted or because he wasn't supposed to be here? Considering Dex couldn't find any information regarding Perry having a child, Dex wondered if maybe Perry wasn't granted access or visitation rights. Well, there was only one way to find out.

Dex got out of his car and set the alarm before casually making his way over. He came to a stop beside Perry who took a subtle step to the side.

"Hey," Dex said with a friendly smile.

"Hey," Perry replied warily.

"My name's Agent Daley. I'm with the THIRDS." Dex showed his badge. He was risking exposure, but he had a feeling Perry wasn't about to go running off to tell the THIRDS. As Dex suspected, Perry's eyes widened, and he took a step back like he was going to bolt. But his gaze moved to the basketball court, and a conflicted expression came onto his face.

"Easy there, Perry. I'm not here to arrest you."

"Look, I didn't have anything to do with the Order. Reyes approached me months ago, and I told him to fuck off. I don't want to have anything to do with him or the others. The whole Humans against Therians shit was a lifetime ago. I was a stupid kid. I made a mistake."

"I don't think Beck Hogan sees it that way. He's looking for you." Dex followed Perry's gaze to the court, surprised when a little girl waved at Perry with a big, dimpled smile. From here Dex could make out a black tattoo on her neck. Shit. No wonder Perry didn't want to get mixed up with Reyes. He had a Therian child.

"Is she your daughter?" Dex asked.

"Yeah. Her name's Beth."

"She's adorable." Dex couldn't help his smile as the little girl screeched and laughed with her fellow students, her pigtails bouncing with her. His smile faded when he once again spotted the tattoo on her neck marking her as a wolf Therian. He understood the need for Therian laws the same way he understood the need for Human ones, but there were aspects he didn't agree with. Justified or not, marking adults was one thing, but children? The whole classification thing had never sat well with him.

Doctors claimed the process was painless for the kids, but Dex called bullshit a long time ago. He remembered when he and Cael had been kids, the way Cael had screamed and screamed when they'd marked him, big, fat tears rolling down his pink cheeks. He'd cried until his throat was sore and his voice hoarse. The whole thing had been terrifying for them all. Dex had been forced to wait outside the CDC Therian Registration office after trying to punch the doctor for hurting his little brother. Tony had been stone-faced the entire time. His dad had never been big on the whole classification thing either. He'd taken them out for ice cream afterward.

"Beth's my whole world. Lana, her mother, was a wolf Therian. A nurse. I met her ten years ago when I ended up in the hospital after someone hit a gas main at one of the sites I was working at. The explosion knocked me out. When I woke up, I thought I'd died and gone to heaven. She was so beautiful. We started talking and then dating. I couldn't lie to her about my past. I cared about her too much. After everything I'd said and done, she forgave me. Two years later, we had Beth. It was unexpected, but we were so happy. I was going to ask Lana to marry me."

"What happened? If you don't mind my asking." By the look on Perry's face, it was clear Lana was no longer with him.

"Lana was pre-First Gen. She lived through the mutation caused by Eppione.8, but it caused a lot of health issues. Her immune system was slowly deteriorating. She caught an infection after childbirth and passed away a few weeks later."

"I'm so sorry."

"I didn't know what to do with myself. Our relationship was far from perfect, but we loved each other."

"Why isn't Beth registered under your name?"

"I dreaded this day. When my past would catch up to me. I was always paranoid about it. It broke my heart, but I couldn't keep Beth with me. I was afraid someone would try to hurt her. But I was weak and couldn't give her up for adoption either, at least not to a stranger. I took all the savings I had and paid off the doctor at the Therian registration office. My brother is listed as the biological father. He's married to a Therian with a Therian child. I knew Beth would have a good home there."

"Does she know you're her biological dad?"

Perry shook his head. "She thinks I'm her uncle. One day she might find out. But who knows where I'll be then." He turned to face Dex, his expression grim and determined. "I'll do whatever it takes to keep her safe, Agent Daley. There is nothing in this world I wouldn't sacrifice for her. I've made mistakes. Unforgivable mistakes. But Beth shouldn't have to pay for them."

"And I agree with you, Perry. But if I can find you and your family, what makes you think Beck Hogan can't?"

"Beck Hogan," Perry whispered the name, as if saying it too loud might conjure the guy up. "I've been moving around, trying not to stay too long in one place. The moment I saw the news reports about the others, and then Hogan being responsible for the explosion, I knew he'd come after me sooner or later."

"Hogan's looking to finish what he started. He won't rest until you and Jackson are dead. If it means getting to you through your family, then so be it."

"Why are you helping me?"

"I sincerely believe you regret what you did, even if I can't forgive it, but I'm not willing to put your little girl's life at risk. I want Hogan. I'm beginning to think the only way is to draw him out." He couldn't believe he was saying this, but when he thought about it, the answer was clear as day. "If I can keep you and Jackson away from him, he's failed. He'll never complete his revenge. Once he finds out, he'll make his move, and I'll be waiting for him."

"What do you need me to do?"

"Turn yourself in to the THIRDS. They'll take care of the rest."

Perry turned to look at Beth who waved at him again. After several painfully silent minutes went by, Perry let out a weary sigh, and his shoulders slumped in defeat. "Okay. Can I have a moment to say good-bye?"

Dex nodded. He stood by as Perry took the stairs on their left leading down to the court. Beth ran to him and threw herself into his arms. He squeezed her tight and put her down, talking to her and smiling like nothing was wrong. It was almost too much for Dex to watch. Despite the brave face Perry put on, Dex could see the man's heart breaking. After a fierce hug, Perry headed back toward Dex, his eyes red and filled with unshed tears.

"I'm ready."

Dex led the way to his car, unlocking the door for Perry and making sure he was seated inside before going around to the driver's side and getting in. He fastened his seatbelt and got them moving, but he didn't head back toward Manhattan. Instead he pulled onto Fifty-Ninth Street next to a dry-cleaning supply warehouse. It was a dead-end road with a few houses across the supply warehouse. He drove to the end, made a three-point turn, and parked.

"What are you doing?"

"The THIRDS will make sure Beth and your family are safe, but there's something else I need."

Perry looked exhausted. "What?"

"Do you have any information on where I can find Brick Jackson? He's the last guy on Hogan's shit list."

"Brick? Jesus, I haven't talked to him in years. We used to work at the same construction firm a few years ago, but he just up and disappeared one day."

Something in Dex's gut told him Perry wasn't being completely honest. It wouldn't be a stretch to believe the only two Westward Creed members who hadn't become members of the Order would contact each other. If Reyes attempted to recruit Perry, it was likely he'd tried to recruit

Jackson. "Does Jackson have any family? Friends you know of? Something? Whatever you can give me might help keep Jackson alive. You have no reason to trust me, I get it, but if I don't find Jackson before Hogan does, the next time you see your friend will be in the news after he's found mauled to death."

Perry stared at him, horrified. He went silent, turning his attention out the car window. The guy was thinking about it, Dex was certain. After an excruciating amount of time went by, Perry turned back to him, his expression suspicious.

"Why do you want Hogan so bad, Agent Daley?"

"Because he hurt someone close to me," Dex said. "I need to stop him before he hurts anyone else."

Perry was undoubtedly wondering whether he should trust Dex or not. He had no reason to. But Hogan and his crew had already killed several Westward Creed members. The evidence was hard to ignore. In the end, Perry let out a sigh. "Jackson's gone. He knew a guy who could get him a new ID and passport. Official. After Craig ended up dead, Brick freaked, said he was leaving for California. No connection to anyone there."

Shit. "So he's in the wind?"

"Yeah. Brick never settled down. I think the guilt about what happened back during the riots ate away at him too."

Dex started the car and headed for HQ. Well, so much for Jackson. He'd still run it by Austen, see if Austen could confirm the intel. There'd be video surveillance at the airports. Even if he'd used a different identity, he'd pop up on a feed somewhere. Then Austen could send an alert to the THIRDS California HQ, just in case.

Twenty minutes later, Dex was walking Perry to HQ. He'd parked a couple of blocks away and accompanied the guy to the corner wall of the looming government agency. Dex was already risking exposure, and God forbid Seb caught him with Perry. One coincidence related to the case was questionable enough, but two?

"It's important you make them believe it was your idea to turn yourself in, otherwise we get a whole load of questions and red tape we don't need. Not if we're going to move this along quickly."

"You want me to lie to them?"

"No, you're simply withholding certain information. Tell them why you're turning yourself in. They've no reason to be suspicious of you, and since you had nothing to do with the Order or Reyes, there won't be any charges. It's likely they'll put you into protective custody until Hogan is caught."

"Why can't I tell them about you?"

Dex decided to be honest with Perry, even if he wasn't being honest with his own employer. "Because technically, I'm on leave. Hogan put my team out of commission, and he's threatened my family. My partner was hurt badly by the bomb Hogan planted. I'll be honest with you, Perry. Another team was assigned this case, but I can't leave my family's safety to chance."

Perry nodded his understanding, his gaze sympathetic. "You're protecting your family. I get it."

Dex wished him luck and watched him approach the guards at the gate. He must have stated his name because the guards jumped to action, talking into their earpieces and quickly escorting him inside. Dex didn't waste any time. He turned and headed back toward his car. As he walked down the block, he felt good. Like something was finally going his way. Talking to Perry had made him realize the quickest way to finding Hogan was to make the guy come to him.

Hogan was obsessed with getting revenge, but if there was no one left to get revenge on, he'd take it out on whoever had relieved him of it, like he'd tried to do with Ash. It was insane, but how the hell else was he supposed to find one Therian in the whole of New York City?

Dex fished his keys out of his pocket and hit the alarm button, but when he opened his car door, the alarm went off. Hadn't he turned it off? He hit the button again. Weird. He sat back, ready to turn on the ignition, then stilled. The hairs on the back of his neck stood on end. He quickly recovered, turned on *Retro Radio,* and when he pulled back, he discreetly went for his Glock. Unlatching the safety mechanism, he swiped up his gun and turned, his gun aimed straight at the chest of the huge Therian in his backseat.

SIX

"Motherfuck!" He returned his Glock to its holster and glared daggers at Ash sitting casually in the back of the car like he was waiting to be chauffeured around town. "What the hell, man? You broke into my car?"

"You should really be more careful. Could have been Hogan back here."

Fuck, he was right. But Dex wasn't about to admit it. "Why are you here acting like some horror movie backseat serial killer?" A thought occurred to him. "Are you spying on me? Did Sloane send you to keep tabs on me?" Was he that transparent? Even if Sloane did know, did he not trust Dex to handle this?

"He asked me to keep an eye on you. He's worried." Ash motioned to the front seat. "I'm coming around. If you try to drive off without me, I will beat the shit out of you."

Dex mumbled something unintelligible under his breath about preferring to drive over him but sat patiently while Ash got out and got into the passenger seat. He fastened his seatbelt and motioned for Dex to do the same. Was the guy serious? Ash arched an eyebrow at him. He was serious. Dex fastened his seatbelt as Ash reached over and turned off the radio.

"I don't know how Sloane listens to this shit music of yours."

"It's not shit. And he listens to it because he's a caring partner and not an asshole," Dex replied, switching it back on and lowering the volume. "My car, my music. And I don't need a babysitter."

"Clearly you do. Otherwise you wouldn't be doing what you're doing."

"Which is?"

"Something incredibly stupid."

"You think I'm going to stand back and watch some other team bring in Hogan after all the shit he's put us through? If they even find the guy?"

"We're under direct orders, Daley."

"Fuck orders," Dex snapped. "My family's in danger. Cael is in danger. I'm not going to wait around for Hogan to put my brother in the hospital, or worse, the morgue. Are you?" He expected Ash to argue back, instead his burly teammate sat back with a disapproving frown.

"Pretty shitty move, using your brother to get me to agree with you."

"Not my intention. Besides, it's the truth, and you know it. We're all in danger. That's part of the reason Sparks pulled us off this thing."

"Exactly. And you're proposing we go out there and make it easy for Hogan to finish the job."

"We? I'm not proposing *we* do anything. Jesus, Ash. Your stitches haven't fully healed yet. Go home. Get some rest while you can get it, and not a word of this to Sloane."

Ash let out a humorless laugh. "Are you kidding me? Do you realize what Sloane would do to me if he found out I knew what you were up to, lied to him, and then let you go off on your own? It'll be a hell of a lot more painful to put up with than my fucking stitches, I can tell you that much. He might be my best friend, but he's also my team leader, and he will beat the shit out of me in training. I think it's how he remains so fucking calm all the time. He takes his shit out on us in Sparta."

"Yes, he does. Ash—"

"Forget it, Daley. If you're determined to play John McClane, I'm going to be there to make sure you don't lose your fucking shoes."

Dex held back a smile as he started the ignition. "Actually, John McClane didn't lose his shoes, he took them off."

"Don't correct me."

"But you're wrong."

"Not about you being a pain in my ass," Ash growled.

Dex opened his mouth, and Ash jabbed a finger at him. "I hear one sexual innuendo come out of your mouth, and I swear you won't have to worry about Hogan because I'll kill you myself. Now get me up to speed."

"What makes you think I have anything?"

"Because if you didn't, you wouldn't be on Destructive Delta. I saw you drop that dude off at HQ. Now stop dicking around and fill me in."

"Okay. Fine. Where am I dropping you off?"

"Home. I followed you in a cab."

"How cliché."

"Fuck off. I'm not supposed to be driving yet. Fucking Therian meds are bullshit. It's like they're purposefully trying to tranquilize us or something."

Dex rolled his eyes. It was true Therian medicine had a way to go and a good deal of cures were still under development, but he hardly thought a bunch of painkillers were out to tranq them. As they headed north in the direction of Ash's apartment, Dex brought Ash up to speed, telling him everything he'd done up to this point without filling him in on where he was working from. If Ash decided to rat him out to Sloane, the last thing he needed was either of them showing up at Clove Catering. Lou would have a fucking heart attack. He'd need to be extra vigilant from now on knowing Ash was spying on him.

"I gotta say, I'm pretty impressed."

Dex shot him a glance. "But...?"

"No but. Good work."

"Maybe I should pull over. I feel kind of faint."

Ash actually chuckled. Well, today was just full of surprises. He'd turned onto FDR Drive when his phone rang. He tapped the Bluetooth button on his steering wheel to answer.

"Daley here."

"It's me."

"Austen. Just the guy I wanted to talk to."

"Aw, I feel loved."

Not touching that. It would be like waving a red flag in front of a horny bull. "According to Perry, Jackson's in the wind. Got himself a new name and is heading for Cali."

"I'll have confirmation by tonight. Now it's my turn. I found you a lead."

"Fucking ace. What is it?"

"It's going to take some reconnaissance. Keeler, you up for it?"

Dex and Ash exchanged glances. "How'd you know Ash was with me?"

"It's what I do, baby. Ash, Sweet Cheeks, how's it hanging?"

Dex burst into laughter while Ash rolled his eyes and answered in his usual pleasant growl. "Get on with it."

"Okay, we have a way to possibly get to Hogan. He's got a new second-in-command. Drew Collins. To get to Collins, we've got to get to Collins's boyfriend, Felipe Bautista. *But* you're going to need help."

"What kind of help?" Dex asked. Something told him he wasn't going to like the sound of this.

"The Destructive Delta kind."

"Shit. You want me to bring the team in on this?" Absolutely not. Out of the question. Putting his career on the line was one thing, but his teammates? He couldn't ask them for that. It was his idea. If shit went south, he'd suffer the consequences alone.

"Depends. You got a fully equipped surveillance van?"

"Um, no. You're the super-secret specialist or whatever."

"Squadron Specialist agent. Dude, I can't just pull a vanload of high-tech equipment out of my ass. If we were going through the proper channels maybe, but not on such short notice and definitely not while you're out playing Batman."

"All right, I get it. But I won't bring Cael into this."

"You know any other boy wonder who's got the equipment and the know-how to set up a surveillance van? Kid's got a shit-ton of equipment in his basement."

"How the hell do you know?" What exactly did Austen's job as Super Spy Whatever entail? He might have to ask Sloane at some point. Was part of Austen's job to keep tabs on them? Is that why every squad had one? If it weren't for Sloane's relationship with Austen, Dex wouldn't have trusted the guy not to go running to Sparks.

"Squadron Specialist agent," Austen reminded him.

"Right. Look, I don't want Cael risking his safety or his career because of me."

Ash let out a scoff.

"What?" It was like arguing was as essential to the guy as breathing.

"You know how pissed off Cael will be if we're found out and you didn't tell him? Not to mention how pissed he'll be on top of that because you didn't trust him to make up his own mind?"

Damn it. Why the hell did Ash keep making sense? As much as Dex hated to admit it, his teammate was right. Cael would be pissed off at him if he found out Dex was keeping even more secrets from him. Seemed like lately all he did was lie and keep secrets from his loved ones. It was starting to become a disturbing trend, one he disliked himself for. Dex kept promising Cael he'd stop treating him like a little kid, and yet he continued to make decisions for him, thinking he knew what was best.

"Okay. I'll tell him. No promises, though. What else do we need?"

"Face it, dude. You're going to need backup. As scary and ass-kicking as Ash is, he ain't a hundred percent right now. Hogan is a tiger Therian, Collins is a cougar Therian, and the rest of Hogan's crew is made up of either Felids or wolf Therians. If you insist on doing this, one lion Therian and one Human won't be able to stop them. Plus, you're going to need firepower. Tranqs and shit."

Ash cursed under his breath. "Letty."

"Duuude, have you seen that chick's house? She's got a fucking armory in her pantry. You open any cupboard, and I swear to Santa's jingly balls there's like a half dozen guns in there somewhere. I'm pretty sure she's got grenades in the cookie jar. There's definitely an AK next to the cans of Goya beans. I saw her take it out to clean."

"Oh my God, you *do* spy on us!"

There was a long pause. "No."

"Whatever," Dex muttered. He didn't have time for this. "Okay. Guns. Letty. Fine."

"You'll need a medic. And a huge-ass tiger Therian wouldn't go amiss. And really, it would be stupid not to invite the sniper along."

"Fuck me." Dex stopped at a red light and let his head fall against the steering wheel. "Okay, so basically we need the whole team."

"I think I said as much like twenty curse words ago."

Dex looked over at Ash who shrugged his shoulders.

"Thank you, Ash. What an incredibly insightful shrug. It really helped me."

"Fuck off. Destructive Delta is family, Dex. I thought you'd know that by now. The least we can do is talk to them. Let them make up their own minds."

"Good," Austen stated cheerfully. "We'll meet tonight. I'll text the address." Austen hung up without so much as waiting for a confirmation from Dex. Guess they'd be meeting tonight.

"Shit. We need a van. Where the hell am I supposed to get a van by tonight?" Who did he know—Damn. Lou was going to kill him. Ash must have seen him cringe because he gave him a questioning look. The light turned, and Dex continued up First Avenue. "Lou. He rents space in a garage a block away from Clove Catering where the company vans are parked."

Ash seemed to consider this. "You think he'll let you borrow one?"

Dex pulled up outside Ash's apartment building and turned to look at him. "I sure as hell hope so."

"You do what you gotta do. I'll call the team. Now go home." Ash checked his watch. "Sloane should be waking up soon. The least you can do is bring him breakfast in bed."

"So he won't be pissed at me?"

Ash got out of the car and leaned in to scowl at Dex. "No, jackass. Bring him breakfast in bed because he's injured, and you're his fucking boyfriend. Stop treating him like your team leader and treat him like the guy you're in love with. It's the least he deserves." Ash slammed the door, and Dex sat there gaping. Had he been out-relationshipped by Ash Keeler? What the hell was the world coming to?

"Damn." Ash was right. Again. How messed up was that? Dex drove home hoping he had time to make breakfast before Sloane woke up. He really needed to get his shit together. After everything they'd been through, they were finally starting to build something solid. The last thing Dex wanted to do was fuck it all up. If he hadn't already. Though he'd like to think they'd be able to work through this the same way they'd worked through everything else.

He got home in record time. Standing perfectly still inside the living room, he listened for any movement upstairs. Nothing. Being as quiet as could be, because Therians had ridiculously good hearing, Dex got to work making Sloane's favorite. Double eggs benedict and a side stack of blueberry pancakes. Dex even made the Hollandaise sauce and pancakes from scratch. While the ham cooked, his stomach demanded not to be left out, so Dex made himself an egg and ham breakfast sandwich and munched while he finished cooking Sloane's food. It made him smile knowing

Sloane was upstairs in his bed, sound asleep. How awesome would it be to have Sloane in his bed every night? Lou's words rang in his ear and he frowned. Maybe Dex needed to rein himself in a little. Let Sloane set the pace. In the meantime, he needed to show Sloane how serious he was about them and their relationship, how much he loved him. Feeling a little extra sappy, he used the heart mold he'd bought during Valentine's Day and made the pancakes heart shaped.

With breakfast cooked, Dex carefully arranged the layers of food on one of his Death Star dinner plates. He poured some orange juice in Sloane's favorite *Star Wars* glass and grabbed the folding tray table from the storage drawer under the island counter. With great care, he arranged the cutlery on the folded napkin, placed the Darth and Storm Trooper salt and pepper shakers next, followed by the R2D2 syrup dispenser. My God, he really was an unbelievable nerd. But so was his partner, even if he was still somewhat in the closet about his nerdiness. Dex was working on fixing that.

He carried the tray upstairs and into the bedroom as Sloane was returning from the bathroom. His partner looked at Dex, then the tray, then back at Dex.

"Morning, Sunshine Bear." Dex smiled brightly as he motioned over to the bed.

Using one of his crutches, Sloane returned to the bed, and Dex put the tray down on the dresser to help him.

"I can do it," Sloane grumbled, sitting down on the bed and propping the crutch up against the nightstand. He sat back and brought his left leg up, but he was forced to use his hands to lift his right leg.

"How is it?" Dex asked.

"It's getting better. I've been getting up every few hours and walking around the room, with crutches obviously, but it feels like it's getting stronger. Therapy starts next week." Sloane shifted back, and Dex ran over.

"Hold on. Let me prop your pillows up." He didn't want Sloane twisting his body too much. His Therian body might heal quicker than a Human's, but his stitches still needed more time.

Dex sorted out all of Sloane's pillows, fluffing them up and arranging them before bringing the tray over. Once Sloane was settled, Dex placed the tray over his lap and kissed him, tasting a faint hint of minty freshness.

Sloane stared down at the tray.

"Is it okay?" Dex asked. Had he forgotten something? "Eggs benedict and pancakes are your favorite, right?"

Sloane nodded.

"What's wrong?"

"You made heart-shaped pancakes."

Dex held back a smile. "Are they too unmanly? Should I have made them grenade-shaped? I'm sure Letty's got a mold for those."

Sloane chuckled. "No, hearts are fine. It's real sweet. Thank you."

Dex sat down on the edge of the bed beside him. He ran his fingers through Sloane's hair feeling guilty for having left him on his own last night. Sloane could take care of himself, even if he was injured, but his partner was drugged up and obviously feeling a little out of it, considering his reaction to the heart-shaped pancakes. Maybe it was time he took care of his partner like he'd promised he would.

"Why don't you eat your breakfast while I shower, and we'll watch a movie or something together?"

Sloane gave him a wide smile. "I'd like that."

Dex left Sloane to his breakfast and went off to shower as quickly as he could. Showering wasn't as much fun without his partner. As he lathered himself up, a naughty thought occurred to him. He'd also promised he'd make his partner purr. Finishing up, he could barely hold back his smile or the heat spreading through him. *Easy there, Daley. Don't get yourself worked up yet.* He dressed in his comfy cotton pajama bottoms and a loose faded *Back to the Future* T-shirt before heading out into the bedroom. Sloane was smiling, his plate devoid of any evidence food had ever been there. Wow, his partner had been hungry. Really hungry. Starving. Sort of like after...

"Please tell me you didn't." Dex removed the tray and put it on the floor against the wall. He pulled the blanket back and tried to lift Sloane's T-shirt, but his partner slapped his hand away. "Sloane, let me see, damn it." He grabbed Sloane's wrist with one hand and managed to pull up the cotton shirt, cursing under his breath at the tiny beads of blood seeping through the bandage. "For fuck's sake, did you try to shift?" When Sloane looked away, Dex had his answer. No wonder his partner was out of it. It wasn't just the meds. Sloane hadn't recuperated from post-shift. Dex opened the minifridge and found it empty. "When?" He slammed the fridge door shut.

"Last night. After you called," Sloane mumbled.

"Last night?" Dex put a hand to his head. Veggies and hummus were all well and good for Sloane's Human side, but not for the Felid inside him. He needed meat, protein, and more than the packet of sliced chicken Dex had left him in the fridge. "Fuck. Sloane, you know you're not supposed to attempt shifting. The doctor said so, and it's in the packet. To make matters worse, you do it when there's no one here to perform Post-shift Trauma Care? With no access to the right foods? What were you thinking?"

"I'm thinking I need to fucking heal, and if that's the quickest way to do it, then it's a risk I'm willing to take!"

Sloane's ferocity surprised Dex, and he took a step back. His partner's pupils were dilated and his fangs slightly elongated. Fuck, what the hell was going on? It was like Sloane was having trouble controlling his feral side. Dex could see it. He could see the Felid inside Sloane staring back at him from behind glowing amber eyes. Could the meds be doing this? The recovery packet the doctor had given them specifically instructed Sloane not to shift while he was healing, especially while on his meds.

"Okay, take it easy. It's me." Dex held his hands up in front of him and swallowed hard, aware of the telltale signs. "There's no hurry for you to heal, Sloane. It's okay."

"It's not okay," Sloane snarled, his fingers flexing against the sheets and his nails starting to grow. *Fuck. Oh fuck.*

"Sloane, you need to breathe. Calm down." Dex slowly edged away from the bed. Why was this happening? Sloane had never lost his grip on his Felid side. Not to mention he'd yet to fully recover from his first attempt. "Please, Sloane. Your body's not healed from the first try. Who knows what a second attempt will do?"

There was no reply from Sloane. He was gritting his teeth, his face red, and his muscles straining.

"Sloane, you need to stop."

"I can't." Sloane lowered his head, his fierce gaze on Dex.

"Why?"

"To protect *you*!"

Dex gasped as Sloane let out a roar, his body starting to shift. What the hell was Dex supposed to do? He'd never faced a Therian who'd lost control of his Human side, much less an Apex predator. Quickly, he backed up against the far wall, cringing as Sloane's cries of agony filled the room. Sloane tore at his clothes, pulling his T-shirt and pajama bottoms off before his mass shifted, bones popped, and fur pierced his skin. Dex reached into his pocket and with shaky hands placed a call.

A gruff voice answered. "What do you want?"

"Ash, you have to help me." The panic in his voice must have been clear, because Ash's tone instantly transformed from its usual gruffness to concern.

"What's going on, Dex? Talk to me."

"It's Sloane. He's shifting, but it's not... not normal. He tried last night but couldn't complete the transformation. Then we got into an argument, and it's like he's lost it. I don't think he's in control. How is that possible?"

"Hide."

"What?"

"Hide somewhere he can't get to you. I'm on my way. I've still got my key to your place."

Ash hung up, and Dex shoved his phone into his pocket. Where the fuck was he supposed to hide? When he moved his gaze to the bed, he stilled. There was no time for hiding. The huge black jaguar lay in the center of the bed, his tail thumping against the headboard. He sniffed the sheets, then the air before his gaze landed on Dex.

"Sloane?"

Sloane let out an angry hiss, baring lethal fangs. Fangs capable of piercing a man's skull. He jumped off the bed and howled when he hit the floor, falling over onto his right side. Dex's instinct was to go to him, but he caught himself before Sloane could notice. There was no telling how much of his partner was in control. Had it been any other feral Therian, Dex would have done whatever was necessary to neutralize the threat. But this wasn't any feral Therian: it was his partner, his best friend, his lover. Dex didn't want to hurt Sloane, but what if Sloane tried to seriously hurt him, or worse? Dex quickly shoved the thought aside. He'd figure a way out of this. He had to.

Sloane twisted and craned his neck to look back at his right leg, hissing at it. When he stood, his leg trembled, and he ended up balancing on his other three legs. It wasn't enough to slow him down. He hissed at Dex and limped toward him.

Okay, calm down. You can do this.

The THIRDS Therian-Human Relations class had prepared him for this. Sort of. Oh my God, no it hadn't! The class had taught him about bonds between Human and Therian agents. It hadn't taught them what to do if their partner went feral. It wasn't something that happened. Any problems with a Therian agent's psych evals were immediately addressed, and as far as Dex knew, Sloane's evals were unquestionable.

Dex quickly considered his options. Sloane was hurt, which meant his response time wouldn't be as quick. There were several Post-shift Trauma Care kits with sedatives around the house, none of which were within his reach right now. Awesome. The bathroom was too far away for him to run to, and it was behind Sloane, so that was out of the question. He'd never make it to the closet in time, and it would mean taking the chance of turning his back on Sloane, which was a big no-no. There was only one option. Slowly, he edged toward the bedroom door, backing away through it and into the hall with his hands in front of him. Sloane watched his every move but remained still. If Dex could make it downstairs, he could hide in the pantry or the basement. Hell, even jump on the counter. *Jump.* With Sloane's back leg still weak, his partner might not be able to jump as high as he normally would.

There was a series of growls and screams from downstairs, followed by a roar that reverberated through the house. Ash.

Dex made the mistake of glancing toward the stairs, and he paid the price. He was knocked onto his back by Sloane's heavy mass, and he banged his head hard against the carpet. Quickly, he tried to scramble back, only to have Sloane claw at him. Dex rolled out of the way, though not before the tips of four razor-sharp claws brushed his forearm, leaving behind a painful sting and tiny beads of blood. Shit, Sloane had clawed him! There was another roar from Sloane when a huge body landed over Dex. Ash stood over him in his lion Therian form, his amber eyes following Sloane's movements. Some sort of hissing contest followed with Sloane looking mighty pissed off as a result.

Sloane clawed at Ash, catching him on the side of his jaw and drawing a thin line of blood. Ash roared, but he didn't swipe back at Sloane. Instead he ducked his head and moved out of the way every time Sloane pawed at him. Ash let out a series of low growls and mewls, but he didn't roar or bare his fangs at Sloane. He also didn't back away from Dex, who was feeling like a tiny kitten among huge lethal Felids. Was his partner finally backing off? The rest happened so fast, Dex almost got whiplash. Sloane lunged at Ash, managing to knock him off Dex and over the first step. With a series of roars and growls, Ash went rolling down the stairs.

"Ash!" Dex managed to get himself to his feet and checked the stairs, relieved when he saw Ash push himself to his paws at the bottom of the stairs, shaking his massive head and mane. Thank God he was okay. Dex wished he could say the same thing about himself. A low growl behind him had him turning slowly. He backed away from the stairs with Sloane following.

"Sloane, stop," Dex stated firmly.

Sloane ignored him, corralling Dex and backing him up toward the wall like he was Sloane's prey, which considering the circumstances and Sloane's possible cognitive absence, was likely true.

"Stop it right now!"

Sloane hissed, and Dex freaked out. In one of his momentary brain farts, he smacked Sloane across his muzzle. *Oh. My. God.* What the fuck had he done?

Sloane sneezed and shook his head. His ears flattened and a low feral growl rumbled from deep inside his chest. Dex stood motionless, holding his breath as he watched Sloane. A roar shook the hallway, and Sloane clawed at Dex's pajama bottoms, tearing through them and jerking him off his feet. Ash roared from the stairs as he approached, but Sloane was already looming over Dex, fangs inches away from his neck.

"Stop." Dex's voice came out shakier than he'd intended. A part of him knew Sloane wouldn't hurt him, but the other was feeling the sting left behind by Sloane's claws. Dex forced himself to look into Sloane's glowing amber eyes. With a shaky hand, he reached out and put it to Sloane's soft fur. "I know you're in there somewhere. It's me. It's Dex. You remember me, right? The crazy guy who eats Cheesy Doodles and makes you heart-shaped pancakes? Who quotes Indiana Jones movies with you, drives you up the wall with his big-hair-band music and thinks you're the most amazing guy he's ever met? Remember him?"

Something flashed through those pools of amber before

Sloane nudged his head against Dex's, and he let out a low mewling, almost wailing. It broke Dex's heart. It sounded almost pained. Dex wrapped his arms around Sloane's thick neck and held him, patting him gently as he murmured words of comfort. Sloane dropped down onto the floor beside him, one paw over Dex's chest as he nuzzled him and bumped his head against Dex's. A big sandpapery tongue proceeded to lick Dex on the side of his head, making him chuckle. At least until Sloane licked his ear.

"Dude! Again with the ear!" He shoved Sloane playfully away, then rolled over to scratch Sloane's belly, laughing when Sloane wiggled on the carpet and pawed at him—without the claws this time, purring like a big housecat. Sloane rolled over and pushed his wet kitty nose against Dex's, his eyes shut in contentment. They bumped their heads together, unmoving for a few breaths. Dex wondered if Sloane was as relieved as he was. It had been one hell of a close call, but he was too glad to have his partner back to turn Sloane away. He got up and saw Ash sitting serenely by the stairs watching them.

"Thanks, Simba."

Ash let out a chuff and padded into the bedroom with Sloane limping behind him. Dex followed the two inside, smiling at the two friends as they playfully bumped heads and pawed at each other. Sloane nuzzled his head under Ash's chin, both purring like chainsaws.

"You two are so adorable," Dex said, as he walked over to the bathroom to get his Therian first-aid kit. He left the two Felids to make up and tended to his arm. The scratches weren't deep, but they were definitely going to leave a mark. Was it weird he kind of liked the idea of being marked by Sloane? There were a lot of Therian chasers out there who loved getting clawed, sporting Therian scars proudly. But

Dex didn't see it as a kink. More like... he was bonded to Sloane's Felid side now as much as he was bonded to his Human side.

Once he'd finished disinfecting the scratches and applying a bandage, he walked out and sat down on the bed, his legs feeling shaky now that the whole ordeal was over. Two huge Felids sat in his bedroom watching him. Sloane padded over and leapt up beside him. He put his head on Dex's lap and mewled.

"It's okay, buddy." Dex scratched Sloane behind the ear. Checking his partner's injured side, he was relieved to see there was no blood. Actually, he couldn't see any sutures. Had the shift healed Sloane's wound? It hadn't healed his leg, though it seemed a little stronger than before. But as far as the surgical incision, Dex couldn't find any trace of it. Of course, inside it might be another matter, but on the outside, there was only a long thin scar.

"Okay, guys. I think it's time to shift back." Ash made to leave when Dex got to his feet. "Whoa there, mister. Where do you think you're going?"

Ash turned his big furry head toward Dex and hissed.

"Hell no. You're not going home in your state. You need Post-shift Trauma Care, and I'm going to give it to you." He jutted a finger at the bathroom. "Get your Aslan ass in there. There's towels and a couple of robes behind the door."

Releasing a huff, Ash headed for the bathroom. Dex followed to make sure he was all right. Before he closed the door, he knelt down in front of Ash.

"Hey, thank you."

Ash wrinkled his muzzle before looking away, as if he was thinking. Then he turned his head and snuggled Dex's face, giving his chin a lick.

"Ew, gross," Dex laughed. "Don't worry, big guy. It'll be our secret. No one would believe me anyway." Dex petted Ash before getting up and closing the door behind him. With hands on his hips, he shook his head at his partner who was rolling around on the sheets. "Seriously dude? 'Cause your scent isn't already all up in here?"

Sloane purred, and Dex rolled his eyes. He walked over to the bed whose sheets were now a rumpled mess, and playfully tugged at his partner's ear. "You. Shift. Now."

With a moan, Sloane stopped frolicking, and Dex headed downstairs. Between the screams in his bathroom and the ones in his bedroom, his neighbors either thought someone was getting killed, or he was having one really fucked-up orgy. While Sloane and Ash shifted back to their Human forms, Dex quickly gathered supplies from his pantry and fridge. In a reusable shopping bag, he chucked bottles of Gatorade and some protein bars. He grabbed a couple of huge steaks from the fridge and cooked them up rare the way Sloane and Ash liked them. While those were cooking, he gathered up Ash's discarded clothes from the living room and stuck them in a second grocery bag.

The steaks were done in no time. With a bag of supplies hanging off each arm and a tray containing a plate with two steaks weighing about as much as Cael did, Dex headed up to the bedroom. Sloane and Ash were sitting on the edge of the bed in robes looking like they had bad hangovers.

"All right, guys. Time for munchies." He made his way over to Sloane first and helped him drink down his bottle of Gatorade before he helped Ash do the same. As soon as they were done, the protein bars came next, followed by the steaks. Dex sat on the floor with his legs crossed watching the broody and surly agents acting like a couple of big kids who'd gotten ouchies. They were grumpy and moaning, telling each other off as they ate. Dex found the whole thing incredibly amusing. Sloane would definitely need a good rest after this, and Ash looked like maybe he could do with a few *z*'s himself.

As soon as the two were done eating and Dex had cleared the plates away, he came in with the Therian first-aid kit and took out a couple of disinfecting pads. He tried to put one to Ash's jaw where Sloane had nicked him with one of his claws, but Ash swatted Dex's hand away.

"Fuck off, Daley. You're not my nursemaid."

"No, he's *my* nursemaid," Sloane grumbled, giving Ash a weak push before taking hold of Dex's wrist and pulling him over to stand in between his legs. He wrapped his arms around Dex's waist and held him close. "Get your own."

Ash shook his head in shame. "You're so whipped, man."

Sloane let out a snort. "Whatever. Like you're not wrapped around Cael's little finger."

"Shut up."

"No, you shut up."

"You pushed me down the fucking stairs," Ash grumbled.

"I said I was sorry," Sloane huffed. "What do you want, a cuddle? Do you want a cuddle, Ash?"

"No."

"Good, because you're not getting one." Sloane rubbed his face against Dex's T-shirt. "Mm, you smell good."

Right. Clearly the two hadn't fully recovered. "Children, please." Dex ran his fingers through Sloane's hair and gave his brow a kiss. "Finish your juice boxes, and then it's time for a nap."

"I'm going home." Ash got up, grabbed the bag with his clothes, and started to get dressed. Having Ash naked in his bedroom was beyond disturbing. The guy had absolutely no modesty. When he was done, he called Dex over. "Help me downstairs. I'll call a cab outside."

"I can drive you," Dex offered, receiving a shake of his head from Ash.

"Just help me downstairs."

Weird, but okay. He accompanied Ash out of the bedroom, wondering why Ash had asked for his help if every time he tried to take Ash's arm, the guy told him to fuck off. Giving up, he followed Ash downstairs and to the door, startled when Ash pulled him closer.

"Um..." Hello, Weirdsville.

"Keep an eye on him," Ash said quietly. "If it happens again, call me."

Dex eyed him. "You know something."

Ash looked like he was considering not telling Dex, but something in Dex's expression must have made him change his mind because he let out a heavy sigh. "It happened once to a Defense agent years ago. First Gen. He lost it while in his Therian form. Ended up injuring some of his teammates. Almost killed one of them."

"Jesus, what happened to him?"

"These huge-ass dudes tranqed him and took him away. We were told he was fine, recuperating somewhere, but I don't know. We never heard from him again. Either way, I'm not letting the same thing happen to Sloane. You might want to consider talking to Shultzon at some point. The guy knows more about First Gens than anyone, especially us."

"Okay." Shit. He hated to admit it, but there was still so much he didn't know about the THIRDS or First Gens. Their DNA was supposed to be stable. First the purring while in Human form, now this.

"And if you insist on going through with tonight, call

Rosa. Ask her to come stay with him. I don't think he should be on his own."

They finally agreed on something. "I will. See you tonight."

Ash gave him a nod and was off.

Dex was glad he had the rest of the day to spend with Sloane before the meeting. He really didn't want to leave tonight, but he was eager to get this damn case over with. He'd give Rosa a call later. Right now, all he wanted was to be in Sloane's arms. He took the stairs two at a time and stopped in the doorway. Sloane was lying against his pillows, dressed once again in his pajama bottoms and T-shirt. The bed was still rumpled, but Sloane had obviously smoothed the sheets as best he could. He was gazing up at the ceiling, his eyebrows drawn together with worry. At least he'd recovered from post-shift trauma. Seeming to sense him, Sloane met his gaze and patted the mattress beside him.

"I'm sorry."

"No." Dex shook his head and climbed onto the bed. "We're not going down that road, okay? Clearly whatever happened was because of me. I'm not surprised I pushed you that far."

"Not funny," Sloane muttered, frowning at him.

"It wasn't meant to be. You've got enough shit going on without me stressing you out even more." They both knew what he was alluding to, but Dex was grateful when Sloane didn't get into it. Sloane had to know what he was up to, though Dex couldn't fathom why he was pretending otherwise.

"What if I'd hurt you? What if I'd—" Sloane lowered his gaze to the bandage on Dex's arm and his eyes widened. "I did hurt you."

Dex shrugged. "It's okay. I kind of like it." Sloane narrowed his eyes, and Dex quickly held a hand up. "Not in a kinky I-want-you-to-use-me-as-a-scratching-post sort of way. It's like you've left your mark on me." Dex reached out and ran his thumb over the tattoo on the left side of Sloane's neck marking him as a jaguar Therian.

"It's not the same thing at all."

"Isn't it?" Dex continued to stroke the black tattoo. "This tells others what's inside of you." He took Sloane's fingers and placed them over the bandage on his arm. "This tells them what's inside of me." Dex let out a soft laugh, feeling embarrassed. Man, he was such a cheeseball. "That probably sounds stupid."

Sloane pulled Dex close against him. "Not as stupid as you think."

They were both quiet, and Dex had no doubt Sloane was thinking along the same line as him. "Do you want to talk about what happened?"

"Not right now. But soon. I promise. I'm just really tired right now." Sloane looked it, and Dex felt guilty. Even if he hadn't caused Sloane's rogue shifting, he'd played a part in it. His partner didn't need any more stress. His thoughts went back to what he'd been considering after his shower. His partner needed to relax. To feel good.

With a wicked grin, Dex ran a hand up Sloane's leg, slipping it under his soft cotton T-shirt. He placed a gentle kiss to Sloane's neck under his ear, hearing his partner's sharp intake of breath. Another kiss soon followed lower down. He trailed kisses down Sloane's neck as his fingers traveled up firm muscles until they reached one of Sloane's nipples. Dex gave the bud a squeeze, and he smiled against Sloane's skin as his partner moaned, a low, deep sound rumbling from somewhere inside Sloane's chest. Encouraged by the sound, Dex moved his mouth over his partner's, kissing him, pressing his tongue against Sloane's lips and demanding entrance.

Sloane relinquished and parted his lips, allowing Dex to slip his tongue inside, tasting Sloane's mouth and releasing a low groan. God, he loved how Sloane tasted. How his firm body felt against Dex's. His scent, which was a delicious mix of body wash and male, drove Dex crazy. They kissed languidly at first, at least until Dex's hand traveled south, and he cupped Sloane through his loose pajama bottoms.

"Mm, I missed this," Sloane breathed against Dex's ear.

"Me too." Dex massaged Sloane's cock through his pants, enjoying the way it hardened underneath his touch. He felt his partner's hands move to the hem of his T-shirt and he sat back as Sloane pulled it off him and tossed it onto the bed behind Dex. He loved having Sloane's strong hands on him, roaming his torso, gliding up and around his middle, fingers digging into Dex's skin. It felt like forever since they'd had sex, though it really hadn't been long. Damn it felt good.

Dex slipped his hand under the waistband of Sloane's loose pajama bottoms and started stroking him. He watched the way his partner closed his eyes and let his head fall back against the pillows. His back arched slightly, and he groaned. After a heated kiss left them both panting and eager for more, Dex pulled back so he could drag Sloane's pants off him. Sloane made to remove his shirt, but Dex stopped him. "Let me. You just relax." He removed Sloane's T-shirt for him and leaned in to whisper in his ear. "I promised I would make you purr. I hope you're ready." When he pulled back, the fiery look in Sloane's eyes sent a shiver through Dex from head to toe.

"You better get to it, then."

Dex smiled and rolled onto his ass so he could swiftly remove the rest of his clothes, chucking them on the floor. He crawled back to Sloane, his dick getting hard at the sight of Sloane's pupils dilating in anticipation. His partner remained still, watching his every move. Dex gave Sloane's thigh a playful smack. "On your back, sexy."

Sloane licked his bottom lip, his eyes remaining on Dex as he shimmied down to lie flat on the bed. God, his partner was hot. From his intense gaze to the tiny specks of silver growing in his stubble. Dex traced his fingers down the side of Sloane's thick neck, over his smooth muscular chest, tight abs, strong thighs and legs. Jutting up from a nest of dark curls, a mouthwatering treat waited for him. Having raked over every last inch of Sloane's body with his eyes, Dex straddled Sloane with his back to his partner. He bent forward, his ass all but inches away from Sloane's face. With a lusty smile at his partner from over his shoulder, Dex took hold of Sloane's wrists and moved his hands onto his ass cheeks.

"How about an early lunch?"

Sloane's gasp was music to his ears. "Fuck."

"For now, how about lick me, suck me, fuck me with your tongue?" He arched his back and stretched, a delicious shiver going through him when he felt Sloane's fingers brush along the curve of his spine.

"I... Wow. Yes. Okay."

Dex bent over, aware of every ragged breath, every gasp, and whispered curse his partner let out as Dex took hold of Sloane's cock and swallowed it down to the root. His partner bucked beneath him, and Dex tried his hardest to concentrate on giving Sloane pleasure while his partner's tongue turned him into a trembling mess. Sloane was putting his all into it, making a meal out of Dex's ass. Okay, maybe Dex had overestimated his sexual prowess. His intention had been to make Sloane squirm and melt with pleasure, but it was Dex who was squirming. He whimpered around Sloane's cock and squeezed the base when Sloane's tongue entered him again. He popped off Sloane with a curse and glared at his partner over his shoulder.

"I'm supposed to be the one making you curse."

"And you are, sweetheart." Sloane wriggled his eyebrows and ran his tongue up one of Dex's ass cheeks before giving it a bite. He pulled back with a groan and gave Dex's ass another squeeze. "This ass. I have dreams about this ass. It's amazing." He gave it a smack, and Dex let out a surprised yelp before laughing. Sloane smoothed the sore spot on Dex's ass cheek with his palm before giving it a kiss.

"What about what's attached to it?"

Sloane shrugged, amusement sparkling in his eyes. "It's okay, I guess."

"Oh, you dick!" Dex laughed and tugged at Sloane's cock, making him suck in a sharp breath. Some form of unspoken challenge seemed to have passed between them because they both doubled their efforts, doing their damned hardest to make the other come first.

His partner was close, Dex could feel it. Sloane pulled Dex back and swallowed his cock, his spit-slick finger entering Dex and hitting Dex's prostate. Oh shit. Dex was so going to lose this one. Their pace quickened, and their movements grew erratic. Dex's muscles tightened, and with a low groan he came inside Sloane's mouth. Seconds later, Sloane followed, and Dex swallowed around Sloane's cock. He continued to suck Sloane off until his partner went soft in his mouth. Pulling back, Dex flopped onto his side, his chest heaving and his leg muscles twitching. The only sounds filling the room were of their own heavy breathing.

"That was... that..." Sloane let out a soft laugh. "Damn that was hot."

Dex couldn't form a coherent sentence in his head much less out loud and ended up nodding as he stared at the ceiling. He heard his partner's deep sexy laugh and felt Sloane's hand on his stomach. With a smile, Dex closed his eyes. When he opened them, it was dark. Shit. What time was it? He carefully sat up, making sure not to jostle Sloane who was fast asleep. Glancing at the alarm, he was relieved to see he had enough time to get dressed and take a cab over to Lou's for the van he prayed Lou would lend him.

Man, he felt like such an asshole. Turning on the lamp, Dex stood at Sloane's bedside watching him sleep, looking so peaceful and content. He couldn't leave Sloane on his own like this. Right now, it was getting pretty damn hard to look at himself in the mirror. He quickly changed into an all-black outfit. Black jeans, boots, long-sleeved T-shirt, and black leather jacket with a black scarf and beanie. It was getting pretty chilly since they were halfway through October. He was looking forward to spending another Christmas with Sloane, Tony, and Cael. Maybe even Ash. With one last look at Sloane, Dex covered his partner with a blanket before he turned off the lamp and headed downstairs. On his way out the door, he called Rosa.

She answered in two rings, her voice filled with concern. "*¿Qué pasó?*"

"I need a favor."

"Sure. Is it about the meeting tonight?"

"Sort of. I need you to skip the meeting. I can fill you in tomorrow. Right now I have something more important to ask of you." He locked up the front door and took a seat on the top step.

"Okay."

"Can you come over to my house and look after Sloane? He hasn't been feeling well, and I don't want to leave him on his own. He probably won't wake up for a while. I'll leave the key under the potted plant to the right of the door."

There was a long pause before Rosa answered. "So he's not part of the meeting?"

"No, and it's important you don't tell him about it either."

"Dex—"

"Please, Rosa. I need to do this. Trust me."

Rosa sighed. "*Está bien*. I'll be there in a few minutes."

"Thank you. I owe you one."

"You owe me several for this."

"Whatever it is, it's done. Good night, Rosa."

"Be careful."

"I will." He hung up and slipped the key under the pot before calling for a cab. Walking down the stairs, he stopped at the bottom as a little old lady walking her tiny dog went past. Dex gave her a wave and a smile. "Hi, Mrs. Bauman."

With a huff, she continued on her way. At least this time she hadn't caught him in his underwear or lying on the sidewalk in his uniform holding his tranq rifle. As he waited on the sidewalk in front of his house for the cab, he looked up at the bedroom. He thought about how much fun he and Sloane had had in bed earlier. He also thought of Sloane's words before he'd lost himself to his feral side.

"To protect you!"

Protect. It's what Dex was trying to do. He hoped Sloane understood. Most of all, he hoped Sloane would forgive him.

SEVEN

"Seriously? What are we, the fucking A-Team now?"

Dex ignored Ash and addressed the team gathered inside the sleek black catering van with fancy white scripted letters that he'd borrowed from Lou. Thank God it was Therian-sized, or they never would have fit. It was pretty tight as it was with three Humans and four Felids. Lucky for Dex, Lou had been in a good mood. In fact, he'd been floating high. Dex assumed his date with Bradley had gone well. Lou had been all too happy to give Dex whatever he wanted, handing the keys over while he rambled on at full speed about how sweet and funny Bradley was, how handsome, smart, business savvy, and about his tattoos, how maybe Lou would get a tattoo—which had knocked Dex for a loop considering how squeamish Lou was about needles.

Ash had put in a call to everyone and given them the location of the van they currently occupied. They were in a parking garage a block away from Clove Catering next to the fire station. Everyone sat on the benches on either side of him waiting to know what they'd been called out for.

"Why are we in a catering van?" Cael asked, eyeing Dex suspiciously.

"I asked you guys to come because I need your help." In reality, on the drive to pick up Ash, Dex had started to have second thoughts, but Ash insisted they needed backup on this. The two of them had argued—as usual—but in the end Dex had conceded, and not because Ash threatened to go ahead with the meeting anyway, but because the guy was right. Dex wouldn't be able to do this on his own. Hogan and his crew outmuscled him. Ash had also admitted he felt like he'd been followed on his trip to the grocery store the other day. It had sealed the deal for Dex.

"Is Sloane okay?" Letty asked him.

"Sloane's fine. He, uh, doesn't know we're here."

"I'm not sure I like the sound of this," Cael muttered.

Calvin looked around the van. "Is anyone going to tell us what's going on? Is this Lou's van?"

Dex was trying to come up with the right wording when Ash did his Ash thing and blurted it out. "Dex has decided to put his career on the line to track down Hogan."

"What?" Cael jumped to his feet and faced Dex. "Are you crazy? You can't go against Sparks's orders."

"I don't expect any of you to join me, but at least hear me out. Hogan's not going to stop with the Westward Creed. He sent two of his followers to case Sloane's apartment, and we're pretty sure he sent someone to keep an eye on Ash."

Cael turned his worried gaze to Ash. "Someone followed you?"

"Yeah," Ash answered quietly. He gave Cael a shrug and a small smile. "It's okay. Don't worry about it."

Cael looked like he was about to argue but instead let

out a sigh and turned his attention back to Dex, who carried on.

"If he's sent his goons after Sloane and Ash, what makes you think he won't send his crew after the rest of us? I'll do whatever it takes to keep my family safe. As Ash pointed out to me recently, Destructive Delta is my family. Hogan's caused enough damage and ruined enough lives." He turned to Hobbs and met his troubled gaze. "Your brother's a great agent, and I'm sure he's gonna be one hell of a team leader, but he's on the outside looking in. We're already knee-deep in this shit. It's our family that asshole tried to kill."

"I'm in."

Calvin's declaration caught everyone off guard, especially Dex. He'd never seen his teammate look so determined. "Cal?"

"You're right. We've always had each other's backs. This is on us. We should be the ones bringing his ass in. The most Sparks can do is suspend us." Calvin turned to Letty who scoffed.

"Like you have to ask."

Hobbs nodded his agreement, leaving only Cael who gaped at Dex as if he'd lost his marbles, which he possibly might have.

"Dad will kick our asses."

"Yeah, he'll be pretty pissed. But we're all grown up, Cael. We need to stop worrying about what Dad would want us to do. It's our choice."

Cael worried his bottom lip as he thought about it.

"It really is okay if you don't do it," Dex assured him. "I'd kind of prefer if you didn't, but it's your choice."

Cael shifted his gaze to him before nodding. "I'm in."

"Cael—"

"You said it was my choice, Dex." Cael folded his arms over his chest. "And I choose to join you and make sure you don't do anything stupid."

"Stupider," Ash corrected.

Cael sat back down on the bench, keeping his gaze everywhere but on Ash, and he shifted uncomfortably when Ash took a seat beside him. These two were going to drive him out of his freaking head. Putting his brother's relationship drama aside for later, Dex addressed the team.

"Perry's handed himself in to the THIRDS, and we believe Jackson's hauled ass to California. I doubt Hogan's realized his prey's flown the coop. There's a good chance relieving him of his revenge will draw him out, but I'd rather we get to him first. If he doesn't bail, he might try to regroup. Thanks to Austen, we've got some useful intel. Hogan only has a handful of reliable members left, and the rest are just muscle. With Merritt dead, Hogan has promoted Drew Collins to be his second-in-command. Collins is a cougar Therian. He's a tough son of a bitch to track down, which means we need to work around him to get to him."

"In other words, go for someone close to Collins," Cael said, nodding in agreement. "Who's the target?"

Austen stepped forward and held a tablet out in front of him displaying a high-definition image of a wolf Therian with dark hair and silver eyes. "This is Felipe Bautista, Collins's boyfriend of ten years. Collins is crazy about the guy, but his loyalty to Hogan keeps him away a good deal of the time, and poor Felipe gets lonely. They argue a hell of a lot. Collins is never there, and Bautista resents being told to stay home and wait like some lapdog. I'm still unclear whether Bautista knows what his boyfriend is up to. If he does, he's playing dumb. So while Collins is busy playing wanted terrorist, Bautista is at Candy Bar picking up cute boys."

"So what's the plan?" Ash asked.

"Send someone in undercover." Austen removed a small transparent baggie from his jeans pocket and held it up. It contained some kind of white powder. "Then slip a little something in his mojito, get friendly with him, and let the pixie dust do its thing. You ask and he'll answer."

"What is that?" Dex asked warily. He wasn't sure about drugging Bautista. "Is it safe?"

"It's a special formula. Don't worry, when he wakes up, he won't remember a thing. The only side effect he'll feel is the hangover from hell, which is why it's important whoever goes in gets him nice and tipsy. He'll think he had too much to drink and—"

Dex snatched the bag from Austen. "What's in this?"

"Hey, man, take it easy." Austen held his hands up. "You don't want to drop that shit in here, or we're all fucked."

A cold chill traveled up Dex's spine. It couldn't be. "Is this made with scopolamine?"

Austen's stunned expression said it all.

"Fuck me." Dex handed the bag back to Austen, his insides twisting. "Who gave it to you?"

"What the fuck does it matter?" Ash growled.

"It fucking matters!" Dex snapped, giving Ash a start. He turned his attention back to Austen who was studying him. "Did the THIRDS give it to you?" For the first time since Dex had known Austen, he saw the cheetah Therian's expression turn grim and his dark eyes cloud over. Something told him there was a whole other side to the cheetah that wasn't so cheeky.

"It's not relevant to this investigation."

"It's not relevant? We're about to put it in someone's drink, and you're telling me it's not relevant? Pearce injected me with that shit and fucked me up, almost got me to kill someone, and you're telling me it's not relevant?"

Cael got to his feet. "Hold on. It's the same drug from the lab? The lab that technically never existed which has been decommissioned?"

Austen casually returned the baggie to his pocket before folding his arms over his chest. His hard gaze moved from one Destructive Delta member to the next. "Are you G.I. Joes done pretending like fucked-up shit don't happen on both sides of the law? If you want to back out, now's the time to do it. You brought me into this, not the other way around. I have enough shit on my plate without putting my neck out on the line for an unauthorized mission." His dark eyes landed on Dex. "Right now, your partner's in Hogan's sights. You gonna wait around for him to finish what he started, or are you going to put an end to this bullshit?"

Dex gritted his teeth. He should have known the whole mess with the Therian Research Facility wasn't behind them, but he had other worries right now. "Fine. Let's do this."

With a wink and a smile, Austen patted Dex on the arm. "That's more like it. Now, as I was saying. We get Bautista to talk. He's a talker. He's also a cuddler. If he really doesn't know anything, we cut him free, put a tail on him, see if he leads us to Collins, though it's unlikely. I've been tailing the guy for days, and Collins is always the one who finds him, not the other way around."

"What kind of guys does Bautista go for?" Letty asked.

"Cute guys."

Letty rolled her eyes at Austen. "Thanks for narrowing it down."

"Ash is out of the question. You'll just scare the shit out of him." Austen moved on to Hobbs. "You're cute, darling, but too big." He gave Hobbs's bicep a squeeze and a wink. He turned to Cael and gave his cheek a pinch. "Sorry, my friend, but you and I are too adorable. Bautista has a type. And it's not just willing and able." Austen spun on his heels and jutted his fingers at Dex and Calvin. "The guy's a sucker for the classics. Blond and blue-eyed."

"I'll do it," Dex said. It wasn't fair for him to expect Calvin to take such a risk when it was his idea to go after Hogan.

Ash's protest descended swiftly. "Hell no."

"You don't agree?" Dex gasped. "What a fucking surprise."

"For one, I don't like the fact we're lying to Sloane. It's bound to blow up in our faces. But more importantly, if anyone from Hogan's gang shows up, including Collins, we're screwed because they've seen your face. They saw you at the exchange. In fact they've seen all our faces."

"No they haven't." Calvin held a hand up. "I wasn't at the exchange. Well, technically I was, but I was up on one of the containers. No one in the group saw me. I'll do it."

"Do you even remember how to pick someone up? When was the last time you had a date?"

"Screw you, Ash." Calvin turned to Dex, his expression unwavering. "I can do this."

"Are you sure about this, Cal?"

Calvin gave him a stern nod, and Austen rubbed his hands together gleefully. The guy really enjoyed his job way too much. "All right. We'll meet up a block away from Candy Bar at ten o'clock." He checked his watch before winking at Calvin. "You have three hours to make yourself look pretty.

Wear something nice." He turned to Cael and threw an arm around his neck. "You've got two and a half hours to turn this van into something James Bond would be proud of." Austen waved at them and slipped out of the van. Dex braced himself.

"Are you fucking kidding me?" Cael rounded on him. "You want *me* to turn a catering van into a surveillance van in *two and a half hours*? Are you out of your mind?"

"Come on, Cael. You can do it. You're awesome at that stuff."

"That *stuff* isn't like hooking up your home theater system, Dex! Especially without access to my equipment locker at work."

"Your brother's right, Cael. You can do it," Ash said gently, bringing Cael's tirade to a screeching halt. Cael's cheeks went pink, and he frowned down at his sneakers while Ash continued. "If anyone can pull this off, you can. You're the smartest, most capable guy we know. We have faith in you."

Dex noticed how Calvin and Letty exchanged glances. They weren't stupid. It was only a matter of time before the rest of the team figured out something was going on between his brother and Ash, even if technically nothing was going on.

"Fine. But you need to drop the van off at my apartment, like, yesterday." He stormed to the end of the van and slipped out. Calvin soon followed, leaving a confused-looking Hobbs behind. Dex threw him the keys.

"You mind driving?" Keeping Hobbs busy would probably be a good idea. He had a feeling this mission wasn't going to be as straightforward as Austen made it out to be. Aside from the fact Calvin was taking a risk going undercover, there was the question of how far he was willing to go to get any useful information. There was no telling how Hobbs would react.

"What do you need me to do?" Letty asked.

"I need you to get some equipment ready. Tranq guns, vests, whatever you can get together under the radar, but I want to keep the real firepower minimal. The last thing we need is to start a shootout and draw attention to ourselves. I'll fill Rosa in, and if she agrees, I'll ask her to have her medical kit ready. Ash will call you and keep you informed. We'll let you know the moment we locate Collins. No sense in having everyone here tonight."

"Got it." Letty headed for the door when Ash followed her.

"I need a ride."

"Well let's go, then, partner. What happened to your face?" Letty inspected Ash's jaw on the way out, and Dex heard him grumble about how he cut himself shaving or something, which made no sense considering his jaw was full of stubble. With only Hobbs left, Dex motioned toward the front of the van.

"We can drop it off and catch some dinner. What do you say?"

Hobbs gave him a nod as he slipped in behind the wheel and buckled up. Dex took a seat beside him and did the same. He turned the radio to his favorite station, though he kept the volume low.

"I'll call you after it's over and let you know what information we get. I can take care of the surveillance with Austen tomorrow."

"No."

Dex blinked at Hobbs. "I'm sorry?"

"I'm going to be here."

"Hobbs, why are you torturing yourself, man? You know

he's going to have to... get close to Bautista." Dex studied his teammate. It was hard to tell what Hobbs was thinking. Despite his inability to speak most of the time, Hobbs was one of the most expressive guys Dex knew, but it only applied when Hobbs wanted you to know something; otherwise his poker face had those Easter Island dudes beat. His stern expression gave away nothing, but his white-knuckled grip on the steering wheel as he drove told another story.

"I know."

"So why torture yourself?"

"He's my partner," Hobbs said solemnly. "I need to make sure he's safe."

"We've got his back."

They stopped at a red light, and Hobbs sat quietly. Seconds ticked past before Hobbs spoke up. "I've had his back longer. And I always will."

There was no point in arguing. Felid Therians were some of the most stubborn around. Dex gave in, telling himself he needed to be on alert. Every time he was around Calvin and Hobbs, it felt like a storm was brewing. One of these days, one of them was going to snap, and Dex had no idea what kind of fallout it would lead to. He hoped the two would find a way to work it out before it started hurting their friendship. As they headed for Cael's apartment, he realized he wasn't the only one whose relationship was at risk during this mission. By the end, it would either strengthen their bonds or destroy them.

It was time.

After they'd dropped off the van and left Cael to do his thing—which meant staying far away since his little brother had his fur all bristled—Dex and Hobbs had gone out for some dinner. It wasn't any more pleasant, with Hobbs spending most of the time brooding. Dex did his best to cheer Hobbs up and distract him, but the tiger Therian always ended up lost in thought. It didn't take a genius to figure out what—or rather *whom*—he was thinking about.

A couple of hours later, they all sat in the back of the van while Hobbs drove. Everyone was dressed in dark colors except for Calvin who was looking all smooth and ready for a night on the town in his trendy jeans, white shirt, and preppy gray vest.

The surveillance console Cael had installed was impressive, complete with two flat-screen monitors, digital drives, keyboard, earpieces, a wireless digital printer, a carbon monoxide and oxygen level alarm, and a joystick for controlling the periscope in the roof. Speaking of roof...

"Holy shit!" Dex's hand flew to his head. Oh my God, Lou was going to kill him. "Bro, you cut a hole in the roof of Lou's van!"

Cael blinked at him. "Yeah, but it's retractable. From the outside it looks like a small fan."

"You cut a hole in the roof of Lou's van!"

"You wanted a surveillance van," Cael grumbled, "you got one. Give me your phone?"

"Why?" Dex reached into his pocket and took out his phone only to have his brother snatch it away from him.

"Because I forgot something." He tapped away at Dex's phone, not bothering to ask Dex for his secret code to get past the main screen. Damn computer nerds. Several speedy taps later, and he was shoving Dex's phone back at him.

Calvin looked the console over and whistled. "Damn, Cael. You had all this in your apartment?"

"Well, yeah. Where else would I have it?"

Hobbs parked the van a few doors down from Candy Bar, then came to join Dex, where Cael proceeded to go through all the equipment with them before testing it out. His little brother had "borrowed" several camera feeds from local businesses using encrypted coding, so every time Dex or Hobbs moved one, it would seem like it was part of the camera's regular rotation.

"Okay, we've got eyes and ears," Cael said and handed them each an earpiece. They were exactly like the ones they used while on the job.

"These aren't THIRDS issued, are they?" Dex asked.

Cael gave him an uninspired look. "Yes, Dex. I'm using standard THIRDS issued earpieces to do surveillance for an unsanctioned mission." Well, someone got up on the snarky side of the bed this morning. Speaking of snarky, Ash had barely said a word since they'd picked him up.

"A simple 'no' would have sufficed," Dex muttered at his brother while discreetly glancing over at his gruff teammate. Ash was sitting on the bench lost in thought. He sure as hell wished Ash was ready for this. The guy was providing Calvin backup along with Austen in case something went wrong. He turned back to the console's screens showing the perimeter around the van, as well as Candy Bar. Being a Friday night, it was already getting packed. Using one of the sleek joysticks, he could switch between cameras, move them around, zoom in, and out. One of the cameras was directly across the street, allowing him to zoom right in through Candy Bar's large front window to the bar and a portion of the seating area.

Austen clapped his hands together. "Okay, guys, let's get this porno started."

Dex heard Hobbs growl beside him. Let the fun begin.

"What do you think?" Calvin asked, holding his arms out at his sides.

"Sexy, but a little too neat. We need to scruff you up a bit. And you gotta lose the jacket."

Calvin looked down at his jacket with a frown. "What's wrong with it?"

"Too boy-next-door. Daley, give him your jacket."

Dex removed his belongings from his leather jacket before handing it over to Calvin. It was a little longer on Calvin since Dex was taller but still looked good. Austen fussed with Calvin's shirt collar, opening the top button and wriggling his brows.

"Seriously man, you need to get laid," Calvin grumbled, slapping Austen's hand away from his collar. Austen puckered his lips and blew him a kiss.

"You offering, Cal? Maybe a little dessert after dinner?"

"Can we get on with this?"

"I'm trying, man, but your hair's like... How the fuck do you get it to stay down?"

Hobbs let out a huff and nudged Austen aside. Well, it was a nudge for Hobbs. It all but sent Austen hurtling across the van. Austen didn't seem bothered. He brushed himself off and took a seat behind the makeshift console while Hobbs straightened out Calvin's clothes and ran his fingers through his bud's spiky hair, giving it the right tousled look.

"Sexy and a stylist," Austen teased Hobbs, "Is there nothing you boys can't do?"

"For fuck's sake, Hobbs. You gonna braid his hair next? Get on with it." Ash got to his feet, ignoring Calvin and Hobbs's glares while Cael leaned against the van's wall next to the bench, pretending he wasn't watching Ash, at least until he seemed to notice Ash's face. He walked around the bench and stepped up to Ash, who stood stock still when Cael reached out to stroke his thumb over the small nick.

"What happened to your face?"

Ash touched his jaw, his hand partially covering Cael's. "It's nothing," he replied quietly. "Just a scrape. Don't worry, okay?"

A buzzer sounded in Dex's head. *Wrong answer*. Obviously, Cael was getting tired of Ash's refusal to let him in. Dex could see it in his brother's eyes, the way they turned from sparkling gray to steel. He pulled his hand back, swiped his messenger bag off the floor, and headed for the back doors.

"Fine. I've gotta go. I've got plans."

"With Seb?" Dex asked.

"Yeah."

"Seriously?" Dex motioned toward the console. "We're in the middle of an undercover op, and you're going to leave it to go on a date?"

"It's not a date. Besides, he called this afternoon. What was I supposed to do? Call him up and say, 'Hey, Seb, sorry I can't make it. I'm with my brother helping him shake down a guy who's part of your investigation, the same one we're supposed to stay away from?' I'll call you tomorrow, Dex." He grumbled a quick good-bye to the rest of the team before slipping out of the van. Refusing to let his brother walk away like this, Dex followed, catching up with him before he could disappear down the street. "Hey, hold on a minute."

Cael stopped and turned, his cheeks flushed with anger. "What, Dex?"

"When did you stop talking to me? We used to tell each other everything." His brother was always so cheerful, always smiling and sweet. Dex hated seeing him like this.

"We're not little kids anymore. *I'm* not a little kid anymore."

"But we're still brothers. That hasn't changed." Dex pulled him to one side, closer to the doorway of a closed business so they weren't out in the open. No sense taking any chances. There was plenty of foot traffic with pedestrians on their way to one of the many restaurants and bars lining the street opposite them. "What's going on?"

Cael leaned against the brick façade and shrugged. "It's just..."

"Ash?"

"Yeah. I thought being on leave would help, but it's almost worse because I can't stop thinking about him. Hoping..." He let out a frustrated groan. "You saw him. He's shutting me out, and I don't know why."

"So you think going out with Seb is the answer? You think that's fair to him?" He told himself not to meddle in his little brother's love life, and although Cael wasn't the kind of guy to lead anyone on or use them, his brother wasn't exactly thinking clearly. He'd hate for Cael to do something he'd regret later on. And Cael would certainly regret it. The guilt would eat away at him.

"I'm not going out with Seb. Seriously, Dex. You really think I'd do something like that? I was up front with him. The night of your birthday party, he took me home. We spent a long time sitting in his truck, talking. I told him I liked him and wanted to spend time with him, but it couldn't lead to anything long-term because... I was in love with someone else. It turned out we had a lot more in common than I thought."

"Seb's still in love with Hudson."

"Yeah. But Jesus, Dex. It was like, years ago." Cael looked up at him, the heartache in his big silver eyes squeezing Dex's heart. "He keeps holding on. Is that what Ash expects me to do? Hold on, waiting for however long it takes? I know he said he has issues to work out, but what if he can't work them out? At the very least, I thought he'd care enough about me to confide in me. Why can't we work our problems out together, like you and Sloane? Maybe he doesn't feel the same way about me."

"Dude, he took a bullet for you," Dex reminded him. "Plus, this is all kind of new for him. Even if something were to happen, you have to consider Ash might not be ready to leave his closet."

"But no one's going to care. Hardly anyone cares about it anymore. I've never gotten shit for being with guys. The douche-baggery is reserved for my being a Therian."

"Maybe no one else cares, but Ash clearly does, so there must be a reason for it."

"Yeah, I guess you're right." Cael nodded, and a small hint of a familiar smile came onto his face. "Thanks, Dex. Be careful tonight, okay?"

"You too, bro. And thank you for the van. I couldn't have done it without you."

"Duh, of course," Cael teased. "I'm the genius of the family. And the cute one. You're the weird one with the cheese obsession."

Dex chuckled and poked him in the ribs, making him squirm with a laugh. "I'm not weird, you little nerd." He gave Cael a playful push. "Go on. Get out of here. Have fun. Get your mind off all this for a while."

"Thanks, Dex." Cael gave him a quick hug before running off, waving his arm. Dork. Chuckling to himself, Dex headed back to the van and after a quick look around, climbed in. It felt good seeing his brother smile again. Inside the van was a different story. Everyone stood around looking like someone had told them they were doing another THIRDS calendar shoot. Luckily, he hadn't had to do one yet, but he'd heard stories. Horrible stories.

Austen looked around. "Wow. You need a chainsaw to cut through the tension in here." He turned to Dex. "What's up with your bro? He's been acting kinda like he's got a stick up his ass."

Dex cast Ash an accusing glare. "He's going through a tough time."

Austen gave a lazy shrug as he leaned against the console. "Well, it's probably not such a bad thing he's got a date with Seb. Means he'll keep him away from the investigation for tonight. Getting laid will do him good."

Ash launched out of his chair and pushed Austen up against the wall. "Watch your fucking mouth, you little shit. No one asked you for your fucking opinion, so shut the fuck up." The van fell into silence with Ash resuming his seat. Austen held his hands up in front of him. When he spoke, he addressed no one in particular.

"Question one: are you all screwing each other? Question two: how can I get in on the action?"

"I'm going to check on Sloane and Rosa before heading into the bar," Ash growled.

Shit. Dex hadn't texted Sloane with an explanation of where he'd gone. He still had no idea what he was going to tell his partner. Kind of hard to use PR as an excuse this late in the evening. "What are you going to tell him?" he asked Ash before the guy could stomp his way out the back.

"That you're sitting in your ex's catering van which your brother set up like the fucking Pentagon to do surveillance on Calvin while he seduces Collins's boyfriend to get intel."

Dex's eyebrows shot up to his hairline. "You're kidding, right?"

"Ask a stupid question, get a stupid answer."

"I think adding some more fiber to your diet might help."

"Fuck you, Daley." Ash stormed out, slamming the van door behind him. That went well. Way to keep things on the down low. This whole night had the makings of a spectacular clusterfuck.

"Is it me, or is he grumpier than usual?" Calvin asked.

Austen looked thoughtful. "How can you tell?"

"Cut the guy a break. He's been through a lot of shit recently." Dex sat down at the console and put in his earpiece. It was time to get this dog and pony show on the road. He didn't even know what the expression meant, but screw it. Screw this. Screw everything. Dex was getting bored of all this asshattery. The silence that had engulfed the van was most likely due to his defending of Ash. "Austen, you going in or what?"

"Yep. Give me five minutes; then send Cal." Austen slipped out of the van, and they watched him on the small flat screens as he appeared from behind a Ford Fiesta two cars down. He strolled across the street and headed into Candy Bar. Dex switched cameras, following Austen as he walked to the bar, took a seat, and ordered a drink.

Hobbs stepped up to Calvin, and Dex turned away, pretending to be busy with the equipment in front of him like an extra in one of those cop TV shows. From the corner of his eye, he could see Hobbs leaning in to whisper in Calvin's ear, his hand squeezing his arm.

Calvin nodded and replied with a quiet, "I'll be careful." The five minutes were up, and Calvin left. Hobbs sat down in the chair beside Dex and put his earpiece in. This was such a bad idea, but who the hell was going to get Hobbs to go home? Dex hoped Calvin managed to get some useful information from Bautista without having to put himself in a compromising position.

Speaking of Bautista...

"There he is." Dex pointed to one of the screens where a dark-haired Therian in a white shirt and jeans walked into Candy Bar. They watched as he headed for the bar and took a seat on the barstool next to Calvin. Go Cal. Check out the sassy smile. Damn. Calvin was better at flirting than Dex had given him credit for. He'd given Bautista a flirty smile before turning away to look at something else. *Make him come to you. Nice.*

Bautista placed his order and turned slightly toward Calvin. "Hey."

"Hey." Calvin smiled, showing his dimple and the cute boy-next-door look Austen had mentioned. His voice was throaty and came off as kind of shy.

"You here with your boyfriend?"

Wow. Bautista didn't waste any time. Dex kind of felt bad for the guy. What was the point of being in a relationship with someone if you were never going to be there for them? A little voice in the back of his head waited for an answer, and Dex promptly told it to shut its trap. His situation wasn't the same as Bautista's and Collins's. For starters, Dex wasn't a psychopath. Then there was the fact Sloane was hanging around indoors due to medical reasons, not because Dex had tried to keep him locked away like some princess in a tower, which Collins seemed to be trying to do with Bautista. *Concentrate, Daley.*

"Nah, he's busy working," Calvin answered somewhat wistfully. "Seems like he's always too busy." He took a sip of his beer and shrugged.

"Mine too. Don't get me wrong, he loves me. I know he does. I just wish he were around more."

"At least you know he loves you," Calvin muttered.

Uh-oh. Danger, Will Robinson! Danger!

Bautista took a sip of his drink and swiveled his chair around so he faced Calvin. "Your boyfriend hasn't dropped the L bomb huh?"

Calvin shook his head. "We've been together a long time, and I was happy with our relationship."

"But now things have changed?"

"Yeah. Well, for me they have. He's amazing, warm, and the nicest guy ever. He's fun and silly, makes me smile with his dopey grin. We've been through so much together. Is it wrong of me to want more?"

"Do you love him?" Bautista asked.

Dex swallowed hard, his gaze landing on Hobbs whose eyes were glued to the screen in front of him. His pupils were dilated so wide his eyes were more black than green, and if he leaned over any more he was going to fall into the equipment. Dex turned his attention back to the screen where Calvin's blue eyes moved up, as if he were thinking, but he was actually looking past Bautista and straight at the camera.

"Yes."

Hobbs inhaled sharply at the confession and sat back, his gaze not moving from the screen.

Man, his team was so fucked. Dex turned his attention to Calvin once again. The two continued to talk about their guys, the good and bad parts. The drinks continued, though Dex could tell Bautista was getting thoroughly merry while Calvin was pretending to. For a Human of Calvin's size, he could outdrink the toughest Therian. It's like the guy had been weaned on whiskey.

Bautista laughed at Calvin's jokes and flirted back when Calvin teased him. Dex was seeing a whole other side of Calvin he'd never known existed, and he wondered how much of it was an act. Calvin was energetic, telling funny childhood stories about him and his best friend and all the mischief they got into. He listened when Bautista needed him to listen, was attentive, and when he smiled it reached his eyes. Bautista leaned in to whisper something in Calvin's ear and Calvin nodded. Bautista stood and took hold of Calvin's hand.

"Shit. They're moving out." He jumped to his feet and slid in behind the wheel of the van. Watching the rearview mirror, he watched Bautista hail a cab. As they were getting in, Dex turned the engine on and turned the van around, grateful the street was wide enough. In the mirror he saw Ash and Austen catching another cab. Dex made sure to stay at least two cars behind Bautista's cab whose plate number he mentally jotted down. The cab traveled for ten minutes before reaching a quiet street of brownstones. Dex parked the van a few feet away, thanking his lucky stars he managed to find some space. At least something was going his way. He spotted a cab stopping at the end of the block, and two figures got out. Austen and Ash. The two disappeared into the shadows, undoubtedly to case the joint.

Bautista emerged from the cab with Calvin in tow. He pulled him up against him, gave him a kiss, and laughed before heading to his front door where he dropped his keys twice. Calvin teased him and took the keys from him. He opened the door with Bautista's arms wrapped around his waist. They disappeared inside, and although Dex lost visual contact, they could hear everything in super-clear surround sound.

Things started to get hot and heavy between Calvin

and Bautista, resulting in plenty of heavy breathing, groaning, and moaning. Hobbs removed his earpiece and tossed it on the console's surface.

"Take it easy, big guy. You know he's just doing his job."

Hobbs let out a huff and crossed his beefy arms over his chest, his frown deepening.

"You really need to say something to him."

Hobbs's reply was a lazy shrug of the shoulders, but Dex wasn't buying it.

"Come on, man. It's bugging the hell out of you knowing he's making out with another dude. The guy just admitted he's in love with you, and all you've got is a shrug?"

When Hobbs refused to look him in the eye, acting like he didn't care, Dex decided it was time Hobbs snapped out of his moping and pulled his shit together before he lost Calvin for good.

"I know you kissed him back." Dex watched Hobbs's eyebrows shoot up near his hairline. He turned in his seat toward Dex and jabbed a finger at his discarded earpiece.

"Yeah, he told me. About what happened at the Fourth of July party, how things changed. I get the feeling you're not big on change."

With a dejected pout, Hobbs shook his head.

Dex could understand. Hobbs struggled every day with his selective mutism and anxiety. It was rough on the guy. Dex couldn't begin to imagine what it was like for him, being unable to speak no matter how much he wanted to. Hobbs was also a tiger Therian and a Defense agent. There were expectations, and falling short of those types of expectations was never easy for anyone, much less someone who was in a position where confidence was a requirement. Hobbs could be as intimidating as Ash or Sloane, but the problem started when the time came to deal with people. If there was one guy who understood, who'd been there from the beginning, it was Calvin. The same guy Hobbs was pushing away with his inability to accept change.

"How long do you expect to keep him waiting? Have you addressed it at all?"

Hobbs shook his head and turned around.

"You know, for a big, scary-ass Therian, you can be such a child."

Hobbs gaped at him. He pointed to himself in question.

"Yes, you."

With lips pressed thin, Hobbs poked Dex in the chest.

"Ow." Dex rubbed the sore spot. "I'm not childish." That earned him a scoff. "Either way, we're talking about you, not me."

With a roll of his eyes, Hobbs turned around again. Well, that had gone well. Dex lowered the volume on his earpiece. He really didn't need to hear what was going on, especially since it was starting to sound too much like a porno without all the cursing and begging.

Dex checked his watch some time later, finding it was nearly four in the morning. Fuck. What the hell was Calvin doing in there? Then again, it was probably best he didn't know. Hobbs was looking like one wrong move could send him into feral territory. His jaw was clenched so tight he was ready to break something, and his pupils were dilated. Despite being in his Human form, he resembled a tiger ready to pounce and tear the shit out of whatever he could get his claws on. Dex checked his earpiece. It was quiet. A series of soft knocks on the door told him why. Hobbs shot to his feet so quick his chair almost toppled over. He opened the back door and pulled a startled-looking Calvin in before shutting the door and looming over his friend.

"What happened?" Hobbs growled.

Calvin's eyebrows shot up before his expression darkened. He looked pissed. "What do you think happened?"

This had the makings of turning ugly. Dex sat quietly. Should he try to contain the situation? Anger flashed in Hobbs's green eyes, and Dex decided it was best he let them work it out. Hopefully it wouldn't lead to something he couldn't handle on his own. Calvin he could restrain, but Hobbs? It would be like the time he'd tried to jump on the merry-go-round at the park while it was going full speed. He'd ended up flying across the yard and losing a tooth.

"What, Ethan? Did I let him fuck me? Did I fuck him? What if I did? It's not like you have a say in the matter. You don't get to be pissed off."

"Stop," Hobbs snapped.

"Or what? For fuck's sake, make up your mind. You either want me or you don't. Whatever you decide, we'll still be friends, but stop dicking me around. I can't take it anymore." He stepped away from Hobbs and removed Dex's jacket to hand it over to him, followed by a piece of paper. "The church Collins goes to. He attends early-morning Mass every Saturday. Let me know what our next move is. I'm out of here. I need to go get a drink or get laid or something." Calvin headed for the door when Hobbs pushed him against the side of the van.

"What the fuck, Ethan?"

Dex couldn't agree more. What the—*Oh*.

Hobbs grabbed Calvin by the waist, hoisted him up, and pushed him up against the van's wall, pinning him there with his body as he took hold of Calvin's face and kissed him. It took Calvin all of two seconds to catch on, and when he did, he threw his arms around Hobbs's neck and eagerly returned his partner's searing kiss. Years of pent-up sexual frustration seemed to be let loose. The two went at it like nobody was watching. Except someone *was* watching. Dex was watching.

Should he remind them he was still here? Should he have brought some popcorn? Should he turn away? Dex sat there for a moment too stunned to do anything but watch. He wasn't exactly turned off either. Did it make him a perv? It was like watching porn. Two hot dudes going at it. He felt kind of guilty but had trouble looking away. Who in their right mind wouldn't find this hot? Damn, he was starting to sound like Austen. Calvin and Hobbs were in their own world, oblivious to anyone or anything else around them, swept up by the fierce emotions which had undoubtedly been driving them to the brink. Their movements grew frantic and desperate. Calvin threw his head back with a gasp for breath as Hobbs moved his lips onto his partner's neck.

"Oh God, Ethan." He dug his fingers into Hobbs's cropped hair, and the two started rutting up against each other, their breaths growing heavy. Hobbs let out a low feral growl, his hand going to Calvin's crotch where he massaged his partner before pulling down the zipper of Calvin's jeans. Oh shit. They were going to whip them out.

"Please, Ethan. You don't know how long I've been waiting for this. I want you so bad."

Calvin's pained words snapped Dex out of it.

Dex swiftly swiveled his chair around to face the console, hearing the soft groans and Calvin's whispered pleas for Hobbs to make him come.

Not. Awkward. At. All.

Dex snatched up the two earpieces and stuck one in each ear. He went online and quickly connected to *Retro Radio*'s online station. His face was red, and he felt relief flood through him when the familiar sounds of an electric keyboard drowned out all the sex sounds. Hold up... *Are you fucking kidding me?* He dropped his head into his hands. In his ears ZZ Top's "Rough Boy" played with its glorious electric guitar and slow drums, its sensual rhythm and innuendos not what he needed to be hearing right now.

Normally, he would have walked out, but he was afraid to interrupt them during such an intense, intimate moment. This had been a long time coming, and poor Calvin had been on the verge of losing his shit. Dex doubted whatever was going on behind him would solve the pair's relationship issues. It might have just complicated the shit out of everything. For an explosives technician, Hobbs wasn't great at handling these kinds of volatile situations, though he seemed pretty damned good at starting them.

Dex hoped the two were getting each other off with a couple of handjobs at most, and considering how long they'd been holding out, he doubted the two would last all that long. Tentatively, he removed one earpiece, relieved to hear soft heavy breathing and kissing rather than the audio file to *Raiders of the Lost Arse.*

Dex removed the second earpiece and turned around. Thankfully, the two were fully clothed and tucked away. Calvin was on his feet and being held in Hobbs's arms as he brushed his fingers down the side of Calvin's face. Dex had no idea what was going through Hobbs's mind. A series of emotions played across his face before he cupped Calvin's cheek, the look on his face heartbreaking.

"What happened?" Hobbs asked quietly.

Probably not the best thing the guy could have said after having done what he'd done. Judging by Calvin's expression, he thought so too.

"Please."

Calvin pressed his lips together, and Dex could see how uncertain he was. With a heavy sigh, he gave in. "Nothing happened. We made out, I slipped what Austen gave me into his drink, and got the information I needed out of him. I waited for him to fall asleep before putting him to bed and getting out. Okay?"

Hobbs's thumb started stroking Calvin's cheek, his head cocked to one side as he patiently waited for Calvin to say whatever it was he obviously wanted to say.

"Come home with me?"

To Dex's relief, Hobbs didn't hesitate. He gave Calvin a nod and pulled him against him, squeezing him tight. Hobbs lifted his head and froze, his eyes meeting Dex's and widening when realization set in.

Dex waved. "Hey. How's it going?"

"Holy fuck!" Calvin spun around and stared at Dex. "Oh my God." The pair turned to each other, their faces turning crimson. "Did we just..."

"Get off in front of one of your teammates?" Dex said, feeling equally mortified by the whole thing. "Yep."

Calvin gasped, his attention on Dex again. "Did you watch us?"

The nerve of the guy. "Who do you think I am? Austen?" He considered lying, but his team knew how shitty he was at it. "I watched a little."

"Oh God." Calvin turned and buried his face against Hobbs's chest, his voice muffled when he spoke. "We jacked each other off in front of Dex! Someone shoot me."

"Hey, how do you think I feel? I'm never going to be able to listen to ZZ Top again without thinking of you two playing knuckle shuffle." And he'd really enjoyed ZZ Top.

"I can't even look at you right now," Calvin said holding a hand out to cover Dex's face as he headed for the back of the van with Hobbs in tow. "Call me when we're moving out. And I swear if you tell Ash I will snipe you."

Dex gave them a salute. "Understood." He held back a smile when Hobbs narrowed his eyes at him and pointed a menacing finger—that really wasn't so menacing—in his direction. "Yep, I get it. Lips are sealed." He made like he was zipping his lips, waiting for them to leave before letting out a sigh of relief.

It was nearly six in the morning by the time Dex parked the catering van back in its garage. Not wanting to disturb Sloane, Dex decided to crash on the couch in his base, but not before he used his smartphone to find out what time the morning Mass at Collins's church was and notify the rest of the team. He received a text from Ash simply stating:

Rosa's in. She's pissed at you. Good luck with that.

Fuck. He could think of a million reasons why Rosa would be pissed at him, but he didn't have the energy right now to start listing them or the many ways he was going to have to grovel in order to make it up to her. And Sloane. And whoever else he happened to piss off on any given day. He lay down on the couch, not bothering with his shoes. In three hours he'd have to get up and head out to pick everyone up. *Shit.* He'd forgotten to text Sloane. Damn it. He thought about what he was going to say and sent a text apologizing for not being there, how Cael had called him with some relationship drama, and Dex had gone off to hang out with him when he'd lost track of time, and he ended up falling asleep at his brother's. He then texted Cael to let him know. His brother's response pretty much said it all.

You're a giant dick.

EIGHT

"I've got eyes on Collins. I'm following him down Adam Clayton Powell Jr. Boulevard."

Dex made sure to keep his distance as he walked down the street Drew Collins's church was on. Thanks to Calvin, Collins was exactly where they expected him to be on Saturday morning. At least until Collins walked right past the church where he was supposed to be attending Mass. Dex tapped his earpiece. "Collins went straight past the church. He's heading into the old Renaissance Ballroom." This couldn't be good. The ballroom was derelict. It had been abandoned for years and was sealed off to the public.

Ash's voice came in over his earpiece. "Wait for backup."

"Sure." He continued walking, speeding up when he saw Collins jump the fence. "He's on the move." Damn it, he couldn't lose him. The team was only a block over, but by the time they all arrived, Collins could be gone.

"Goddamn it, Dex. You—"

Dex hung up and put his phone on silent. If only he'd

be able to do the same to Ash later on when the guy ripped him a new one. Holy Shit! He'd hung up on Ash!

"Shit." In an attempt to soften the blow, he quickly shot off a text saying he was sorry.

Dex strolled past the Abyssinian Baptist Church and lingered by the chain-link fence. The church had a sign outside saying early Saturday Mass had been cancelled until further notice. If Collins wasn't attending church on Saturdays like he told his boyfriend he was, then what was he doing around here? Dex stopped and leaned against the fence, his hands shoved into his jacket pockets and his foot propped up against the fence. The woman who'd been walking behind him with her kid gave him a warm smile as she walked by. He waited for them to round the corner and disappear before swiftly climbing over the fence, cringing at the noise made by the shuddering metal.

His Chucks skidded slightly on the gravel, and he wished he'd invested in some biker boots like Sloane had suggested. He remained crouched down close to the fence for a few heartbeats before slowly rising and peeking through the droop in the tarp zip-tied to the fence. Coast was clear. He made a dash for the block-wide brick building. The windows were too high for him to climb, and all the doors were either boarded up or bolted shut. He could kick in one of the flimsy compressed boards covering one of the entrances, but if Collins was in there, Dex didn't want to spook him.

He came across an entrance with a sheet of plywood that was loose from the bottom. Looked like he'd found someone's secret entrance. Crap. He'd have to crawl in. He kneeled down, removed his tactical flashlight from his jacket pocket, and stuck it between his teeth. Carefully, he pulled at the base of the board and squeezed through. Good thing he wore his busted-up leather jacket. He would have scratched the shit out of his new one. Once inside, he released the board and gingerly turned, his flashlight now in his hand.

The Renaissance Ballroom had once been a bustling casino and theater back during the days of the Charleston and Lindy Hop, with performances by some of the most renowned jazz musicians of the time. Now all that was left were the decaying remnants of an era long gone. The skeleton of the ballroom was shrouded in shadows and dimly lit with its only source of light filtering through the hollow windows and collapsing ceiling.

Dex removed his tranq gun from the holster concealed by his jacket, and silently ventured farther in, making sure to watch his step. What appeared to have been a dance floor was nothing but dirt and rubble, colonized by patches of stinky mushrooms. The place was filthy. God only knew what else was in here. He listened for any sounds and tried to keep to the shadows. If Collins was in his cougar Therian form, he'd be stalking and hunting Dex by sight. Maybe he should have listened to Ash and waited for backup.

Trying to keep an ear out for movement would have been a lot easier if the place didn't creak and rustle all over. He warily shifted his gaze up to the corroded ceiling beams. The whole damn roof looked like it could collapse at any moment. All it needed was for a pigeon to come through one of the open windows and take a shit on one, and the whole place would come crashing down over him.

Slowly, he moved from room to room, the walls crumbling or in piles of rubble. There were faded sketches of musicians playing their instruments on some of the walls, and a few of the chandeliers still had bulbs in them. A piece of debris snapped under his sneaker, and he froze. *Shit.*

Staying perfectly still, he heard nothing but the sound of his own breathing. There was enough light for Dex to see around him, and so far, there was no movement. Leaving the room and entering another, he almost didn't see it. A shadow moved, and the hairs on the back of his neck stood on end. Collins leapt at him with a fierce roar from a pile of what Dex had assumed had been debris. Dex bolted, running as fast as he could while trying not to trip on all the scattered rubble. He made for a set of rickety stairs he doubted would even hold his weight, but he had little choice. Before he could make the stairs, Collins came at him from another angle, slamming him into the old concrete bandstand and knocking the gun from his hand. He cried out as his ribs hit at an odd angle, and he fell onto the dust-covered floor, writhing and holding on to his side.

An angry hiss caught his ear, and he raised his head in time to see Cael claw at Collins's neck. Collins retaliated, but Cael was too quick. He sped off with Collins on his tail, giving him the runaround, leaping and skidding, making sharp turns Collins's much bulkier frame had trouble with. Cael led Collins away from Dex when a leopard Therian jumped out from the shadows, tumbling into Cael.

"Cael!" Dex held on to his ribs, snatched up his gun, and tried to scramble to his feet, the lack of air filling his lungs making it difficult. Two or more Felids emerged from the shadows, all roaring, hissing, and surrounding his little brother. Dex forced himself to his feet and took aim, firing off rounds into as many of the Felids as he could catch. One got shanked with three darts, and he hobbled drunkenly away. Dex kept a grip on his side as he headed for Cael, firing into the roaring Felids until his gun was empty. A roar shook the rafters, scaring the shit out of Dex, but he was relieved to see it had come from Ash with Hobbs close behind. A Felid Therian battle ensued with sharp fangs snapping and claws grazing flesh. Ash roared at Cael, and Cael took the hint. He sped toward Dex when more of Collins's crew crawled out of the woodwork.

Dex cursed under his breath. One of them caught him in his sights, and Dex wished he'd brought more than one tranq gun. He should have been more prepared, but he'd been expecting reconnaissance work, not a goddamn ambush. Dex turned to run only to find himself knocked to the ground. He was getting really tired of being pushed around like some Felid chew toy. A roar louder than Ash's brought everything and everyone to a screeching standstill, and for a split second, Dex thought Hogan had joined the party, but he was way off, though no less screwed. Seb collided with Collins, sending the smaller Felid rolling across the floor into a mound of mushrooms. Seeing himself outmuscled, Collins bolted with the rest of his crew fast on his heels.

"You have to go after him!" Dex yelled at his teammates. Hobbs turned to do as Dex asked when Seb let out another roar, bringing Hobbs to sit. He lowered his head and flattened his ears back with a chuff. Seb was having none of it. They'd been so close. Dex sat where he was and let out a frustrated growl. No point in arguing. Collins and his crew were long gone.

Hobbs padded over and bumped his big furry head against Dex's. At least one of his Therian teammates wasn't pissed at him. Dex gave Hobbs a reassuring scratch behind the ear as he returned his gun to his holster.

"I'm okay, pal. Thanks."

The low mewl Hobbs let out said he wasn't too convinced. Cael soon appeared beside Dex and started grooming him, licking his face and hair.

"Bro, seriously, I'm fine."

Cael sat on his haunches and proceeded to tell Dex off in cheetah Therian, despite knowing Dex couldn't understand what the hell his chirps meant. Intimidation really wasn't his little brother's strong suit. Seb on the other hand...

The huge tiger Therian loomed over Dex, his green eyes flashing with fury. The dude was even bigger in his Therian form than he was in his Human form. What the hell did these guys eat? He held up a hand. "I know you're pissed—"

Seb roared, the sound terrifying enough to startle Cael and Hobbs who both ducked behind Dex. Ash kept his distance, his tail and ears saying he was aware of what was going on but trying to keep out of it for everyone's sake.

"How about we discuss this in a language we can both understand." Not that "pissed off" was difficult to understand. Dex preferred it when he could argue his case. He slowly put his hands up in front of him. "I'm going to call Rosa and have her bring the van around. You can shift there." Seb sat back, and Dex reached for his phone. He called Rosa and asked her to drive up to the chain-link fence on 138th Street. Returning his phone to his pocket, Dex waited. "Letty's going to bring everyone their clothes, so..."

Seb let out a chuff and got up. After a quick lick to Dex's face from his little brother, Cael trotted after Seb with Hobbs slowly trailing behind. "This is going to be fun," Dex muttered, cursing under his breath as he struggled to get up. Ash appeared beside Dex and pushed his head against him. He shook his mane, and Dex grabbed a fistful of it. "Thanks, man."

Ash pulled and Dex stood. He brushed himself off as he headed for the boarded-up door he'd come in through. It was bigger now that his Felid teammates had forced their way in. Teeth gritted, he crawled through. Man, his ribs were killing him. At least he hadn't broken anything.

Out on the street, Lou's catering/surveillance van was parked, and his Felid teammates were leaping in, including Seb. It was going to be even more packed than usual.

"He's going to tear me a new one, isn't he?"

Ash let out a loud huff before climbing into the van. Dex waited on the steps of the closed church as his team shifted. How the hell had Seb found out they were here? Cael wouldn't have told him, Dex was sure. Checking his watch, he saw it was almost noon. Shit. Sloane had to be up by now. His thoughts were interrupted a few minutes later when he saw Seb thundering over to him. Although not at one hundred percent, considering post-shift trauma, he was still intimidating as hell.

"You have every right to be pissed."

"Is this why you were glad Sparks gave me the case? So you could make an asshole out of me?" Seb demanded.

"What? No. Jesus, Seb. Of course not."

"Really? Because it sure as hell feels like it. I can't even begin to list the number of protocols you've broken. And worse, you roped our brothers into this? You put your whole team in jeopardy. For what? Ego? What are you trying to prove, Dex?"

"I'm not trying to prove anything." Dex rose, the step he stood on making him the same height as Seb. "The guy tried to blow up my team! He had Ash shot and Sloane..." Dex shook his head and did his best to keep his emotions in check before he said or did something he would regret. Just because the guy was Hobbs's brother didn't mean they were best buds.

Seb's expression softened, and some of his anger seemed to have shifted. "Hey, Sloane used to be my team leader too.

He's a great guy and a damn good agent. What happened was fucked-up. I know how you feel."

"Then you know why I have to go after Hogan."

"It's not your job! I'm sorry, Dex, but I have to report this." Seb reached for his phone and Dex caught his wrist, his eyes pleading.

"You would have done the same."

Seb frowned at him and shook his head. "I'd be pissed as hell, but I wouldn't go against orders, put my team in danger, or risk disciplinary measures."

"You did once."

Something flashed through Seb's eyes and he straightened. "That has nothing to do with this."

"It has everything to do with this."

A puzzled look came onto Seb's face as he studied Dex, then realization dawned on him. "Shit." He wiped a hand over his face and shook his head before his eyes landed on Dex again. "Shit."

"Tell me something. If you had it to do over, knowing what would happen, would you let him die so the boy could live?"

Seb looked away as he thought about his answer. Finally, he shook his head before meeting Dex's gaze. "No. I'd take the bullet myself so they could both live." The conviction in Seb's voice left no doubt about how serious he was.

"I'm sorry. I wasn't trying to fuck with your case. I couldn't sit on my ass doing fuck all after what Hogan did to Sloane. I'll take full responsibility for this. Report me, not the team. They did it for me," Dex pleaded. He watched with bated breath as Seb mulled it over.

"I know I'm going to regret this. I'm not going to report you, but you stop investigating immediately."

"I can't."

Seb threw his arms up. "Jesus, are you always this fucking difficult?"

"Only on days ending in y." Dex's attempt at humor fell flat, and he decided the hell with it. He wasn't too proud to beg. "Please. Let us work with you off the books. If anything happens, none of it will get back to you, and you can disavow all knowledge of us working with you. I'll take whatever heat comes down. But if we catch Hogan, you can take the credit. I just want to see his ass nailed to the fucking wall."

Seb eyed him. "You're not going to let this go, are you?"

"No."

"I must be out of my damn mind," Seb muttered. "Fine, but I want to know everything you know so far, and you don't make a move without me. Got it?"

"Deal." He held his hand out, and Seb shook it. Having Seb on their side certainly evened the odds. "Ash will fill you in. I need to speak with a contact. Anything I find out, I'll call you. Collins won't be coming back here. I hope we don't have to start from scratch." Dex followed Seb to the van where his brother and Felid teammates were back to their Human forms and dressed. The girls had taken care of their post-shift trauma, and now they all sat waiting. "Hey, how'd you know where to find us anyway?"

Seb climbed up and helped Dex in. He looked embarrassed. "Cael tried to sneak off this morning without waking me up, and I was worried, so I followed him."

Dex never saw it coming. One minute Ash was sitting on the bench, the next he had Seb pinned against the van's wall with his forearm against Seb's throat. Ash's pupils were dilated and his fangs growing.

"You son of a bitch! You slept with him?" Ash growled.

"What the fuck, Keeler?" Seb threw his arms out and shoved Ash away from him. The two Felids advanced on each other when Cael squeezed himself between them.

"Enough!"

Ash balled his hands into fists, his pained gaze on Cael. "How could you sleep with him?"

"I didn't," Cael hissed angrily. "You assumed I did. We had dinner last night. I had too much to drink, and Seb kindly took me to his place. We talked, and I crashed on his couch. Is that okay with you, Ash? Or do you assume every guy I hang out with is fucking me?"

The fight went out of Ash and he deflated. "All right, I get it. I messed up. I'm sorry."

Seb opened his mouth, but Dex elbowed him and shook his head. If Seb wanted to keep his stripes, it was best he not get in the middle of an argument between Cael and Ash. He motioned to the bench, and Seb took a seat. Dex slid in next to him, catching Letty and Rosa's worried expressions as they whispered to each other. Hobbs discreetly pointed to the front of the van and Dex nodded. He and Calvin practically tripped over each other trying to escape to the front seats.

"You know what, Ash?" Cael closed his eyes, took a deep breath, and let it out slowly. "I'm exhausted. I can't do this with you right now." He marched over to the bench and dropped down beside Dex, snuggling in close. He twisted his body slightly so he was facing Dex, his head resting against Dex's arm, and his eyes closed. The van fell into awkward silence, and Dex saw Seb pull his phone out. A few seconds later, Dex's phone buzzed. He pulled it out and read Seb's text.

Should I be worried?

Dex texted back. *About what?*

Your team.

It's fine. We'll handle it. It was all he was going to say on the matter. After texting Seb, he texted Hobbs, telling him to drop him off first. Dex needed to call Austen and fill him in. They had to approach this from another angle now that Collins was gone.

Half an hour later, after Cael reassured him for the hundredth time that he was fine and didn't need Dex babying him, Dex was back in Lou's basement. *Damn it.* They'd been so close. Austen was doing reconnaissance, and everyone else was waiting to see what Dex would come up with. But the truth was he had nothing. He'd been bent over this table for hours, searching through all his notes and reports. His back was killing him, his head hurt, and a sharp pain went through his side every time he inhaled.

"Dex!"

"Hm?" Dex looked up wondering how long Lou had been standing there. "What, Lou?" He opened several map windows on his tablet, all filled with abandoned buildings. Fuck, it was like finding a needle in a haystack. New York City was littered with old buildings waiting to either be torn down, sold, or restored. Hogan, Collins, and the rest of those assholes could be anywhere.

"I can't believe you're still here. Did you go home last night?"

Dex followed Lou's gaze to the couch. "I crashed here."

"Have you been home at all today?"

Dex let out a noncommittal grunt. Couldn't Lou see he was trying to get some work done? Had Collins and the rest of his gang been hiding out in the ballroom all this time? Had Hogan been there? Dex would be mighty pissed if he found out Hogan had been hiding out there and they'd missed him.

"You need to go home, Dex."

Dex waved a hand dismissively. "I will. I just need to figure this one thing out." Considering where they found Collins today and Austen's intel on previous Coalition sightings, not to mention the group's need to stay hidden and their penchant for abandoned buildings—

Lou grabbed Dex's arm and jerked him back, surprising the hell out of Dex.

"Stop it."

"What the hell, Lou? It's fine. Go home." He checked his watch. Jesus, it was almost ten o'clock already?

"You're doing it again."

"Doing what?" Didn't Lou understand how important this was? It wasn't like the guy didn't know Dex. They'd had four years together. Then again, Lou had never been a fan of Dex's career choices. The job was always at the heart of all their arguments.

"You're putting the damn job before everything and everyone else."

"Did you come down here to lecture me?" He really didn't have time for this.

"Dex, your boyfriend was almost killed. He's at home, in pain, needing you, and you're here obsessing over this case."

"I'm doing it for him," Dex argued. "I've been working my ass off for Sloane, for my family, my friends. To keep them safe."

"Bullshit. You're doing it for you!"

"What?" Dex didn't like where this argument was going. It sounded too much like all the other arguments they'd had about his job. The ones always resulting in Dex sleeping downstairs on the couch and then having to somehow find a way to make it all okay again the next day.

Lou's hazel eyes pleaded with him. "When you get obsessed over a case, you're like a different person. You push your family away, your friends, everyone who cares about you. I know you want to see this through. You want justice. But it shouldn't come at the cost of what you love."

Dex frowned, not liking the way Lou's words cut through him. "It's not." He wasn't pushing Sloane away. Was he?

"Oh, really? So, Sloane knows you're here? He knows what you're doing?"

Dex opened his mouth but quickly closed it. What could he say? There was no point in lying. Lou would see right through him. Lou's stunned expression made him feel all the worse.

"Wow." Lou shook his head in disbelief.

"Lou, don't." He watched a familiar blazing look come into Lou's eyes. The one he used to say he inherited from his mother, along with her temper. It was usually followed by a flurry of hand gestures and finger movements.

"No, you know what? We're not together anymore, Dex. You don't get to 'don't' me. You're going to hear this whether you like it or not."

Dex tried to pacify his ex, but there was no point. When Lou was truly fucked off about something, all you could do was weather the storm and hope you made it through without a cow dropping on your head.

"You're a good man and a good agent, Dex, but let's face it. We know what this is really about, what it's always been about."

Dex arched an eyebrow at him. This should be interesting. "Enlighten me."

"It's about your parents."

"What the fuck?" Of everything he'd been expecting

Lou to throw his way, ego, stubbornness, general fuckery, he'd never expected Lou to bring up his parents.

"They're the reason you went into law enforcement. They're the reason you're terrified of losing anyone close to you, of letting the bad guys win. The idea there are criminals out there who haven't been brought to justice eats away at you, and if someone hurts someone you love, you won't stop until they're either behind bars or dead, no matter what it costs."

"And that's a bad thing?"

"You being dead?" Lou's temper flared. "Of course it is, you jackass!"

Dex had never seen Lou so worked up. "I didn't mean the dead part. The rest of it. What good cop doesn't want the same thing?"

"Yes, but what are you willing to give up for it, Dex? Your family deserves to have you in their lives. Sloane? You love him. Do you want to give up the chance at a future with him before it's properly begun? This isn't just you risking your life while on the job. This is you obsessing and taking unnecessary risks. You can't save the world. You can't save your parents."

"You know what? I don't have to stand here and listen to this bullshit." Dex turned away only to have Lou get in his face again. What the hell had made him think this was a good idea. When Lou got something stuck in his craw, he was relentless.

"You're pissed off because you know it's true. You play tough guy, making jokes to hide the anger you feel in your heart because they were taken from you, the men responsible never found. And this?" Lou motioned around him. "This won't make the pain go away. It won't bring your parents back or change what's happened. Stop living in the past and think about your future. Your parents are gone, Dex, and it's tragic, but you're lucky enough to have found a new equally loving family. You have an adoptive father who would give his life for you. A little brother who looks up to you like you're the greatest hero who ever lived, and a brooding Therian who needs you more than he's ready to admit. Don't take them for granted, Dex, or one day you'll turn around and find them gone, and you'll regret it for the rest of your life."

Dex was too stunned to speak, his heart and ego feeling as bruised as his ribs. Did he really take his dad and brother for granted? He loved them more than anything. There was nothing he wouldn't give for them. It wasn't about his parents; it was about justice. It always had been, hadn't it? A tear rolled down his cheek, and he stood numbly as Lou wiped it away with his thumb.

"Go home, Dex."

Dex nodded, his voice quiet when he spoke. "You're right. I should go."

"SLOANE?"

Sloane was surprised to hear Lou's voice on the other end. He'd finished washing up after his takeout dinner when his phone had gone off. Stupidly, he'd thought it was Dex. "Lou? What's wrong? Are you okay?"

"Yes. I'm worried about Dex."

Carefully, he lowered himself onto the couch, his gut twisting at Lou's words. "What happened?" Was it the reason Dex hadn't called or texted? Had something happened? Sloane told himself not to panic.

"I know he's going to be pissed at me, but I can't watch him do this to himself. Not again."

"Talk to me, Lou."

"He's been working and sleeping from an empty office in the basement of Clove Catering. I swear when he asked me if he could use it, I didn't know what it was for. He's barely sleeping, barely eating, comes in at all hours. Living off sandwiches, donuts, and coffee, if that. He's been crashing on the couch. It's heartbreaking."

"Damn it. I can't believe he dragged you into this." So that's where Dex had been hiding himself. He remembered Dex's text stating he'd stayed over at Cael's last night. It wasn't bad enough he was lying to Sloane, now he was getting everyone else to lie for him.

"Wait, you know?"

Sloane let out a sigh. "Yeah."

"Why haven't you told him?"

"I'm sure he knows."

"But you haven't discussed it?"

"I've been wondering how long he's going to keep on lying to me. After everything he's said and done, he comes home, and he lies to me, Lou." Had Lou and Dex's relationship fallen apart because they'd not been right for each other? Or had this been the reason? Lou said he couldn't watch Dex do this to himself again. So it wasn't the first time. Dex was stubborn, no doubt about it, but he was also reasonable. Was this a side of his partner he hadn't known existed? Sloane had seen how dogged Dex could be when he was working a case, and he admired his partner's determination. But what if this was something different altogether?

"He loves you, Sloane. I don't know how you feel about

him, but I'm guessing you really care about him. Don't let your pride come between you."

"His lying is what's coming between us," Sloane replied angrily. Part of his anger stemmed from Dex lying, but it wasn't what bothered him most. It was Dex putting the job before them, his family, and everything else after how fiercely he'd defended the point following the whole mess with the Therian Youth Center bombing. How the job could be replaced but not someone he loved. And then he turns around and does this?

"So your solution is to act like everything's okay? To meet his lie with yet another lie? *Dios mío*, I want to smack you both upside the head." Lou let out a frustrated growl, stunning Sloane. Damn, he didn't even know Lou could get that pissed. Sloane heard the rumble of Dex's Challenger coming up the street.

"I have to go. He's almost home. Thank you for calling."

"Sloane. You two have found something special. Don't throw it away. I could never get through to him. Maybe you can. For both your sakes."

"Thanks, Lou." Sloane hung up and put away his phone. He sat on the couch and waited. By the time Sloane heard the keys jingling outside the door, he'd worked himself up. Lou was right. Meeting Dex's lie with another lie would get them nowhere, and it wasn't how he wanted their relationship to go. This had to stop before it got any more out of hand.

The door opened, and Sloane waited with his jaw clenched so tight he might break something. Dex appeared in the doorway to the living room, hair needing a cut, scruffy beard growing in, his clothes disheveled, dirty, and he was pretty sure there was some kind of fungus stuck to his jeans. He was also carrying a bouquet of roses in one hand.

Sloane blinked dumbly. What the hell?

"Hi." Dex lingered in the doorway. He rubbed his free hand over his hair before shoving it into his pocket. "I'm sorry I missed dinner. And lunch. And um, breakfast."

Sloane's gaze went to the flowers. "Are those for me?"

"Yeah. I know it's kind of cheesy, but..." Dex shrugged, looking embarrassed.

"It's not cheesy. It's sweet. Come here," Sloane said softly, holding his arms out. God, if this was any indication of how their relationship was going to progress, Sloane was screwed. He'd talk to Dex, straighten this mess out, but right now, his partner was clearly in need of some care. Dex looked like he was ready to collapse.

His partner put the flowers on the coffee table, kicked off his sneakers, and climbed up on the couch to curl himself up against him, his arms wrapping around Sloane's waist. Sloane returned the gesture, wrapping his arms around Dex and holding him.

Dex sucked in a sharp breath and winced. "Shit."

"Dex?" Sloane pulled his arms back and looked down at him. "Are you okay?"

"It's nothing."

"We'll see." Sloane reached for the hem of Dex's T-shirt.

"Babe—"

Anger flared through Sloane. "Oh, fuck no."

"What?" Dex sat back, his eyes wide.

"This is the first time you've called me that, and you use it to get yourself out of trouble?" To his credit, Dex looked offended.

"I didn't say it to get out of trouble. It just came out." He shrugged, his cheeks going pink. "It felt right."

"Fine. Just show me." Sloane told himself he was an idiot for wanting to smile at the endearment. No one had ever called him anything resembling a pet name. It sounded sweet coming from Dex. Natural. Hell, if he weren't so pissed off at Dex right now, he *would* be smiling. When he carefully lifted the hem of Dex's shirt to reveal blotches of nasty looking purplish-pink bruises, he cursed under his breath. "Jesus, Dex."

Sloane's fierce urge to protect Dex was battling it out with his growing desire to strangle him. With deliberate care, he brushed his fingers down Dex's ribs, watching his partner wince. The appropriate swear words eluded him, and as much as he wanted to growl and yell, he ended up talking quietly. "You promised me."

"I know," Dex said, looking like he was about to shatter. What the hell had his partner been putting himself through? Sloane didn't have the heart to be angry at him. Tomorrow. Tomorrow he'd be angry. Properly fucked-off angry.

"What happened?"

"Can we not talk about it?"

"Dex—"

Dex gave him a small smile. "It looks worse than it is."

"Have you taken ibuprofen?"

"Not yet."

"Come on." He grabbed his crutch and allowed Dex to help him to his feet. They walked around the couch, and Sloane motioned to the kitchen. "Grab the icepack from the freezer." He waited for Dex to grab the icepack before his partner helped him up the stairs. As soon as they were in the bedroom, Sloane nodded toward the bathroom. "Hot shower. Make it quick."

Dex didn't argue, and while his partner showered, Sloane turned down the bed. He switched on the lamp and turned off the bedroom light, leaving only the warm glow of the lamp. Placing his crutch by the nightstand, he sat on the edge of the bed and waited, wondering how best to approach this situation. They couldn't continue the way they were, and it had gone on far longer than it should have. Each day with Dex was an adventure, and Sloane loved it, but sometimes he wished the two of them could have a little normalcy like any other couple. Was it too much to ask to have some peace and quiet, without the world going to hell, bombs exploding, bullets flying, or his partner running around looking to punish all the wrongdoers?

Sloane wasn't about to simply dismiss Dex's fixation with this case. There was obviously something under the surface, something driving his partner other than a need for justice. Dex was smart. Too smart to be risking everything he'd worked so damn hard for when there were other agents capable of handling the case.

The door to the bathroom opened, and Dex walked out in only his pale-blue-and-white-striped pajama bottoms. He was a yawn away from falling asleep standing up. Sloane patted the bed next to him.

"Lie down."

"Sounds like the beginning of a porno," Dex said as he climbed onto his side of the bed. He let out a fierce yawn and ruffled his hair.

"Zip it, wise guy. I'm still mad at you." Sloane picked up the icepack and settled in next to Dex facing him. Gently, he placed the ice pack to Dex's ribs. His partner winced but remained still. "Did you take the ibuprofen?"

"Yes."

"Don't," Sloane warned.

"What?"

"Make that 'I'm too cute, you can't stay mad at me' face." Sloane was going to find a way to be immune to that face. He might need to ask Ash for some pointers.

"I have one of those? Why didn't you tell me?" Dex teased, though he yawned in the middle of it, so half of it was garbled.

"Close your eyes." Sloane knew as soon as Dex closed his eyes he'd be asleep. A few seconds later, and his partner was out. Or at least he thought so when he heard Dex's sleepy voice.

"They never caught them you know."

"Who?" What on earth was his partner talking about? Was he talking in his sleep?

"The men who killed my parents."

"Oh, Dex..." Sloane placed a kiss to Dex's brow. "I'm so sorry, sweetheart." He hadn't been aware. It was something Dex rarely talked about. Sloane understood grief all too well, so he never pushed the matter. When and if Dex wanted to discuss it with him, Sloane would be there to listen. Dex mumbled something else under his breath before falling asleep, and Sloane wondered if his parents' deaths had something to do with Dex's obsession with catching Hogan. If it did, Sloane had to put a stop to it now, or Dex would continue to spiral down the darkened path.

Dex's lips were slightly parted as he slept like the dead. His partner was generally a heavy sleeper, but this was pure exhaustion. With Dex asleep before him, Sloane could take a good look at his partner. Besides the nasty bruising over his ribs, he was covered in various tiny nicks and scratches.

There were a few smaller bruises on his arms, and heavy bags under his eyes. Sloane couldn't let this continue.

The room was warm from the heat he'd turned on earlier in the evening. Soon it would be Thanksgiving, then Christmas. Fanciful images of him with Dex and his family at Christmas entered his thoughts. He'd joined them for dinner last year and had had a great time. It had been the first time he'd had a Christmas where he'd felt... at home. This year it would be slightly different. Cael knew about them, and Sloane had to wonder how much Maddock knew. His sergeant was too sharp, too world worn to be oblivious to what was going on in his sons' lives. Well, he'd worry about it later. Right now, he had to work out how to deal with the man lying beside him. A man Sloane was daring to hope would always be at his side.

NINE

SLOANE SAT ON THE COUCH, brooding. His gaze followed Dex around the room as he looked for his messenger bag. The one Sloane had stuffed under the couch cushion next to him. They'd had a great morning. After waking up in each other's arms, they'd made love before their stomachs demanded nourishment. Dex made Sloane his favorite—eggs benedict and pancakes. Sloane had even gone as far as to ask for the heart-shaped ones again. For a moment he thought maybe Dex had given up this madness. Sometime between his going to sleep and now, Dex's resolve to find Hogan seemed to have strengthened.

"Damn it. I know I left it here this morning. You sure you haven't seen it?" Dex scratched his head, then waved a hand in dismissal. "Forget it. I don't need it. I'll call you later." Dex headed for the door so lost in thought, he hadn't even remembered to kiss Sloane good-bye.

"All right, that's it. I can't take this bullshit anymore. Get your ass back here," Sloane growled.

Dex turned with a deep frown on his face. "Excuse me?"

"I know everything, Dex. I know about your Batcave in Lou's basement, the stakeouts, Bautista, the ballroom, Seb, everything."

"It was Ash, wasn't it?" Dex curled his fists at his sides. "I knew he was narcing on me."

"No, he was being honest, unlike you. How could you look me in the eye every day and lie to me, over and over?"

Dex opened his mouth, and Sloane quickly held up a hand.

"And don't you dare tell me you did it for me, or you didn't want to worry me. You lied. I asked you not to go after Hogan, and not only did you completely ignore me, you lied about what you were doing. You brought the team into it, your brother. Seb? Jesus, the guy just got his career back, Dex."

"You of all people should understand why. I almost lost you!" Dex's pale-blue eyes pleaded, but Sloane stood his ground.

"So you run around the city like you've got a death wish, throwing yourself into the line of fire, without so much as the proper equipment? You work yourself ragged, sleeping on a goddamn couch in your ex's basement living off sugar and caffeine? I understand how important this is—"

"Do you? Because if you did, you'd be supporting me. It's *my* job."

Sloane grabbed his crutch and pulled himself to his feet. "No, it's *our* job because we're part of a fucking team. It's not the Dexter Daley show. You don't get to run around doing whatever the hell you want, flash your smile, and then expect everything to turn out okay. Because while it may turn out okay for you, the rest of us have to run around behind you picking up your shit and making sure you don't get yourself fucking killed."

Dex stormed farther into the room. "What the fuck? Since when? Is that how you feel? That you have to run around behind me picking up after me? Babysitting me like I'm some fucking asshole who doesn't know his left from his right? Am I that much of a shitty partner?"

Sloane shook his head. This wasn't going at all like he'd hoped. "Don't put words in my mouth."

"Then don't make it sound that way. I might act like the class clown, but I'm a damn good agent. No, I don't always follow the rules, but sometimes to get results, the rules have to be broken."

"Oh my God, how can you say that? You were arguing with Ash against the same thing weeks ago!"

"I have to go. We'll talk about this later."

"Dex, stop." Sloane couldn't let him walk out of there. His desperation got the better of him, and he didn't think, stepping forward with his right leg instead of his left. His leg gave out, and he went crashing onto the carpet.

"Sloane!" Dex rushed over and dropped to his knees beside him, his arms embracing him and helping him sit up. "Damn it. What the hell were you thinking?"

"I was thinking, 'I can't let him leave. I can't watch him walk out the door for what could be the last time.' I was thinking I need to do whatever it takes."

"For what?"

"To keep you with me." Sloane took hold of Dex's arm, needing someone so badly it hurt.

"I'll call Ash—"

Frustration, anger, and something else he couldn't explain bubbled up inside him, erupting furiously. "I don't want Ash, goddamn it. I want you! I fucking love *you*!"

Dex stared at him, and Sloane realized what he'd said. He swallowed hard, allowing Dex to help him to his feet and over to the couch where he sat down, trying to get his thoughts and emotions under control. Inside him, his Felid roared and clawed to get free, and Sloane could feel him. Could feel him trying to tear through, to claim Dex and show him the raw need he had for him. His eyesight sharpened, and he felt Dex's hand on his cheek as he murmured soft words.

"Hey, it's okay. Tell him it's okay. I'm not going anywhere."

Sloane didn't know how Dex knew, though it was likely because his pupils had dilated. He breathed deeply and exhaled slowly.

"Is it true? What you said? Because if it's to make me stay—"

"It's not to make you stay," Sloane snapped. "Do you really think I would say something like that to make you stay? I can't make you do anything, Dex. No one can make you do anything because you're fucking Dexter J. Daley, and no one makes you do shit you don't want to do. No one can stop you from doing what *you* want. I've seen you beat up, bloodied, bruised, shattered, at the mercy of a madman, and goddamn it, I can't—" His words caught in his throat, and he let out a shaky breath. "I know the job is dangerous. But for you to go out looking to face a force you can't handle on your own. To disregard your safety when there are plenty of capable agents to do the job... Fuck you. Fuck you for putting yourself before the rest of us. Before your dad, and your brother, and *me*."

"I... didn't know."

"Well, now you do. I won't sit here waiting for Ash or Calvin to tell me you've been fucking mauled to death.

Maybe I am being selfish, but you know what? Fuck it. I'm going to be selfish. You wanted a future for us. Well, this is it. Us. You and me. No lone-cowboy shit. Every time you think of doing something stupid out there, you think about *us*." He took hold of Dex's face and looked into his pale-blue eyes, hoping his words would get past his partner's thick skull.

"I know you're a capable agent, Dex. You're a great agent. You're smart and sharp. You adapt quicker than any other rookie I've seen. You're determined, loyal, resilient... but you're *Human*. I'm not saying you're weak because you're one of the strongest men I know. You need to accept there are forces out there stronger than you. It's okay to walk away. I spend all day worrying about you, about what you're getting yourself into. Do you know what it feels like to watch you walk out the door, wondering if it's going to be the last time?"

"I'm sorry, Sloane."

"From the moment I met you, you've been driving me out of my fucking mind. I've never known anyone who makes me want to laugh and scream at the same time. When you asked me to stay with you, I thought it would expose the faults in our relationship. And now? When you're not here, I wish you were. God, I even miss your stupid music. I want the Dex that drives me crazy. The one who laughs at his own jokes and eats snacks at inappropriate times. And I want to wake up with him every day. I want his beautiful eyes and breathtaking smile to be the first things I see when I wake up and the last things before bed."

Dex's eyes widened. "Are you... are you saying what I think you're saying?"

"I think I should move in. Someone needs to save you from yourself, and I'm the only one qualified."

"Is that the only reason?" Dex asked quietly, a small smile on his face.

"What? That and my wanting to because I love you isn't enough of a reason?"

"That's all the reason I need." Dex brought Sloane in and kissed him, sending a shiver through him. Maybe he was losing it, but nothing in a long time had felt so damn good or made him this happy. He held Dex to him, savoring every passionate kiss, every gentle touch, and lingering smile. As Dex's tongue sought his, Sloane gave himself over to his partner. How could one man, one Human, have so much power over him? Sloane's Human side wanted to relinquish everything to the man in his arms, while his feral side wanted to possess him.

Sloane's fingers brushed over the four thin claw marks on Dex's arm, and a fierce heat threatened to consume him. He deepened his kiss, and pushed Dex onto his back, his heavier weight pinning Dex to the couch cushions beneath him. He slipped his hand over Dex's forearm and pulled back, his partner's kiss-swollen lips and flushed face drawing his feral side closer to the surface. What the hell was happening to him? Lately the beast inside him seemed to stir at the slightest provocation, especially when it concerned Dex. Sloane couldn't explain the sudden ferocity. When had his need for Dex become so great that the thought of him with someone else had Sloane growling with anger from deep in his chest? He wasn't one to be possessive, and he'd always maintained a firm grip. But now...

Dex arched his back, and he placed his free hand to Sloane's heart. "What's he telling you?"

"You don't want to know," Sloane replied roughly.

"Yes, I do."

Sloane shook his head. His partner didn't know what he

was asking. Dex might have grown up with a Therian brother, but the dynamics of that relationship compared to the one with a Therian lover were completely different, outside of the obvious. "You won't like what you hear. He's not... civil. I think he knew how I felt before I did. Everything I feel, he feels ten times stronger. It can be a little... disturbing."

"Try me." There was no mistaking the sincerity in Dex's voice.

Sloane pressed his hard body down against Dex's, his voice low as he tried to keep his grip on his feral half. "He wants me to mark you so that every Therian will know you belong to us." His finger circled one of the faint lines on Dex's arm.

Dex swallowed hard, his blue eyes moving to his arm in Sloane's grip. They widened slightly as Sloane's nails slowly elongated. Sloane hissed at the pain, but he held his feral side at bay. Dex moved his eyes back to Sloane, the lust in them taking Sloane's breath away.

"Do it."

"Dex, you don't know what you're saying." Even as he whispered the words, he could feel his feral side demanding he go through with it. Sloane's blood felt hot inside his skin, his eyesight remained sharp, and his fangs began to grow. "Please, Dex. I don't want to hurt you. I can't." The thought alone frightened Sloane. He'd never done anything like this before. His Human side desired Dex. His Therian side wanted to claim him.

"I love you. Please. I want you to. I *need* you to." Dex cupped Sloane through his pajama bottoms and Sloane hissed. He was so hard it was painful. Dex didn't know what he was doing.

"Dex," Sloane pleaded. He gritted his teeth against the pain of his claws growing in.

"Do it," Dex urged, slipping his hand inside Sloane's pants and stroking him. "Make me yours. I want to be yours in every way possible."

Sloane's hold on his feral side was tremulous at best, and Dex kept pushing. How could he make his partner understand? "This is serious, Dex. You'll have this mark for the rest of your life."

"Good. Because that's how long I want you with me."

Sloane inhaled sharply, and he relinquished control to his Therian side without any further thought. His claws came out, and his painful cry drowned out Dex's as the tips of Sloane's claws pierced his lover's skin. Dex clutched at Sloane, his finger's digging into his bicep and his jaw clenched as he tried desperately to keep himself quiet. His eyes grew glassy and red, but Sloane could see Dex fighting to keep himself from screaming. Darkness encroached on Sloane's vision, his senses sharpening. Slowly and deliberately he sliced at Dex's arm, making sure to go deep enough to leave his mark permanently but not enough where Dex would need stitches.

Sloane's heart pounded, the scent of Dex's blood filling his nostrils. He ground his hips against Dex as he finished leaving his mark around Dex's forearm. As soon as he was finished, he pulled off his T-shirt and wrapped it around his partner's bleeding arm, tying it firmly in place. His eyes landed on Dex, and Sloane was taken aback by the heat in his amazing eyes. They clawed at each other's clothes the best they could with Dex's arm and Sloane's leg. Desire and love turned into desperation, sending them both into a frenzy of need and lust. Sloane spit into his hand, making it good and wet, then wrapped it around his cock, stroking himself before he pushed a finger against Dex's entrance.

"Yes," Dex hissed, his fingers slipping into Sloane's hair and grabbing fistfuls of it. "Please, fuck me."

Sloane quickly prepped Dex, his dick soon replacing his fingers inside his lover. The feral beast inside him rejoiced. Dex was his. Would always be his. Any Therian who laid eyes on Dex's arm would know what the deliberate claw marks meant. Would know the pain they'd both endured for their bond. Dex gasped and moaned, his back arched up, and his fingers pulled at Sloane's hair. His amazing lips were plump, pink, and slightly parted. They kissed with a hunger and fervor that left them gasping for air. Sloane's movements were awkward at first because of his leg, but he used his arms to steady himself, to give him the momentum he needed to drive himself deep into Dex over and over. Dex cried out beneath him as he came, and Sloane wasn't far behind, his teeth gritted as he thrust into Dex several more times before collapsing on him.

Their breaths steadied, and their skin began to cool as the minutes passed. Sloane was afraid to get up, fearing Dex might be regretting it now. Did his partner truly understand the significance of what they'd done?

"It's okay."

Dex's soft words met his ear, and Sloane closed his eyes, relieved. He pulled back, and his heart squeezed at the warm smile on Dex's face.

"Are you having second thoughts?" Dex asked hesitantly. "I didn't want to push you into doing something you didn't want to do."

"I wanted to do it," Sloane said confidently. "But..." He gently took hold of Dex's arm wrapped in his T-shirt. "I've scarred you."

"How about if once they're fully healed, I get a tattoo? It'll look cool. I've always wanted a tattoo."

"A tattoo?" Sloane liked the idea of that. He carefully sat up and pulled Dex with him, wrapping him up in his arms.

"Yeah. Therians will still know your mark is there, but Humans will only see the tattoo unless they're close enough."

"You really want to?"

Dex smiled brightly. "It'll be awesome."

"Okay." Sloane sat there for a moment, his hand tenderly holding Dex's arm. Any Therians who saw it would know. "You'll have to keep it covered at work." The gossip would run rampant through their unit, especially since Dex was supposedly not seeing anyone. This wasn't the kind of thing you did with a casual hookup or even a long-term boyfriend. This was the real deal. Sloane swallowed hard. How'd he go from flipping his shit over the word *boyfriend* to being in a committed relationship to... this?

"No problem."

Speaking of work... "You see this?" Sloane held Dex's arm up. "When you're unsure, when we're not together, when you're scared, or about to do something you know you shouldn't, you look at this, and you remember you have more to think about than yourself. I'm a part of you now, got it?"

Dex nodded.

"I want to hear you say it," Sloane growled.

"You're a part of me."

"Good. Now, get the Therian first-aid kit. We need to patch you up. While you're there, could you bring me a T-shirt?"

"Sure." Dex gave him a quick kiss before getting off the couch and pulling on his pants. Although his partner did his best to hide the pain he was feeling in his arm, Sloane knew better. He dressed while Dex fetched the kit, and when his partner returned, Sloane went to work cleaning his wounds and dressing them. As soon as his arm was bandaged, Dex popped a couple of painkillers and pulled his long-sleeved T-shirt over his head, mindful of his bruised ribs.

"Okay. We're dealing with Hogan as a team. No going off on your own."

"I promise."

"And we're going to stop acting like a bunch of fucking idiots and talk things through. No lies, no withholding information, no nonsense. Communication."

Dex arched an eyebrow.

"Yes, that goes for me too, wise guy."

"Okay." Dex's smile grew wide before he planted a kiss on Sloane's lips. "Have I told you I love you?"

"I wouldn't mind hearing it again," Sloane teased, releasing Dex's arm and returning the kiss.

"I love you."

Sloane did his best Han Solo impression. "I know."

"You dick," Dex laughed. "Come on."

"Okay." Sloane grew serious. "I... kind of like you. Sometimes."

Dex pressed his lips together trying not to laugh. He shook his head.

"No? Okay, how about, I like you, but more than like. You make me feel like there's a party in my pants."

Dex burst into laughter. "Oh my God, what are you on? Is it the meds talking? It's the meds isn't it?"

"I have no idea. No, it's not the meds." He drew his partner up against him and put a hand to his cheek. "I love you." If those three little words were all it took to bring that glorious smile to Dex's face, he'd never stop saying them. "And I'm sorry it took me this long to realize it."

"That's more like it."

They kissed until they could no longer hold off on the inevitable. It was time to deal with this case and put an end to it so he could concentrate on the insane spur-of-the-moment decision he'd made to move in with Dex. The thought alone should be scaring the hell out of him, but like several other choices as of late, it wasn't. He had no idea what the hell they were going to do about work, but they'd sort it out later.

"All right. From the beginning."

Ash had filled Sloane in on what he knew, but Ash obviously hadn't been with Dex every step of the way, so he needed Dex to fill in the blanks. He sat silently listening as his partner recounted everything he'd done from the day he'd asked Lou to use his basement up until their team's most recent undercover job. Sloane had to admit he was impressed. His partner had done all of it without Themis, without algorithms, or fancy gadgets. When Dex finished, he gave Sloane a few minutes to think quietly. They were getting close.

"Good job. Okay, I need you to set up a meeting with the team."

"You got it. Where?"

"I want them here in the next half hour. And get Austen to set up a safe house. Nothing fancy, just somewhere out of the way where we can bring someone in. I want it equipped for an interrogation. Make sure there's a nice restaurant within a few blocks."

Dex gave him a puzzled look but got right to it. He phoned Austen first, then the rest of the team. In less than half an hour, they were all present and accounted for in Dex's living room, including Seb. Man, his team looked like shit. Most of them had bags under their eyes, were in serious need of sleep, and the rest looked grumpy as fuck. The worst part was the grumpy ones weren't the usual suspects. Cael, who was more often than not cheerful and enthusiastic, looked like he was ready to hiss and claw at someone. Ash looked... beat. Seb looked worried. Calvin and Hobbs looked... uncomfortable. Sloane would have to work that one out later. Rosa was most definitely pissed, and her glare was aimed at Dex. Letty was the only one who looked like everything was cool.

"Thank you all for coming." Sloane sat on the couch with Dex beside him. "First, I know all about this insane unsanctioned mission."

"Are you pissed?" Cael asked worriedly.

Sloane smiled at him. "No, I'm not pissed. In fact, I don't think I've ever been prouder." His team stared back at him with surprised expressions, so he elaborated. "We're a family, and when one of us needed help, you all stepped in. You put everything on the line to back Dex up. I'm not thrilled you kept it from me, and it better not happen again, but you came through for him."

"So Dex fessed up," Rosa said, wrinkling her nose at Dex. "You should have kicked his ass."

"Yes, he fessed up," Sloane said with a chuckle. He motioned over to his crutch. "Kicking is out of the question, but don't worry. Sparta will still be there when I get back."

Dex groaned. "Man, I thought you were going to let this one go."

"Aw, that's cute." Sloane gave his partner's knee a pat. "Not a chance. I'm going to remember every detail, and then I'm going to remind you why it's a bad idea to withhold information from me." He smiled brightly at the rest of his team. "That goes for the rest of you. Except Ash, because he was the only one who actually did what he was supposed to do."

There was a collective groan followed by several colorful expletives in multiple languages.

"I thought you said you were proud of us," Cael whined.

"I am, but you should know better than to keep secrets from me. Especially when it concerns the safety of one of your teammates."

Everyone glared at Dex who went to remove some imaginary dust from the couch cushion next to him.

"You can all thank Dex later. For now, let's get this show on the road." Sloane turned his attention to Calvin. "Cal, you did recon on Bautista. Do you think he'd turn?"

Calvin didn't hesitate. He gave Sloane a firm nod. "I genuinely believe he doesn't know what his boyfriend is up to. He's a nice guy. No criminal record or priors, not even a parking ticket. He's a grade school teacher with a perfect record. Visits his grandmother every Sunday. Spends time with his family. Does charity work. I think if we showed him who his boyfriend really is, he might be willing to help us."

Ash nodded his agreement. "Cal's right. We've done surveillance on him. Poor sap has no clue what Collins is up to. The guy genuinely believes Collins attends church every Saturday morning."

Sloane mulled it over. This was their best lead. "All right. Let's bring him in. Austen's getting us a safe location. Cal, it's time for another date with Bautista. Call him up. See if he's free for dinner tomorrow night. If he asks you where, tell him it's a surprise. Everyone else, wait for my instructions. In the meantime, help yourself to whatever's in the kitchen."

"Drinks and snacks, *mi amigos*!" Dex carefully pushed himself off the couch and motioned to the kitchen. Rosa, Letty, Cael, and Hobbs followed while Calvin fished his phone out of his pocket and headed outside to call Bautista. Ash hung back, his gaze somewhere over Sloane. It didn't take a genius to know who his eyes were following. He really hoped his friend sorted himself out. Sloane had no idea how much longer Ash could go on like this. Seb was heading for the kitchen when Sloane reached out and took hold of his arm.

"Hey, can I talk to you a moment?"

"Sure." Seb came around the couch and sat down next to him. "How are you feeling?"

"Better. Thanks." He glanced over his shoulder to make sure Dex was still in the kitchen and occupied. The team was currently surrounding his partner and tossing Cheesy Doodles into his open mouth for him to catch. So far he hadn't missed one. Man, his partner was such a loveable dork. Looked like he'd be busy for a little while. Sloane turned back to Seb. "I really appreciate what you're doing. If anything goes south, it's on me."

Seb sat back, his arms folded over his broad chest and his legs crossed at the ankles. "Interesting. Dex told me the same thing."

"Yeah, well, I have a higher clearance level. So whatever happens is on me."

Seb gave him a smile. "You haven't changed, you know."

"What do you mean?"

"Since I was on the team. Still protective. I always admired that about you." Seb looked remorseful. "I don't know if I ever apologized, or if I did, I'm sure it wasn't enough. I'm sorry I fucked up, Sloane."

Sloane shook his head. "You gotta stop beating yourself up about what happened, Seb. You made a mistake, paid the consequences. If Weidman had been on the ball, it could have been prevented." He was quiet for a moment. "I'm sorry I was such an asshole to you about it. You needed a friend, not another officer chewing you out." At the time he'd been furious. They'd had a huge fight over it, and Sloane had said some things he regretted. Seb had needed a friend, needed Sloane to be understanding, but at the time, Sloane hadn't been able to see past the breach in protocol. He'd never been invested in anyone emotionally and couldn't understand Seb's fierce instinct to protect Hudson.

"No, you were—*are*, a good team leader. You had every right to be pissed off at me. My Felid side clawed for dominance, and I allowed it. I relinquished control to him." Seb met Sloane's gaze, his intense emerald stare pinning Sloane to the spot. He could see the Felid behind his friend's eyes. See the ferocity in the tiger Therian watching him. "I'm not excusing what I did, but when your Felid side has found his mate, he will fight you with everything he's got, Sloane. You might think you're in control, but..." Seb glanced over his shoulder, and Sloane followed his line of vision to Dex who was laughing and teasing his brother. Something stirred inside him, and he turned back to face Seb, who continued, his voice grave. "When his life is about to be ripped away from you, you'll see what you really are, what's inside of you. I guarantee you, it's terrifying."

Shit. Did Seb know?

"I hope your Human side is stronger than mine was."

Sloane didn't know what to say. He wanted to say he'd be able to make the difficult choice, but he wasn't so sure.

His thoughts went to the other night when he'd lost control for the first time in his life. He remembered thinking how angry and scared he was at Dex for putting himself in danger. Wondering what he'd do if something happened to him. Before he knew it, his Felid side had taken over to the point his memory was fuzzy in several places. He couldn't remember being present the whole time, and it had scared the hell out of him.

"You know," Sloane said quietly.

"Yes. He didn't come out and say it, but he made me understand why he was going through with this insanity." Seb let out a heavy sigh. "I thought simply being Therian was challenging enough. Now I know it's only the beginning. There's so much we don't know about what we are, Sloane."

Sloane wanted to continue the conversation when Calvin came in from outside waving his phone. "We're in. I'm picking him up at seven thirty tomorrow night." His phone beeped and Calvin frowned at it. "How did Austen get my number?"

Dex shrugged as he walked back into the living room. "Dude's like a short annoying ninja spy. Who the hell knows how he does anything?" He sat down in the armchair with Cael propping himself on the armrest next to him.

If Dex only knew the kind of spying Austen had been doing on him.

"Anyway," Calvin said, sending a text. "Austen sent a location. I'm forwarding it to you guys."

"Great." Sloane looked up at Calvin. "We'll meet at the safe house two hours before. Austen will have everything set up. Bautista trusts you, so this is your show. You up for it?"

Calvin gave him a firm nod. "Yeah."

Sloane knew Calvin well. His friend was feeling guilty for what he was about to do. "We're just going to talk to him, okay? If he's really innocent in all this, there's nothing to worry about."

"I know." Calvin tapped Hobbs's shoulder, and the two headed for the front door. "Call if anything changes."

The rest of their team said their good-byes, all promising to keep their eyes on their phones for any additional intel. There was nothing left to be done until tomorrow night. Hobbs would be the driver as usual, and he'd pick everyone up in the surveillance van they'd made out of Lou's catering van. Sloane did not want to be around when Lou discovered what Dex had done to his shiny, expensive van. He might have to get Bradley to intercept and soften the blow.

After everyone had gone, Sloane had been left somewhat winded. It was more activity than he'd had in ages. Dex told him to go upstairs, that he'd clean up the kitchen. Nearly an hour later and still no Dex. Sloane was settled in bed against his garrison of propped-up pillows, trying not to doze off when Dex called up from downstairs.

"You in bed?"

"Where else would I be?" Sloane teased. "Why? What are you doing down there?" The kitchen hadn't been *that* messy.

"I've got something for you. To say I'm sorry for acting like a jerk."

"Okay, then come up here." Sloane crossed his arms over his chest and waited to see what craziness his partner was about to spring on him. He heard Dex's voice getting closer as he spoke.

"Do you need me to take your temperature?"

"What?" What the hell was he talking about? "What

are you—" The words died on his lips, and his jaw dropped when Dex stepped into the doorway.

"I said, do you need me to check your temperature, Mr. Brodie?"

"Sweet Jesus." It took some effort for Sloane to close his mouth, but eventually he managed it. Dex strutted into the room dressed in nurse's scrubs made of white latex so tight it was all but painted on his body. The V-neck top exposed his collarbone and emphasized the curve of every muscle, from his lean sculpted torso to his muscular legs and the prominent outline of his hard dick. The white was a stark contrast against his tanned skin. Holy hell, his partner looked like something out of a porn magazine.

Wait.

"Are those..." Was it too much to hope for?

Dex gave him a cocky smile and turned around, the sight making Sloane gasp. His gorgeous round ass was exposed, perfectly cupped by the tight latex. Sloane was in danger of coming in his pants just looking at it. He loved Dex's ass. It was plump and perky, and Sloane couldn't resist sinking his teeth into it, kneading it, pounding into it. Fuck, he was so hard right now.

Dex snapped his fingers, and the sound of several electric guitars filled the room, followed by the beat of heavy drums. Sloane threw his head back and laughed. How the hell did his partner do it? Then, of course, there was the choice in music. Trust Dex to choose a Def Leppard song to strip to. Sloane could barely contain his glee as Dex started moving, slowly at first. He ran his hands over his body, slipping them down his chest to his crotch, which he cupped. His hips thrust forward in time to the drums, his sexy voice singing along with the '80s rock song as he gyrated his hips while lyrics went on about him being sticky sweet.

Sloane sat mesmerized by his partner's body and his sensual, fluid movements as he made his way to the foot of the bed. Then the show really got started. Sloane had never seen anything more gorgeous than his partner in tight white latex dancing for him.

"I'll give you sticky," Sloane growled, spreading his legs.

His partner crawled onto the bed and knelt at the foot of it, his knees spread as he ran his hands down his thighs and slid them back up the inside of his legs to his crotch where he rubbed himself and moaned before he got on his feet and started dancing again, this time with his back to Sloane. Damn. Where the hell had his partner learned to move like that?

Sloane had to adjust himself. Not only was he getting uncomfortably hard, but when Dex got on his knees and arched his back, his ass in the air just out of reach, Sloane was in serious danger of coming in his pants. He might have even let out a whimper. As if sensing his need, Dex turned and crawled over to him. He straddled Sloane with a sexy lopsided grin.

"I'm all sweaty. How about you help me out of this and I get *you* sweaty?"

Speech had completely eluded him. With a nod, Sloane took hold of the hem of the latex shirt and pulled. It took some effort, considering how tight it was, but Dex did his part, and soon it was on the floor. Dex took his turn, carefully undressing Sloane, pulling off his sweatpants and socks, followed by his T-shirt. He shoved everything off the bed before he removed the chaps and threw them onto the floor with the rest of the clothes. With a naughty smile, Dex straddled Sloane's lap, a small bottle of lube in his hand. Sloane had no idea where his partner had conjured it up, but he wasn't about to ask questions. Dex handed him the lube before he turned around and bent over.

"Lube me up and make me slick. I want to take a ride on your pogo stick."

Sloane peered at him. "Are those song lyrics?"

"This is waiting for you," Dex said with a chuckle, smacking his own ass cheek.

"Right." Sloane got to work lubing Dex up and stretching him, trying not to lose it at all the sensual moans and soft gasps his partner let out while Sloane was fingering him. Dex reached back and took the lube from Sloane and poured some onto his hand. If Sloane had found it difficult before to not jizz himself, it was doubly hard with Dex spreading the lube over his rock-hard cock.

"Fuck. Dex."

"Easy there, handsome. The fun's just beginning." When Dex was done, he turned, lined Sloane's cock up, and slowly started pushing himself down onto it.

Sloane hissed and let his head fall back against the pillows. His fingers dug into Dex's thighs as Dex lowered himself onto Sloane's cock with deliberately slow movements. Inch by inch until he was sitting on Sloane.

"I love this," Dex groaned.

Sloane nodded and swallowed hard. Why did he feel like a damn virgin? Like he was having sex for the first time? Wait... weren't those song lyrics too? Or something like it? Dear God, he was spending too much time listening to Dex's music. He ran his hands up Dex's legs, loving the feel of his partner's muscles and his soft hair. Dex might not be as big as him, or as muscular, but he was all male and sexy as fuck. He watched Dex let his head fall back and moan as Sloane explored with his hands, sliding them up smooth skin, over flat abs and a defined chest. Dex moved one hand over his own cock and started stroking himself. A low growl rose up from Sloane's chest at the sight.

"You're so fucking gorgeous." Sloane watched Dex jerking himself off, his movements slow and matching the subtle rocking of his hips. Damn, it felt so good. Dex continued to rock his hips, his leg muscles flexing as he did his best to control the excruciatingly slow movements. He leaned forward and pressed his lips to Sloane's, his tongue poking out, and running along Sloane's bottom lip before demanding entrance. Sloane opened up, his skin beading with sweat as Dex sucked on his tongue. His fingers dug into Sloane's hair, holding on tight as he pulled almost all the way out before impaling himself down on Sloane's dick.

"Oh shit," Sloane gasped.

Dex started to bounce, his ass cheeks slapping against Sloane's groin. Again he leaned forward so he could pull almost all the way out before impaling himself down again on Sloane's cock. He did it over and over.

"Dex."

"You okay?"

"Other than feeling like I'm going to pass out from how fucking amazing this feels? I'm fine."

Dex let out a breathless chuckle and alternated between impaling himself, rotating his hips, and forcing himself down deep against Sloane. Beads of sweat formed on Sloane's brow, and a drop rolled down the side of his cheek. Dex leaned in and lapped it up with his tongue.

"Oh, fuck yeah." It was like the more time they spent together, the bolder Dex grew in the bedroom. Sloane could hardly contain his excitement. His muscles strained, and his blood all but boiled over. God, he wanted to fuck his partner senseless.

"You like that, handsome?"

Sloane couldn't help his smile. "Yeah, I like it a lot." There was so much he liked. Dex's plump lips parted, releasing moans, whimpers, and groans as Sloane took hold of Dex's cock and started pumping it. Dex thrust his hips up and down, his movements picking up as Sloane's hand did the same.

"That's it. Fuck yourself on my dick."

"Oh God, Sloane." Dex's movements grew erratic, his face pained with the need to release. Sweat beaded his skin, and Sloane thrust his hips up as Dex came down, making his partner cry out in surprise.

"Come for me, sweetheart. I want to see your face when you come."

Dex nodded. He rotated his hips, but when his own fingers found their way to his lips and his other hand to his hair, his expression of sheer reckless abandon as he fucked himself on Sloane, it was more than Sloane could endure.

"Fuck. Oh fuck." Sloane sat up, one arm wrapping around Dex and pulling him close against him as his other hand continued to pump Dex's cock. Sloane thrust his hips hard against Dex's ass over and over until Dex cried out, his fingers digging into Sloane's shoulders as he came in Sloane's hand. The hot, sticky feel of it had Sloane thrusting hard and deep one last time, causing his partner to let out a half cry, half moan before Sloane came deep inside Dex. He held on tight to Dex, thrusting until he'd emptied himself of every last drop. Carefully, he rolled over with Dex, pulling out of him as he did.

Sloane hadn't even realized the music was still going. Except instead of a hot sexy tune, it was a sweet romantic ballad about love. Kissing Dex, Sloane held him close, wondering why the hell it had taken him this long to realize what he had.

"I love you," he whispered against Dex's ear. His body was going to be sore, but it was worth it. He nuzzled Dex's neck and smiled when he felt Dex slip his leg between Sloane's. He huddled close, his arms around Sloane's waist as he whispered back.

"I know."

TEN

THE SAFE HOUSE was like any other. An empty, secure location with several vacant rooms all painted the same drab gray. Nothing particularly interesting to look at. One room had been set up with a table and a chair to either side of it. Digital microphones and recording devices were in position, ready to feed everything back to the digital drive in the next room where Dex and Sloane sat watching the medium-sized monitor on the table in front of them.

Calvin had managed to blindfold Bautista, and Dex felt a little sorry for the guy. Either Bautista was as innocent as he seemed or an exceptional actor. He'd trusted Calvin to blindfold him and lead him who knew where. They watched Calvin escort Bautista into the brightly lit room and remove the blindfold. Bautista blinked at the lighting, his smile fading when he realized something wasn't right. He spun toward Calvin, eyes wide with fear.

"What is this?"

"I'm sorry, Felipe, but... I'm not who you think I am." Calvin reached into his pocket and presented his badge. "I'm an agent for the THIRDS. Please, sit." He motioned over to one of the chairs, and after some hesitation, Bautista did as he was asked.

"I should have known. I thought you were too good to be true."

"I'm really sorry," Calvin said sincerely. "It wasn't my intention to hurt you."

"I haven't done anything wrong. I'm registered. What do you want with me?" Bautista had his hands on his lap, his fingers clutched tightly together. He was anxious, showing all the signs of genuine fear and apprehension.

"That's not why we've brought you in. Have you heard of Beck Hogan?"

Bautista frowned thoughtfully. "He was in the news, wasn't he? Something about an explosion a few weeks ago."

Calvin nodded. "He's the leader of an extremist group calling themselves the Coalition. Have you heard of them?"

"They were at war recently with a Human group. I can't remember their name. It was horrible. There was a bombing in the youth center, then the Coalition killed those Humans. But the news said it was over. The THIRDS arrested them. Or what was left of them." Bautista's gaze wandered around the room, momentarily landing on the steel door before coming to rest on Calvin again. "It's all very tragic, but I don't understand what it has to do with me."

"I need to show you something. It might be shocking and difficult to look at, but I need you to look, okay?"

Dex watched Calvin open the folder containing photographs of the Order members Hogan and his crew had killed. Some of them shot, some mauled to death so badly they were barely recognizable as Humans.

"Oh my God." Felipe's hand went to his mouth, and he

turned away, his eyes shut tight. "Why are you showing me those?"

"Because your boyfriend was involved in these murders."

Bautista stared at Calvin. He almost looked like he'd been frozen in time. After what seemed like a lifetime went by, he shook his head. "No. It's not possible. Drew couldn't have had anything to do with this. He might be an insensitive jerk sometimes, but he's not a murderer."

"I'm afraid he is." Calvin showed Bautista photographic evidence taken from street cameras capturing Collins heavily armed. "He's a part of the Coalition, along with Beck Hogan. We've been after them for months."

"But... how? I mean, he..." Bautista kept shaking his head, tears welling in his eyes.

"When he wasn't with you, do you know where he was?"

"He was busy with work. Meetings. Church." Something seemed to dawn on him, and his expression fell. "He lied to me."

The irony was not lost on Dex, and he squeezed Sloane's hand under the table. He would be spending a long time groveling and making it up to Sloane. He looked forward to it. Sloane deserved to be treated a lot better than the lousy job Dex had been doing lately.

"I can't believe this."

Bautista's shaky voice caught Dex's attention, and he turned back to the screen. Tears pooled in the wolf Therian's eyes and several escaped. His bottom lip quivered, but he tried his hardest to get himself together. He continued to shake his head, as if doing so would make everything he'd seen and heard untrue. Calvin offered him a tissue, which

Bautista took with a muffled "thanks." "Do you have proof of what he's done? I need proof."

"I have a whole team of agents who he attacked. My team leader is next door on crutches. Your boyfriend helped Hogan plant a bomb that nearly killed him." Calvin showed him a picture of Sloane.

"I saw him on the news," Bautista said quietly. "What do you want from me?"

"We'd like you to have him meet you. Somewhere familiar to the both of you, but preferably with not a lot of foot traffic. Out in the open. We'll clear the area, set it up with our own agents. You just meet with him. We'll handle the rest."

Bautista let out a heart-wrenching sigh and nodded. "Okay. I know it sounds ridiculous, considering everything he's done, but you won't... you won't kill him will you?" Bautista covered Calvin's hand with his, his eyes pleading.

"We'd prefer to arrest him," Calvin said gently, removing his hand from under Bautista's. His job had been done. He'd made the connection and gotten the information. Now it was time to put it to use and cut Bautista loose. It was shitty, but it was what had to be done, and Calvin seemed to be all too aware of it. "But if he becomes dangerous, we can't risk any civilian casualties."

"I understand," Bautista conceded.

Calvin stood and gave him a small smile. "I'll give you time to get yourself together before you call him. It's important he meets with you tomorrow. Preferably early in the day." Calvin left the room, joining Dex and the rest of the team next door.

"You okay?" Dex asked him.

"Yeah, I feel kind of shitty. He's a nice guy. I can't imagine what must be going through his head right now.

Finding out his boyfriend of ten years is a murdering scumbag."

Hobbs put his arm around Calvin's neck and gave him a reassuring squeeze, receiving a pat from his friend before Calvin moved to the monitors to watch Bautista. The wolf Therian wiped his eyes, took a deep breath, and removed his phone from his pocket. It was now or never. They all watched on the edge of their seats as Bautista called Collins, his voice sounding far more casual than he appeared. Bautista chatted about nothing in particular before telling Collins he missed him. He asked if they could meet up for lunch tomorrow because it had been so long since they'd gone out for a meal together. With bated breath they all waited, when finally Bautista let out a sad smile.

"Perfect. I'll meet you at our usual spot at noon. I love you."

Seconds later, Bautista ended the call, placed his phone on the table, and burst into tears.

To Dex's surprise, Hobbs appeared beside Calvin and nudged him. He motioned to the monitor where Bautista was crying and nodded.

Calvin smiled at his partner and left the room to comfort Bautista.

"Man, now I hate Collins even more," Dex said through his teeth. "The selfish prick. How could he put the poor guy through this? Telling his boyfriend he was out at church or in meetings while he was murdering people. How could he come home and act like everything was hunky-dory?" At Calvin's signal, the team left the room to join him, with Dex staying behind to help Sloane. As soon as his partner was on his feet, Dex stepped in front of him.

"I'm sorry for being such an insensitive asshole," Dex

said. "For leaving you home on your own while I was out there and lying to you about it."

"Hey, whoa." Sloane put his hand to Dex's cheek. "Now you listen to me. Don't you dare compare yourself to that asshole. You're a good man, Dex. Your heart was in the right place. I admire you for that. This whole situation has made me realize how much I've taken you for granted."

"What?" Dex shook his head. "Sloane—"

"I have. I know I have. You've been nothing but supportive, understanding, and amazing. I've put you through a hell of a lot, and I've hurt you. I swear, I'm going to try my damn hardest to deserve you.

"So no comparing yourself to Collins. However he tries to justify his actions, he's killed people in cold blood. If we don't stop him, Hogan, and the rest of their crew, who knows where this will end?"

"You're right." He kissed Sloane before wrapping an arm around his waist and leading him out of the room. Bautista was in the hall, and when he saw Sloane, he gingerly approached.

"I'm so sorry, Agent Brodie."

"You can't be held responsible for his actions, Felipe. He made his choices, and now he has to answer for them."

Bautista nodded. "Thank you."

Calvin escorted Bautista from the building. He'd be dropping him off, and Austen would take over surveillance from there, making sure Bautista didn't change his mind and try to warn Collins. Dex doubted the guy would try to skip town. From what he'd heard, Bautista loved his job and cared a great deal about the kids he taught. Dex was relieved the Therian wasn't involved with the Coalition. He hoped Bautista would move on from this and maybe find himself someone more worthy of his love than Collins.

As soon as the two were gone, the team gathered around Sloane in the middle of the hall.

"So where's the meet?" Dex asked Seb who checked his tablet.

"Wagner Cove in Central Park."

"Great." Sloane motioned toward the next room, and they all followed him. The room was equipped with everything they'd need for a mission. An unapproved THIRDS one anyway. Between Letty and Austen, they now had enough firepower to go in, arrest Collins, and face Hogan's crew if they showed up. Everything from unmarked uniforms and vests to tranq guns. Two large steel tables were positioned together in the center of the gray room with maps and several tablets. Sloane stood at the head of the tables and grabbed a black Sharpie, along with the huge map of Manhattan.

"All right. Seb, how do you want to play this?"

Seb studied the map before pointing to Terrace Drive in Central Park. "I'll have Theta Destructive on standby here in the BearCat."

"You sure you want to bring your team into this?" Sloane asked.

"Don't worry about my team. I'm not about to let you guys go in there without backup."

"Okay." Sloane motioned for Dex to get closer and pointed to West Drive. "I think we should park the surveillance van on one of these paths here near the lake, off West Drive. You'll be close enough to catch everything, but far away enough not to be spotted by any of Hogan's gang if they happen to be in the area. I'll be in there with Cael."

Dex's head shot up. "No way. You're not even supposed to be exerting yourself as much as you are."

"Dex, I'm not going to send my team into danger and

then sit at home twiddling my thumbs, waiting to hear what happened."

"It's a catering van, Sloane. It's not equipped to handle anything remotely resembling a medical emergency or PSTC. It doesn't have any kind of holding bay either. The only reason we're taking it is so we can make a quick getaway if we need to."

"Okay," Sloane agreed. "Then I'll be in the BearCat with Seb."

"Sloane—"

"I'll be in the BearCat with Seb." Sloane was using his team leader tone, and he'd made his decision. As much as Dex wanted to argue about how Sloane had no business being out in the field in his condition, he backed off. It was up to both of them to know where to draw the line between their personal relationship and professional one.

"Okay."

"I'll watch the van," Cael volunteered. "Give me a call if we need to get lost, and I'll make sure the engine's running. We can get the hell out of there if we need to."

Sloane agreed. "Seb, get some of your guys undercover and have the rest discreetly redirecting any foot traffic that might head Dex's way." He turned his attention to Dex. "You, Ash, Hobbs, Letty, and Rosa will be concealed in the shrubbery nearby waiting. On your call, you move the team in."

"Got it."

"I'll inform Calvin to get Bautista out of there the moment you make your move. I want everyone in their positions at ten a.m. sharp, geared up and ready to go. If you gotta tranq the shit out of Collins, you do it. But try to make it fast and low key. The last thing we need is the HPF calling it in. Everyone clear on what to do?"

Everyone's collective "affirmative" ended the briefing. The girls headed off with their equipment, and Dex handed Hobbs the keys to the van. It would be better if he took the thing home and picked them all up in the morning. While Seb, Sloane, and Ash went over a few details, Dex approached Cael.

"Dad won't suspect anything, will he?"

Cael went over to the equipment and grabbed a vest. "Nah. You know he never asks where we're going. I tell him I'm going out, and he tells me to take care. He's kind of pissed at you, by the way. This morning he was mumbling to himself as he walked around the kitchen." Cael lowered his voice to mimic their dad's deep baritone. "Damn boy can't even pick up a damn phone. What he needs is a good ass whupping."

His brother looked too damn happy about it. Crap, Dex hadn't called his dad in days. Tony didn't expect him to check in, but Dex should have had the courtesy to let him know everything was all right, considering recent events. Tony was probably worried about Sloane, how his recovery was going, whether the two of them were ready to strangle each other, or more likely whether Sloane was ready to strangle Dex. It was never a good thing when his dad mumbled to himself. It usually meant Dex was going to end up paying for it later.

"I'll give him a call as soon as this is over." Hopefully it wouldn't all blow up in his face and his dad wouldn't be kicking his ass. Seb, Ash, and Sloane finished hashing out the details, and everyone grabbed what equipment was left. They agreed to call if anything changed. Seb and Sloane chatted as they headed out, with Dex carrying his and Sloane's equipment. Outside, Ash caught hold of Cael's arm. Since Seb and Sloane stopped to continue their conversation, Dex pretended not to eavesdrop on his brother and Ash.

"Hey, listen, I know things between us are rough, and it's completely my fault, but how about if after this is all over, we sit down and have a chat. Just the two of us? Please. I... don't want to lose you."

From the corner of his eye, Dex saw Cael fold his arms over his chest, his gaze hard.

"You have to have something to lose it, Ash."

Ouch. Dex almost cringed. He kind of felt sorry for Ash. Cael obviously hadn't retracted his claws completely.

"I deserved that," Ash said, "But give me a chance to explain. I'm sorry I've been pushing you away. I want to let you in, I really do. More than anything. I promise to try harder. Give me a chance. If what I have to say isn't good enough, then... well, you decide."

Cael seemed to mull it over, a host of emotions crossing his face, many of which Dex knew all too well. His brother was afraid of getting hurt, even more than he already was, but he also wanted Ash more than anything. Cael was easy to read, always wearing his heart on his sleeve like his big brother.

Damn it, Cael, say yes. Put him out of his misery. You know you want to.

Cael's expression softened and he nodded. "Okay." He met Ash's gaze and spoke softly. "Please don't hurt me anymore, Ash. I don't think my heart can take it."

Ash swallowed hard. He looked like he wanted to reach out but held himself back. "We'll work it out somehow. I promise. Be careful tomorrow, okay?"

"Van sitting isn't exactly dangerous work," Cael teased. "You'll be out there, so you take care. And wear a vest this time."

Ash chuckled and gave Cael's cheek a playful nudge like he'd always done. "Got it." With a wink, he walked off, calling out a grumbled good-bye to the rest of them. Dex pretended to be inspecting the equipment when Cael came to stand beside him.

"You can stop acting like you weren't eavesdropping."

Dex blinked innocently. "Moi?"

Cael rolled his eyes at him. "Please. You are like the nosiest person ever."

"Ridiculous lies."

"I heard Rhonda from PR was hooking up with Josh in Accounting."

Dex gasped. "I thought she had a thing for Mark over in Recruitment?"

"A-ha! I told you. I was totally making it up," Cael replied smugly.

"Damn. All right, I was eavesdropping. You mad?"

"No." Cael's expression turned worried. "Do you think I made the right decision? What if we sit down and it all falls apart? What if things get worse between us?"

Dex bumped his brother playfully with his hip. "What if it works out and you get everything you want?"

Cael smiled shyly. "Thanks, Dex."

"Any time."

"You ready, Dex?"

"Yep." Dex motioned for Cael to follow. "Come on. I'll walk you to your car."

As they left the dimly lit sidewalk outside the boarded-up house Austen had set up for them, Dex tried not to give too much thought to the next day. Finally, after months of frustration, dead bodies, and no leads, they were moving in on Hogan. They were going to get a location on the guy if they had to beat it out of Collins. This time tomorrow, Beck

Hogan would either be behind bars or six feet under. Dex was fine with either one of those.

IT WAS ALMOST TIME.

The day was bright with clear skies, the air crisp and cool. According to Seb, his agents were already undercover and in position around the area.

Dex helped Sloane out of the van, a tingle going up his spine at seeing his partner back in uniform, even if it wasn't his official THIRDS uniform. Then there was the crutch under his right arm. Dex really wished his partner would reconsider and head home, but Sloane was in work mode, and nothing would deter him, injuries or not. Who the hell knew what was about to go down or what would happen at the end of this. What was the likelihood they'd catch Hogan without the THIRDS finding out about it?

"All right, let's all get into position," Sloane said. "Cael, get this van out of sight."

Cael gave him a salute. "You got it. Good luck." He closed the doors to the van, and they all waited for him to drive off before Dex helped Sloane over to Seb's BearCat concealed in the bushes off Terrace Drive. The back doors opened, and Seb appeared with Calvin beside him. They helped Sloane inside.

"We're ready when you are," Seb stated.

"Okay." Dex turned to the rest of his team. "Let's do this." He tapped his earpiece. "Cael, you in position?"

"Affirmative."

"All right, then." Dex signaled forward. The rest of the team followed him, and he disappeared into the bushes.

Time to get this party started.

THIS WAS GOING to be too easy.

Idiots. Going off to hunt their prey while leaving their baby bird in the nest. That's why cheetahs struggled to survive. Why they were the most vulnerable of the Felids. So eager to trust, so innocent, needing someone to take them under their wing. Hogan smiled to himself. This was going to be fun.

He pulled the officer's cap down low over his eyes as he approached the van parked among the trees and dense shrubs, and he knocked on the back door. A few seconds later, the door cracked open, and the young cheetah Therian appeared.

"Is there a problem, officer?"

"You have to move your van, son. There's no parking on the grass."

"Oh. Sorry, I'll go ahead and do that. Thanks." He made to close the door when Hogan grabbed the handle and jerked it open, the kid tumbling out and into his arms. With a toothy grin, Hogan shoved him hard into the van before climbing in and securing the door behind him.

"What the hell?" The young cheetah Therian scrambled to his feet and spun around, recognition dawning on his boyish face. "Shit."

"Afternoon, Agent Maddock. I hear you've been looking for me."

Big silver eyes widened as the kid took another step back, Hogan's name escaping from between plump lips. He inched closer to the side of the van where the equipment was.

"I hope you're not planning on contacting your brother, because it would ruin my surprise."

The young agent glared daggers at him. Brave little shit. Hogan would give him that much. He almost felt sorry for the kid. No doubt he'd been corrupted by his Human family. A Therian should never be raised by Humans. They'd tamed him. Eaten away at the wildness in his heart until there was nothing left but a harmless kitten.

"Well, well. Aren't you adorable?"

"Fuck you, asshole!"

Hogan launched at him, grabbed the young Therian around his waist, and tackled him to the ground. It was over in seconds. The kid was no match for a tiger Therian, much less one of Hogan's size and strength. He used his heavy mass to hold the agent down on his belly against the floor, his arms pinned at the sides of his head.

"And such sharp claws," Hogan murmured, his lips close to the agent's ear. "I bet Keeler loves that feistiness. I knew there was something going on between you two. He pretended so damn hard not to show he cared, but we saw right through him. You should have seen his eyes when Merritt said your name. There was this rage vibrating through him. Your ferocious lion could barely maintain a grip on himself. He might have been able to fool the Humans, but he couldn't hide it from a fellow Felid. He's in love with you. So much so, he would die for you. This time, I'm going to make sure he actually does."

"You'll never beat him or my brother," the kid spat out. "They'll take you down and put you in a cage where you belong. With the rest of the rabid animals."

"There's that mouth again. I hear it runs in the family. Shame. It's a pretty mouth." Hogan held both of the agent's wrists in one hand so he could run the other down his slim neck and sinewy frame. He was soft yet firm. Hogan pushed his crotch up against the young Therian's perky little ass. It would be a waste to get rid of the cheetah Therian so quickly. He slipped his hand under his T-shirt, moaning at the silky soft skin underneath. His hand traveled lower down, the tips of his fingers slipping under the waistband of the agent's tac pants.

"Maybe I should fuck you right here. We could make a little video for Keeler. I would love to see his face when he watches it. When he sees all the ways I defile his precious little chew toy. It'll destroy him. What do you say?" His hand moved to the agent's ass and in between his legs where he pressed firmly down. "Shall we give him a show?"

"You sick son of a bitch! Get off me!"

Hogan chuckled before the unexpected blow landed. The young agent's skull slammed back into Hogan's nose, causing him to roll off with a litany of curses, the wind knocked out of him when a boot kicked him in the stomach over and over. Officially fucked off, Hogan let out a fierce growl and snatched the kid's leg, jerking him off his feet and slamming him down against the van's carpet, making the young cheetah Therian gasp for air. Hogan straddled him, surprised by the kid's ferocity.

Hogan swiped his arm across his bleeding nose, momentarily letting his guard down when a punch caught him in the ribs. With a growl, he struggled to get a grip on the feral young Therian hissing and clawing at him. Silver eyes flashed with indignation.

"You really think you're a match for me?" Hogan snarled. "I'm going to put an end to your lover, your piece of shit brother, and the rest of your traitorous team. They took my revenge from me, now I'm going to take everything away from them. First your brother, then Keeler, then that asshole Brodie, and then I'm coming back for the rest." He snatched a fistful of the agent's hair and jerked him to his feet. "Then after I've had my fun with you and your sweet little ass, you're going to join them in hell."

The kid landed a punch across Hogan's face and kicked at the side of his knee, freeing himself long enough to lunge at the equipment on the console across from them where he managed to hit something on a keyboard. The last of Hogan's patience snapped. He picked the kid up, shoved him against the van's wall, took hold of his head, and cracked it hard against the side. The kid went limp in his arms.

"Fucking little shit." Hogan cursed and winced at his split lip. Fishing the burner phone from his pocket, he put in a call. "Pick me up. Little fucker was more of a pain in the ass than I expected. Don't underestimate those assholes."

"Destructive Delta, on my mark," Dex instructed quietly, his fingers flexing on his tranq rifle from his hidden position in the bushes.

Bautista sat on the edge of the fountain in Wagner Cove a few feet away. Around them were agents dressed as civilians. One in rollerblades, another tending to the grass, a couple walking down the path. Theta Destructive sat in their BearCat several yards away on Terrace Drive awaiting instructions from their team leader. Seb had given them only enough information for them to know another team was working the area undercover. It was all they needed. When a team trusted their team leader, the agents would follow him or her to hell and back, no questions asked, no excuses given.

Exactly at noon, Collins appeared, giving the area a

cursory glance as he headed over to Bautista and gave him a kiss. Destructive Delta listened in on the conversation through the tiny military-grade bug they'd placed on the cross hanging from the delicate gold chain around Bautista's neck.

"Hey, baby. I'm surprised you called."

"I was missing you," Bautista replied, standing to wrap his arms around Collins's waist. "You're always so busy these days."

"Yeah. But it'll be over soon."

Dex's gut twisted. The alarm bells in his head went off, and he listened intently.

"What will be over soon?" Bautista asked, cocking his head to one side.

Collins kissed his boyfriend on the lips before taking a step back, an almost heartbroken expression on his face as he held his hands up in surrender. "I don't blame you for turning me in. You're a good guy. It's why I fell in love with you. Take care of yourself."

Shit. He knows. "Destructive Delta, move in!" Dex held his tranq gun at the ready as he and the rest of his team emerged from the shrubbery and rushed Collins who remained still, his hands up in front of him as he called out to them.

"I'm unarmed, agents."

"How could you?" Bautista cried as Calvin tried to drag him away. "How could you kill all those people?"

"You wouldn't understand," Collins replied, turning away from his distraught boyfriend. Calvin led Bautista to Seb's black Suburban heading their way while Ash removed the Therian-strength zip ties from his belt. He kicked at the back of Collins's knees, forcing him onto the ground before he secured the Therian's ankles, then his wrists behind his back.

"You're going to rot in jail, you piece of shit," Ash said, roughly hauling the Therian to his feet.

Dex frowned. He studied the area around them. Everything was quiet. No telltale signs of an ambush. No Therians hiding in the bushes or reflections from sniper beams. Nothing.

This is too easy.

Collins smiled maliciously, and Dex's blood ran cold. He marched up to Collins and grabbed a fistful of his shirt. "What did you do?"

"Me? I haven't done anything." The smile never left the smug bastard's face. "The question you should be asking, Agent Daley, is what have *you* done?"

Something wasn't right. Dex's gaze shifted to Ash who looked equally annoyed by Collins's cryptic threat. A phone went off, and Dex looked around, the rest of the team shrugging. It took Dex a moment to realize it was coming from Collins. Searching the Therian's pockets, he pulled out a burner phone. There was a text message. He opened it up, and his heart almost stopped.

We'll be in touch. Don't do anything stupid until then, or your cheetah won't be chirping much longer.

On the screen, an image of Cael bound and gagged, his cheek bruised and lip split, popped up. Dex thought he was going to be sick.

"Oh God." He shook his head. No. No way could that sick son of a bitch have Cael. It couldn't be. The phone slipped from his hands onto the grass. It couldn't be. The photo was a lie. It had to be. Dex walked away from Collins before his shaky hand touched his earpiece. "Seb. I need one of your guys to check the van. *Now.*"

"On it."

"What is it?" Ash asked worriedly.

Dex held a hand up, signaling for him to wait. He had to know for sure. A few heart-stopping moments later, and Seb's anxious voice came on the line.

"It's empty, Dex. Cael's gone. Looks like there was a struggle."

"*Fuck!*" Dex put his hands to his head. It had been a trap. The whole thing had been a fucking trap. Had Collins known Bautista would turn him in? He had to have been expecting it. No wonder the guy had turned himself in so easily. It had all been a distraction for Hogan to get his hands on Cael. How long had the bastard been waiting to make his move?

"I'd listen to what he says," Collins called out behind him. "Hogan likes them cute and perky."

"What the hell are you talking about?" Ash demanded, giving Collins a shake. Dex stormed over, his anger reaching the boiling point as he threw a punch and hit Collins square across the jaw, forcing his head to snap to the side.

"You motherfucking piece of shit, where's my brother?"

Hobbs appeared beside Collins, holding him up. Furious, Dex concentrated on Collins, barely aware of the gasp behind him or the lack of Ash's presence. He was about to beat the shit out of Collins if he had to when Ash's claws dug into Collins's neck, drawing a horrible gurgling sound from him. Startled, Dex took a step back. He stared in stunned disbelief as the Felid inside Ash looked out from his amber eyes. His claws had grown out along with his fangs, and he lifted Collins off his feet. Tiny rivets of blood trailed down Collins's neck.

"Tell me where he is, or I'll rip your fucking throat out!" Ash snarled.

Fuck. Dex looked from Ash to Hobbs, who was staring wide-eyed at Ash. So this was a first for his teammates as well.

"Tell me!" Ash squeezed his fingers tighter around Collins's neck, drawing more blood and choking from Collins.

"Ash!" Dex tried to pry Ash's hand off Collins's neck. "We're not going to get any answers if he's fucking dead!"

Dex's words seemed to get through, and Ash lowered Collins, placing him back on his feet, but he didn't let go. He let out a low feral growl as he shoved him into Hobbs. Dex walked up to Collins who was awkwardly holding on to his bloodied neck, glaring at them.

"Tell me where he took my brother, or I swear I will let him beat it out of you."

Collins let out a scoff. "I'm dead anyway, Daley. I'll never fucking talk."

"Have it your way," Dex replied through his teeth. He stepped back and nodded to Hobbs. "Bring him."

Seb's voice came in over his earpiece. "You said you were going to hand him over."

"When I was done with him," Dex said. "And I'm not done."

"Jesus Christ, Daley. What the hell are you going to do?" Seb's irritated voice was swiftly followed up by Sloane's concerned one.

"Dex, what the hell is going on?"

"Hogan has Cael."

"Shit."

"We're taking Collins back to the van to interrogate him." They headed for the van when there was a commotion behind him. He spun around in time to see Collins swipe Ash's gun from his holster. Theta Destructives agents pulled their weapons, aiming at Collins who took aim at Dex. Hobbs was quick, clamping down Collins's arm and twisting it, forcing the man to cry out while Ash threw an arm around Collins's neck. The expression on Ash's face had Dex bolting toward him, shouting out an order. It came too late. Dex watched, horrified, as Ash jerked his arm back, snapping Collins's neck. The cougar Therian crumpled to the ground in a lifeless heap.

Dex dropped to his knees beside Collins, checking his vitals for some miracle. His gaze shot up to Ash whose amber eyes were filled with quiet fury. "What did you do?"

"He was a threat, and I neutralized him." Ash swiped his gun up and returned it to his holster.

Dex jumped to his feet and shoved Ash. "You snapped his fucking neck!"

"They were about to take him out. I saved them the bullets."

Seb and his team came running, stopping beside Collins's body. "What the fuck happened?" He turned to one of his undercover agents who quickly relayed the events as they occurred with no hint of emotion or concern. Collins had swiped Ash's gun, meant to shoot Dex, agents were going to open fire, and Ash neutralized the threat. The agent made it sound like a drill, just a regular procedure. Dex's eyes landed on Ash. His stillness scared the hell out of Dex, but it was superseded by a greater fear.

"How are we supposed to find Cael now? We're running out of time."

"Come on." Ash motioned toward their van. "Your brother's smart. He would have left something behind for us. Seb, take care of Collins. We'll call you."

Before Seb had a chance to answer, Ash walked off. Fuck. Dex's earpiece beeped, and he knew Sloane was calling him, undoubtedly wondering what the fuck had happened. Seb would fill him in, and while he did, Dex wanted some answers from Ash. The team followed Ash to the van, and they all climbed in. Dex stopped cold when he saw all the equipment on the floor. It took everything he had not to lose it. He shook his head and turned to Ash.

"He wouldn't have been expecting Hogan." Dex thrust a finger at the equipment on the floor. "Hogan has my brother, and you killed the only fucking lead we had!" Dex threw his hand out, snatched Ash's gun, and pulled. All it did was tug at Ash's belt. The safety mechanism was in place and secure. He stared up at Ash in disbelief. "You let him take it."

Ash studied Dex, his lips pressed into a thin line before he looked around at the rest of the team. "Hogan has Cael, and if I have to snap the neck of every last one of these murderous motherfuckers to get him back, then so be it. If anyone has a problem, you can join Seb." He turned his attention back to Dex, pupils dilated. "We'll find Cael. So help me, we'll find him if it's the last fucking thing I do."

Dex swallowed hard. He nodded and walked over to the equipment. He didn't want to think about how goddamn bad everything had gone. Collins was dead, Hogan had Cael, and they didn't have a clue where the bastard had taken him. What if something happened to his little brother? It would be his fault. He'd brought Cael into this. What the hell would he say to his dad? That he'd decided to go against orders, play fucking hero, and it got his brother killed? God only knew what Hogan was doing to Cael. Dex's chest started to feel constricted, and he was having trouble breathing. Fuck, he couldn't be losing his shit. Not now. Cael needed him.

"Take it easy," Sloane breathed into his ear, and Dex

stilled. His arms slipped around Dex, and all at once Dex felt himself growing calm. "There you go."

Dex had been so lost in his own anguish he hadn't even heard Sloane arrive. He turned, slightly aware of the rest of his team watching them, but he didn't care. His smartphone beeped, and Dex fished it out of his pocket.

"What is it?" Ash asked, looming over his shoulder.

"There's a weird orange light blinking on my phone."

"Why's that weird?"

"I didn't even know it had an orange light. I've never seen it before." He woke up his phone from sleep mode and tapped through the security screen. A little bluebird wearing a Rebel Pilot helmet bounced on his screen and chirped. Tears pooled in Dex's eyes, and he let out a soft laugh. "You little genius."

"Is that Angry Birds?"

"From the Star Wars version," Sloane offered.

Dex nodded. "The Bluebirds are Cael's favorite." Dex tapped the screen, and the bluebird bounced and spun. An alarm went off on the console, and the screen flickered to life, splitting into two images. On the left was a map with a bouncing Rebel bluebird. On the right an abandoned-looking building beside a canal. "That's where Cael is."

Rosa stepped up to the console. "Cael must have installed some kind of GPS in the system. Looks like he's in Red Hook."

Sloane turned to Hobbs. "You know what to do."

Hobbs jumped behind the wheel and buckled up, the van's engine roaring to life. Beside him, Calvin buckled up in the passenger seat.

"Everyone buckle up. Hobbs, move out," Sloane ordered as Dex helped him sit. He took a seat beside his partner. Sloane took hold of Dex's hand, laced their fingers together, and gave him a reassuring squeeze. It took Dex a moment to realize what Sloane had done. They were holding hands in front of the whole team. No one said a word, and Dex was grateful. All he could think about was getting to Cael.

"We're going to get him back," Sloane promised.

Dex believed Sloane, but as the van sped through Manhattan toward Red Hook, he closed his eyes and prayed they'd get his little brother back alive.

ELEVEN

"I don't like this."

Dex turned at Sloane's words. His partner was as concerned as the rest of the team. Dex would be lying if he said he wasn't worried too. Besides the fact he trusted Hogan about as far as he could throw his hairy ass, the guy had picked the location and not just any location, but something out of a bad horror flick. Dex was certain Hogan had no intention of making it out of this.

How many members of Destructive Delta was he planning on taking down with him?

The Red Hook Grain Terminal loomed in the distance like some haunted Scottish castle on a foggy moor. Its concrete silos and crumbling façade were covered in black mold and graffiti. Sections of the building had collapsed and crumbled into the Gowanus Canal. There was a container terminal nearby along with several other industrial structures. It was all eerily quiet. They were the only thing around for miles. Black specks among stretches of gray. Heavily armed specks. They'd parked the van behind one of several mountains of debris away from the road.

"I don't like it either, Sloane, but that asshole has Cael in there somewhere. I'm not leaving here without my brother."

"Dex is right," Ash said, checking the ammo in his tranq rifle.

Theta Destructive's BearCat arrived on the scene, and when the back doors opened, four agents in their Therian forms leapt out. Two tigers, a lion, and a cougar. They followed Seb, who looked like he was ready to take on an army with enough firepower to bring down the whole fucking grain terminal, which was fine with Dex. He didn't care if the whole place went up in smoke as long as he got Cael out of there. The public would probably thank them for getting rid of the eyesore.

"I thought we should even the odds," Seb said with a grin. "Hogan's likely to have some of his goons in their Therian forms."

"You're right." Sloane turned to Hobbs. "How about it, big guy?"

Hobbs gave a curt nod and headed back to the van to shift, with Calvin accompanying his partner. A shadow swept over Dex, and he gave a start, his hand flying to his chest when Austen materialized beside him in his Therian form.

"For fuck's sake, Austen. You scared the shit out of me." Could the guy not approach like a normal Therian?

Austen chirped and rubbed up against Dex's leg only to get promptly swatted by Sloane. "Knock it off."

Fur bristled and ears flattened, Austen dropped onto his back with his paws in the air.

"No, I'm not mad at you," Sloane grumbled. "But you should know better."

Felid Therians did *not* like having their scents

encroached upon by other Therians. Sloane's scent was all over Dex, and any Therian trying to replace it would get in deep shit with his partner. It was common courtesy. You did not hit on a dude's boyfriend when he was right there. Austen was lucky Sloane wasn't in his Therian form. Suddenly Austen stiffened. He rolled onto his paws and his ears flattened against his head as he sniffed at Dex's arm. He started chirping, and the other agents in their Therian forms hissed and growled. They backed away from Dex and hissed at him.

"What the fuck's gotten into them?" Ash asked, arching an eyebrow at Sloane.

Shit. Was it Sloane's mark? Dex discreetly tucked his arm behind his back.

Sloane's jaw muscles clenched, and he took a step closer to Dex. The feral Therians backed off. "Who the hell knows? Let's get on with this."

"Okay. So what's the plan?" Ash asked.

"The place is fucking huge," Rosa added, scratching Hobbs behind the ear when he padded over to them. "They could be anywhere."

Sloane turned to Seb. "Well, we found Hogan. This is your rodeo now."

Dex tensed and Seb noticed. He let out a sigh. "You can't be here when backup arrives."

"And when's that?" Dex asked with bated breath.

Seb seemed to think about it. He looked from Dex to Sloane and back. "When you get your hands on Hogan or give me the signal. Whichever comes first. If I don't hear from you thirty minutes after breach, I'm calling in the cavalry."

Dex nodded. He couldn't ask for more than that. "Thank you. I appreciate that."

"As for entry, everyone goes in. Teams of two and three with at least one feral Therian in each group to sniff out the others. I think Ash and I should remain in Human form to tranq whoever we can. I'd rather take them in alive if possible. Keep in communication and watch your backs. Priority is to get Cael out safely. The place is falling apart. Watch your step."

"You heard him," Sloane said. "Ash, Austen, you're with Dex. Rosa, Letty, you're with Seb and his team. Calvin, you're with Hobbs. Let's finish this." Everyone broke off into their respective teams, and Sloane took hold of Dex's elbow. "Can I talk to you a sec?"

"Sure." Dex accompanied him behind the van, away from the prying eyes of their teammates. Sloane's pupils were dilated, leaving only slivers of glowing amber around them. It seemed to be happening quite a lot lately. Dex might have to ask his partner about it at some point when they weren't about to walk into what was undoubtedly a giant trap. Knowing what Sloane was going to say, Dex stepped up to him and put a hand to his cheek.

"Hey, I'll be careful. I promise."

"I can't believe I'm letting you go in there, but I know how important this is." Sloane let out a sigh and nuzzled Dex's hand. "Please come back to me alive and bring Cael with you."

"I will."

"You know I would give anything to be in there with you." He glared at his crutch before shifting his eyes back to Dex. "But I'd be more of a hindrance than anything."

"Do you really think I don't know how hard this is for you? It'll be okay." Dex gave Sloane's lips a kiss and followed it up with a wink. "I was trained by the best."

Sloane chuckled and swatted Dex's ass. "Get going."

Dex nodded and joined the others. On Seb's signal, they took off toward the terminal building, one group at a time. Most of the windows and doors were missing, broken, or crumbling. They slipped inside, their rifles ready and Therian teammates silently on the hunt alongside them. Dex, Austen, and Ash were the last ones in on Seb's orders. Inside one of the doorways, Seb signaled silently to Dex, and he made a dash for Seb with Ash and Austen on his heels.

Seb pointed to Dex, then up. Looked like he and his team were heading upstairs. He nodded and carefully started making his way through the cavernous terminal, making sure to remain alert, listening for every sound, peering into shadows while checking on Austen who sniffed the air around him. Despite the daylight coming through all the openings, there were still far too many shadows for Dex's liking. Hogan's crew was most likely in their Therian forms, which meant they would sniff Dex out before he even saw them coming.

The ground floor was filled with rows of white columns—circular silos, stretching up to the ceiling. One of the staircases nearby had collapsed into the canal with all manner of rusted reinforcement—steel bars, chunks of concrete blocks, and bricks. The place was falling apart. Gray concrete and corroded iron girders surrounded them on all sides. Dex found a set of oxidized metal stairs just about strong enough to hold Ash's weight. He motioned over to it, and Ash nodded, testing one slat, then a second. When it didn't give way under him, he started to climb. Dex followed with Austen close behind.

They heard a sharp cry, and Dex's blood ran cold. *Cael!* He pushed past Ash, running up the stairs with Ash cursing behind him. Dex took off toward his brother's scream, the cry that followed shaking him to the core. He was going to tear Hogan apart! A gasp escaped him when the floor suddenly disappeared from beneath him. Two strong hands snatched ahold of his vest and jerked him to one side where he fell into Ash, the two crashing to the ground.

"Fuck," Dex breathed, pushing himself to his hands and knees. He moved his gaze to the large hole in the floor he'd almost fallen through. Crawling over, he peeked in and was met with nothing but a black abyss. The only sign it ended was the tiny dot of white light way down below. Turning his head to one side, he found the floor littered with huge holes leading down into the silos. Fuck, if anyone fell through one of these, there was no coming out of it alive.

"Watch your step," Ash hissed at him. He stood and grabbed Dex's vest before hauling him to his feet. "Come on."

Dex followed when Austen paused ahead of them. His head popped up, and he sniffed the air before he darted off, leaping over huge moveable spouts once used to transfer bushels of grain from the roof into the silos. Ash came to a halt beside a metal door tagged with graffiti, a deep frown on his face. What the hell was he doing? Ash thrust a hand out and mouthed the word "run."

Listening to his gut—and Ash—Dex bolted in the opposite direction from where Austen had gone when he heard the roar of a cougar Therian behind him. He glanced over his shoulder long enough to see Ash fighting off two Therians in their feral forms. Cael's scream echoed around him, and Dex skidded to a halt, turning and frantically trying to find where it had come from. There were so many windows, nooks, doorways, holes, and tubes. It could have come from anywhere. If he called out for Cael, he'd give away his position. Damn it, where the hell had Austen disappeared to? Just as the thought crossed his mind, Austen leapt out from behind a spout, his claws scratching against the concrete as he made a sharp turn away from Dex, two Felids on his tail. Austen jumped and skidded sharply, avoiding the two Therians coming at him from two different angles. He sprung over them, and they smacked into each other. Their dizziness didn't last long, and with roars, they gave chase.

Fuck! Both his teammates were otherwise occupied, but Dex couldn't hang around any longer. He had to find Cael. His brother cried out again, and Dex forced himself to remain silent. This time he'd caught where the shout had come from.

At the end of the floor was the terminal's small tower with iron girders and steel shafts high above his head running in various directions, along with funnels and a set of narrow stairs leading to the grain terminal's storage bins at the top. Dex rushed up the stairs, rifle in his hands and ready to take down any bastard who got in his way. Slowing when he reached the top step, he took a deep steady breath and released it gradually. He stepped onto the wooden floor, the decaying boards protesting under his weight. Dex cursed under his breath.

"Come on out, Agent Daley. I know you're there."

Dex edged farther out onto the rickety floor, hoping one false step didn't send him crashing through it. It would be a painful ride down considering all the girders and steel below. Rifle aimed, he advanced slowly, his jaw clenched. Hogan was in here somewhere with Cael. Problem was there were plenty of places for the bastard to hide, shadows he could see Dex from and at the same time deny Dex the same courtesy. More rusted tubes littered the room, along with pieces of crane equipment not touched in decades.

There were mounds of debris of various sizes scattered about the long rectangular room, and shards of broken glass from the bare and broken windows crunched under his boots.

"Look at you. Ready for war." Hogan's voice bounced off the hollow tubes, frustrating Dex. He stilled, listening to every sound around him. In the distance far below he heard faint roars, shouts, and rifles being fired.

"Your crew is getting their asses handed to them, Hogan. Why don't you give up?"

"Or what? You and your team have been a pain in my ass, Daley, but you're kidding yourself if you think you can beat me."

"Maybe you haven't heard, but I'm not alone. When my team is done with your crew, they'll be coming after you," Dex said as he edged against the far-left wall so he was away from any shadows where Hogan might be hiding, waiting to get the drop on him.

"Your friends are busy. It's you and me."

There was a soft groan, and Dex swallowed hard. His little brother needed him. "What do you want, Hogan?"

"To make you suffer the way I suffered." Hogan emerged from the shadows, dragging a bound and bloodied Cael with him.

"You motherfucker!" Dex aimed his rifle at Hogan's chest, but he jerked Cael up in front of him as a shield before Dex could even think of pulling the trigger. A sniper would have come in real handy right about now, but who the hell knew where Calvin was or how many Therians he was knee-deep in.

Hogan hissed and put his claws to Cael's neck, his fangs elongating. "Watch your fucking mouth!"

Looked like Dex had hit a sore spot. He mentally went

through Hogan's file, remembering the reason for all this. "I apologize," Dex said, doing his best to control his tone and not spit the words out. Hogan's pupils were dilated, and Dex could see the guy was struggling to maintain a grip on his feral side. He was huge with dark hair and nearly black eyes, at least three hundred pounds or slightly over, dressed in a tactical uniform and black vest. He was all bulging muscle. How the hell the guy didn't go through the piss-poor excuse of a floor beneath them was anyone's guess. Dex glanced around the room, taking in all the places he might be able to escape to with Cael if he needed to. High places with narrow spaces. Hogan could still follow, but he was bulkier, and although his Therian form might climb with ease, in this confined space, the Therian's Human form might struggle.

Here's hoping. Now if he could only get his brother away from the guy. Dex swallowed hard, telling himself to concentrate on Hogan and the task before him, not the way his brother's cheek was bruised. Not the smear of blood under Cael's nose or the way he was balancing himself on his right leg which meant Hogan had done something to his left leg.

"I'm sorry about what happened to your family. Believe it or not, I know how you feel."

Hogan let out a bark of laughter. "Oh shit. Are you trying to sympathize with me? Trying to make a connection? Some sort of bond? Negotiating? Are you about to fucking negotiate with me, Agent Daley?" Hogan's grin fell away and he snarled. "Tell me how you understand my pain. How you lost someone important to you as well, but how this isn't the way. Go ahead. Tell me how my family wouldn't have wanted this for me!" Hogan pressed the tip of a claw into Cael's neck, making him cry out.

"Stop!" Dex pleaded, holding a hand up. "Please. Tell me what you want."

"I want all you THIRDS assholes to go to hell!" Hogan hauled Cael off his feet, lifting him over his head and heading for one of the large open windows. Cael flailed, and Dex opened fire, shooting tranq after tranq into Hogan wherever he could get him. His legs, arms, neck. Hogan roared and carried on. Dex bolted forward, slamming into Hogan from the side with all his strength. The three of them went tumbling, the boards beneath them creaking and groaning as they rolled. Dex scrambled to get up when Hogan grabbed his vest.

"Dex!" Cael pushed himself to his knees with a wince.

"Run, Cael!" Dex swung his arm around, catching Hogan on the side of the head with his fist, but the blow only pissed the Therian off even more. Hogan's beefy hands were around Dex's neck, and he squeezed, the tips of his claws drawing blood. Dex gasped for breath. He scratched at Hogan's reddened face with one hand while reaching for the Glock in his holster with the other. If he didn't do something fast, Hogan might decide to snap his neck rather than enjoy stealing the breath from his already burning lungs.

Hitting the release mechanism, Dex snatched his Glock, swiping it before Hogan pulled back, getting to his feet and hauling Dex with him by the neck and dangling him off the ground. *Fuck this.* It wasn't going to end like this. Dex brought his gun up, but Hogan's arm got in his way, so Dex did the only thing he could while hanging in Hogan's grip. He pressed the barrel of the Glock against the side of Hogan's vest and fired one round after another. Hogan stumbled, blood trickling down the side of his mouth, but he refused to release Dex, his expression both pained and determined. Rage, hatred, and anguish were driving Hogan, coupled with Therian adrenaline.

A blow landed across the back of Hogan's head, and Dex was dropped on his ass. He gasped and wheezed for air, his hand going to his neck as he turned in time to see Hogan spin on his heels toward the culprit. Nostrils flaring and fangs bare, Hogan roared at Cael who backed away, a steel rod in his hands.

"Get the fuck away from my brother you piece of shit!"

Hogan lunged at Cael who ducked and swung the rod as if it were a baseball bat like their days back in Little League. Except Cael wasn't so little anymore. He put all his weight behind it, all his Therian strength. He caught Hogan behind the knee, the piercing crack resonating around the room before it was drowned out by Hogan's howl.

Cael hopped over to Dex as he got to his feet, and Dex threw his arm around his brother's waist, helping him quickly move toward the stairs only to have their path blocked by a white tiger Therian. One of Hogan's crew. They were trapped. Dex frantically looked around the room, spotting Hogan getting to his feet. He quickly headed for one of the hollow corroded tubes angled toward some iron girders.

"Come on, Cael. We gotta climb."

Despite knowing the tiger Therian could easily follow and jump, Cael did as Dex said, moving as quick as he could onto the tube. Dex swiped up his tranq rifle on the way there, firing at the hissing and roaring tiger Therian as he advanced.

"Kill them! Tear them apart!" Hogan ordered, limping in their direction. Dex jumped onto the tube, balancing as he followed Cael toward the girders. He emptied what was left of his tranqs into the tiger Therian, grateful to see they were slowing him down. If he made it out of this, Dex was going to have some serious words with Letty about having more potent shit on hand. Fucking tiger Therians didn't go down for anything short of a goddamn explosion.

Cael pulled himself up onto one of the girders, kicking back when a paw swiped at his leg, grazing his tac pants. Another paw swipe, and Dex kicked the tiger Therian in the face, earning himself a fierce roar. Pulling himself up on the girder, he followed Cael, dragging himself on his stomach and praying Hogan was too weak to climb up here. No such luck.

"Fuck. What is this guy on fucking 'roids? He's like the fucking Terminator," Dex growled. They were going to run out of girder. The iron beam trembled beneath them, and Dex looked over his shoulder. The tiger Therian was pushing Hogan up onto the beam with his head, and as soon as he was up, the tiger Therian jumped too. The beam creaked. Cael looked over his shoulder at him, eyes wide.

"Dex..."

"Get to the end! There's a narrow ledge. Hurry up!"

They both pulled themselves as quickly as they could, the terrifying sound of the girder creaking and wood snapping reaching Dex's ears.

"Come here you little shits!"

"Hurry up, Cael!"

Cael reached the end and climbed onto the narrow steel ledge as the beam dropped. With a cry Dex threw his arm out. Cael snatched Dex's wrist, his other hand holding on to a piece of metal piping. He held on tight to Dex as he dangled in midair, the whole fucking place falling apart around them. The girder dropped to the floor with Hogan and the tiger Therian, the combined weight tearing through the wooden boards. Hogan's screams mingled with the tiger

Therian's roars as they fell, until the beam hit the girders and steel shafts below, along with Hogan and his friend. The screams stopped when the two fell through the collapsed set of stairs at the canal's basin, impaled on rusted reinforcement bars.

Cael pulled Dex up, and they hugged, relief causing the both of them to shake in each other's arms for a slip of a moment. Dex closed his eyes and held Cael close before he pulled away and looked him over.

"Are you okay?"

Cael nodded. "I think he fractured something in my leg, but I'm okay."

"Let's get the hell out of here before the whole place collapses on us." They edged along the wall to a thick pipe near the stairs which ran down and through the floor. Dex slid down first, then Cael with Dex's help. There was enough floor left for them to make it to the stairs, and they were as quick as they could be going down. Thankfully the stairs from the roof hadn't been destroyed with everything else. Dex helped his brother down to the first floor.

"Cael? Dex?" Ash came running with Seb on his heels. They both looked like hell. Ash was out of breath, his face smudged with dirt and blood. When he saw Cael, he stopped in his tracks, his expression conveying what Dex could only assume was heartache. It had been rough on Dex seeing Cael smacked around. He had no doubt Ash was feeling something similar.

Ash rushed toward Cael, and Dex stood by as his little brother gently pushed away from him to limp in Ash's direction. Cael threw himself into Ash's open arms where he was lifted off his feet and held tight against Ash, his large hand to the back of Cael's head.

"Are you okay? Are you hurt? I—"

Ash's words were cut off by Cael's mouth on his. It took Ash a moment to react, and it wasn't how Dex had expected. Closing his eyes, Ash returned Cael's kiss. At Ash's response, Cael threw his arms around Ash's neck, and the two kissed like nothing else in the world existed.

Out of breath, Ash pulled back. He smiled at Cael before carefully placing him on his feet. He ran a hand over Cael's head. "Are you okay?"

Cael nodded, a big, wide smile on his face, cheeks flushed. "I'm great. Leg hurts like a bitch, but other than that, I'm good."

Seb walked over to Ash and Cael, his hands held up in front of him when Ash moved in front of Cael, shielding him with a low growl.

"It's okay, Ash." Cael came out from behind him, a hand going to Ash's bicep. He gave it a pat and faced Seb. "I'm sorry, Seb. I wasn't playing you. Like I told you, I really like you, I'm just..."

"In love with someone else," Seb said, smiling softly. "I remember."

"Don't give up, Seb. Find out how he feels. If there's the tiniest bit of hope, try."

"Thanks." Seb turned his hardened gaze to Ash. "Take good care of him, Ash. He deserves it."

Ash nodded when they heard the blare of sirens in the distance.

"Sounds like backup is arriving. You guys better get the hell out of here."

Dex watched stunned as Ash swept Cael off his feet. His brother arched an eyebrow at Ash. "I can walk. Sort of."

Ash gave him a wink. "I know. But this way is quicker."

With a playful smile, Cael wrapped his arms around Ash's neck. "All right, then. What are you waiting for?"

Dex and Ash hurried down to the ground floor and out toward the van, and Dex was relieved to see the rest of their team doing the same. Sloane opened the back door, and everyone climbed in before he slammed the door shut and told Calvin to get them the hell out of there.

Looking around, everyone looked worse for wear—scratched, bloodied, covered in dirt or dust—but in one piece. Ash put Cael down on the bench and took a seat beside him, his arm coming to wrap protectively around Cael.

Dex had no idea what would come next for his brother and Ash, but he hoped whatever it was, they'd work it out. As much as the thought of his little brother being loved up by Ash horrified Dex, he'd deal with it if it meant Cael was happy. Speaking of happy, he smiled when his partner wrapped an arm around his shoulder.

"Are you okay? What happened?" Sloane's amber eyes watched him worriedly. He saw the marks on Dex's neck and cursed under his breath before he reached out and tenderly ran a thumb over his bruised skin. "Jesus, Dex."

"Cael and I handled it. You know what they say. The bigger they are, the harder they fall."

Sloane chuckled and bumped his head against Dex's. His smile reached his eyes, affection and love shining through.

"I couldn't agree more."

TWELVE

"KARAOKE?"

Dex's blue eyes sparkled, his smile wide. Sloane had never seen anything or anyone so beautiful.

"Yep. The bar's all ours tonight." Sloane was grateful to Bradley for the offer. The guy had called Sloane to see how he was doing, and after a brief rundown—because Bradley was as good at listening outside of Dekatria as he was in it—Bradley had offered to close the bar for one evening and open it up just for Destructive Delta. And Lou, of course. Sloane let his partner help him over to one of the tables in front of the stage. After Rosa had patched everyone up and pulled a few strings to get Cael's leg x-rayed and tended to on the down low, they were all in need of some serious relaxing.

Seb was a hero. He'd initially refused to take credit for capturing Hogan's men and the standoff at the grain terminal, but Dex had worked his magic and said if he didn't take the credit, Destructive Delta's cover would be blown, bringing down all kinds of shit on everyone, so it was better if Seb and his team took the credit. It sent Seb flying through his probationary period as team leader. The higher-ups were practically wetting themselves, and the PR department was bringing out the champagne. There was nothing the public loved more than a story of redemption. Poor Seb had paid the price for his past mistakes and clawed his way back to the top. The guy deserved it. They never would have been able to get through this without his support.

Dex took a seat beside Sloane who shook his head. "Well?"

"Well what?"

"Aren't you going to sing for me?" Sloane smiled at the way his partner's cheeks flushed.

"For... *you*?"

"But I get to pick the song," Sloane said.

"Oookay." Dex stood. He was going to help Sloane when Sloane shooed him toward the stage and asked Hobbs to help him. With a big smile, Hobbs wrapped an arm around Sloane and helped him to his feet. Sloane allowed himself to lean on his friend as he was helped slowly onto the stage. His leg was taking a little longer to recover than he liked, no thanks to his putting therapy on hold. The last thing he'd wanted was to leave Dex out there chasing down Hogan with Sloane stuck in some doctor's office every day. He had plenty of time to recover and was enjoying having some time off.

Ash called out at him. "Sloane's going to sing! Woo!"

"Only if you sing a duet with me," Sloane replied.

"Fuck off," Ash laughed.

"Yeah, I thought so."

Sloane scrolled through the list, unable to help his smile. There seemed to be an extraordinarily large amount of '80s songs on the list. He had no doubt Bradley had added them for a certain someone. Finally he found the one he was looking for. It was one he'd heard on the radio recently. It wasn't retro, but it was the kind of song his partner needed, even if Dex didn't know it himself. Sloane wasn't too opposed to the lyrics either. He motioned for Dex to come up on stage, and Dex did. He looked over Sloane's shoulder and arched an eyebrow at him.

"Strange choice for you. I don't think I've heard it."

"It's no Journey, but I think you'll like it. I know how much you like a good beat."

Dex nodded, and Sloane made his way back to the table with Hobbs's help. He thanked his friend and sat down. As soon as Sloane was settled in and smiling at Dex, his partner pressed play.

The stomping and simultaneous beat of the drums reverberated throughout the bar before the piano kicked in. Dex's smooth and sexy voice started singing about being his light and burning sun. Everyone started clapping and stomping their feet in time to the music, making Dex smile as he sang. He started moving with the beat and grabbed the microphone off the stand when the tune kicked into high gear. Everyone erupted in whoops and catcalls. Rosa and Letty jumped to their feet and started dancing, their arms up in the air as they bounced around. Soon Calvin joined in, and the girls even managed to drag Hobbs to dance.

Sloane watched his team having fun, but the warmth in his heart and the smile on his face was for Dex who'd transformed back into the playful, passionate man Sloane had missed more than he originally thought. He had his Dex back, and Sloane had no intention of losing him again.

Rosa came over to Sloane and wrapped her arms around his neck. "Nice choice."

"I missed that smile," Sloane confessed.

"We all did." Rosa leaned in to talk quietly in his ear.

"I'm happy for you. He's exactly what you needed. Even if you were too stubborn to admit it."

Sloane laughed and gave Rosa's cheek a kiss, surprising her. "You are exceptionally wise, Rosita Bonita."

With a chuckle, Rosa went back to dancing. When Dex was finished singing, Lou and Bradley came out with drinks and food. Everyone cheered and crowded around the table. Nothing made his team happier than good food and good company. Dex came to stand beside Sloane, his hand discreetly going to the back of Sloane's neck and his fingers stroking his skin.

"This was a great idea."

Sloane smiled up at him. "It's good to have you back." His partner's expression fell, and he crouched down beside Sloane.

"I'm so sorry for everything I put you through."

"Me too."

"I really wish I could kiss you right now."

Sloane looked around the room, filled with his teammates. His family. They'd all risked everything to help Dex. They never hesitated to do whatever it took to back each other up. They bickered and fought, drove each other crazy, made mistakes, and sometimes had to be put in line, but they never stopped being family. Sloane took hold of Dex's face, his heart fluttering at his beautiful partner's questioning smile. He pulled Dex close and brought their lips together, stifling Dex's gasp. After a moment of hesitation, Dex threw his arms around Sloane and returned his kiss. Seconds later there was cheering and catcalls from everyone around them. Spurred on by their audience, Sloane deepened the kiss, and Dex got up to sit on his lap, their lips never losing contact.

"Well, it's about fucking time," Letty called out, making them both laugh.

Sloane pulled away with a breathy chuckle and turned his gaze on his team. "You all knew anyway."

"We were wondering when you were going to finally tell us," Rosa said, picking up her beer. She held it up for a toast. "To Sloane and Dex. May they have many years of amazing sex and driving each other batshit crazy."

Dex picked up his beer. "I'll drink to that!"

Sloane lifted his pineapple juice. "To Destructive Delta. The greatest family I could have ever hoped for."

"Aw," Letty said with a sniff. "Your meds make you so sappy."

Dex let his head fall back as he laughed.

"Quiet, you." Sloane nipped at Dex's neck making him squirm. At least until his partner saw the huge platter of cheese snacks. He jumped off Sloane's lap and bounced like a kid in a candy store. What was it with his partner's weird obsession with cheese? As everyone munched away and chatted, Dex came to sit on Sloane's lap with a tray of snacks.

"Sloane? I think there's something wrong with me."

"I know, sweetheart, but that doesn't mean I like you any less," Sloane said with a chuckle as he stole one of Dex's cheese cubes and popped it into his mouth.

"Smartass. Seriously, I think I might be sick."

"You're not feeling well?" Were the previous weeks starting to catch up to his partner? He held a hand to Dex's brow. Seemed normal. Then again "normal" was a relative term where Dex was concerned.

"I'm losing weight, but my clothes fit the same. How's that possible?"

"Probably means you're putting on muscle and losing fat."

"But I'm not doing anything different with my workouts or in training." Dex looked thoughtful as he held a Cheesy Doodle up in front of him. "I'm not eating any differently."

"Um..." Uh-oh. The jig was up.

Dex's eyes went wide. "What did you do?"

"Now, keep in mind I care about your health, and I only did what I thought was best for you." If all else failed, Sloane was not above using his injuries to protect himself.

"What did you do?" Dex repeated.

Sloane cringed, and the table went quiet as everyone watched on in amusement. There was no way around it. He'd known his partner would find out sooner or later. "I've been swapping your junk food for healthy food."

Dex let out an exaggerated gasp, and the table erupted into laughter. "Judas! How could you?"

Sloane braced himself. He might as well say the rest. "I've swapped your sugar for sugar substitute, your full fat milk with two percent, your milkshakes for protein shakes, white pasta with whole wheat, your white bread with multigrain—"

"Stop! I can't listen to any more of this... this horror." Dex shook his head, his hand going to his heart. A thought struck him, and he narrowed his eyes at Sloane. "My gummy bears?"

"They're sugar free."

Dex put the tray on the table, jumped off Sloane, and dropped to his knees, his arms raised to the heavens. "Nooo! Not the gummy bears! Is nothing sacred? Oh, the inhumanity!" He jumped to his feet and put his hand to his hips. "How?"

Sloane shrugged. "You don't read labels. You just eat. Which is part of the reason I started doing it."

"How long has this betrayal been going on?" Dex folded his arms over his chest and tapped his foot. "How long has this *deception* been going on?"

"Six months."

"You, sir, are a fiend," Dex declared, his finger poking Sloane in the chest. "A fiend, and a cad, and a... a... sugar thief! Thief!"

Everyone laughed, much to Dex's annoyance. Sloane grabbed his partner's wrist and dragged him onto his lap, despite Dex's sorry attempt at struggling. He huffed and crossed his arms over his chest.

"Aw, come on," Sloane said, nuzzling his face against Dex's neck and delivering kisses. "Don't be mad."

Dex wrinkled his nose. He opened his mouth to say something when ZZ Top played over the speaker system. Dex's eyes went wide, and his face went red to the tips of his ears. "Oh my God."

"What?" Sloane asked, trying to hold back a smile. "You look embarrassed." Sloane happened to look up when he noticed both Calvin and Hobbs had gone stock-still, their eyes as wide as Dex's and their faces equally red. What the...? Calvin jumped to his feet.

"Uh, I have to go to the bathroom."

"Thanks for sharing," Ash teased.

Hobbs stood and pointed to the bathroom. The two darted off. To Sloane's surprise, Lou finished sipping his JD and Coke before declaring, "Those two are totally sleeping together." Everyone around the table gaped at him. Lou blinked at them. "What? You don't see it?"

"They're just close. They've been best friends since they were little kids," Letty said.

Lou grinned wickedly. "Honey, those two are way more than best friends."

"Fuck. Is that why they've been all weird for months?" Cael said.

Sloane turned his attention to Dex who was averting his gaze. "Dex."

"Hm?"

"You know something."

Dex pressed his lips firmly together and shook his head, refusing to look at Sloane.

"Dex." Whatever his partner knew, it was big. Sloane took hold of Dex's jaw and turned his face so he could look into his pale-blue eyes. "Spill." Dex cringed.

"Ooh, bad choice of words."

On second thought, maybe Sloane didn't want to know.

Dex leaned in to whisper in Sloane's ear. "I saw them jerk each other off."

"What?" Sloane's reaction was far louder than he intended, and he clamped a hand over his mouth. He narrowed his eyes at Dex.

"I know that sounds... weird," Dex continued quietly, ignoring their teammates' demands he share with the rest of them. Sloane held a hand up to quiet them. "But I was in the surveillance van, and Cal had come back from undercover work with Bautista, shit went down, and next thing I knew they were doing the dirty up against the van wall."

"And you watched them?" Sloane whispered hoarsely.

"Only in the beginning. I didn't know what to do!" Dex's voice went up in pitch, which meant he was panicked about it. It made Sloane want to laugh, but he restrained himself.

Sloane arched an eyebrow at him. "How about turning away?"

"I did. After I snapped myself out of it, I turned around and put the earpieces in. ZZ Top was playing, hence why I'll never be able to listen to that song again."

Sloane went thoughtful. "Did you get turned on?" His partner's face went beet red and Sloane laughed. "Oh my God! You got turned on. You little perv."

"What? It was like watching live porn."

"Now you sound like Austen," Sloane muttered. He glanced at Dex's red face and couldn't keep himself from laughing. And his partner called him kinky. This was too much. He wasn't surprised Dex had snapped himself out of it and turned away. He could imagine what had been going through his partner's mind.

Dex groaned. "You're not going to let me live this down, are you?"

There was no hesitation on Sloane's part. "Absolutely not."

Calvin and Hobbs returned, took one look at Sloane who was grinning broadly at them, and Calvin let out a wail. "Oh my God, you told him!"

"I'm sorry!" Dex jumped off Sloane's lap, backing away as Calvin approached.

"I'll give you sorry." Calvin took off toward Dex who let out a yelp and made a run for it, with Hobbs worriedly following at a much slower pace. Rosa and Letty joined in the chase, demanding to know what had happened. Bradley and Lou were busy feeding each other pieces of fruit, so Sloane turned his attention to Ash, smiling at his friend's dopey smile as he leaned into Cael who was cheerfully rambling on at him.

"Ooh, and I just got a new shooter game, if you want to come over sometime this week. We can hang out."

"Okay. Tell me when, and I'll be there."

"Great." Cael bit his bottom lip and rubbed his bare arm.

"You cold?" Ash asked.

"A little. These stupid meds. I'm hot one minute, cold the next."

"Here." Ash grabbed his knitted scarf hanging off his chair and wrapped it around Cael's neck. "There you go. It'll keep you warm."

Cael looked down at the scarf and petted it, his face flushed. "Thanks."

"Keep it. I've got another one at home." He gave Cael's cheek a playful nudge.

"I need to go to the bathroom. Excuse me." Cael made to stand, and Ash helped him up.

"Need help getting there?" Ash offered.

Cael shook his head. "Nah. I grew up with Dex. I know my way around crutches." He laughed, took his crutch, and headed for the bathroom, walking right by his brother who waved at him from under the headlock Calvin had him in. With a sappy smile on his face, Ash watched Cael go until he'd disappeared into the bathroom. When he noticed Sloane was watching him, he frowned.

"What?"

"You two are so fucking adorable."

"Fuck off," Ash replied, looking embarrassed.

"So?"

"Come on, man."

"Nope." Sloane folded his arms over his chest and got comfortable. "Talk to me. Dex told me about what happened with you two back at the grain terminal. It was pretty... epic."

"Yeah." Ash shifted uncomfortably. "It kind of took me by surprise."

"Talk to me, Keeler. This isn't just anyone. It's Cael."

A pained look came onto Ash's face, and it worried Sloane. "Which is why I don't want to fuck this up. I shouldn't have done what I did."

Sloane sat up. "You're regretting it?"

Ash tried to hold back a grin but couldn't. In the end he gave in. "Fuck no. I don't regret it. I just mean, I wish I hadn't been so impulsive. I wanted to do it right."

"I don't know about you, but I'd say by the look on Cael's face a moment ago, you did it right."

Ash leaned forward, talking quietly. He looked determined. Sloane was under no illusion his friend was in for a tough time. Not where Cael was concerned. The young Therian was crazy about Ash. This was certainly a step in the right direction, but it didn't eliminate Ash's previous concerns or his troubles. "Look, we have a lot of shit to sort out. Mostly my shit. But we agreed to take it slow and talk first."

"So, are you together or what?"

"That's something we have to work out." Ash sat back with a sigh. "I know the team wouldn't care, and we'd have to hide it at work, but outside, in the open... I don't know if I'm ready to be what he needs me to be."

Sloane reached over and patted his friend's arm. "Whatever you do, do it with him. Be open and honest. Work it out together. He loves you, Ash. Let him help you."

Ash gave him a nod before his expression turned smug. "Dropped the L word, huh? I knew you were in love with him."

"Yeah, well, guess you and I can be stubborn assholes." Sloane couldn't stop the flutter in the pit of his stomach when he spoke. "We're moving in together."

Ash's jaw dropped. "What?"

"Yeah, it was kind of a spur of the moment decision."

"What are you going to do about your apartment? And work?"

"I don't know," Sloane replied with a sigh. "I'll have to keep it for a while, move my stuff into Dex's. We haven't quite worked it all out. Austen says no one suspects anything at work, and I doubt anyone who isn't a commanding officer would butt in. But they're still working on all the reports from the grain terminal incident. We need to be extra careful at work. Especially since I kind of, sort of, maybe, definitely marked him."

Ash's eyes went wide. "You marked Daley? Holy fuck, Sloane."

"I know."

"This is serious shit." Something occurred to Ash and he frowned. "That's why Seb's team went all feral while in their Therian forms back at the granary. They smelled it. Plus your scent's all over him. Always is. That could be dismissed as your partnership, but now this? Fuck, man. You think people aren't going to put two and two together? What were you thinking?"

Sloane's expression became grim, and he met Ash's concerned gaze. "I was thinking he's mine, and I want everyone to know it."

"Fuck. Sloane—"

"I know." Sloane let out a heavy sigh. "Like I said. I don't know what we're going to do yet. Luckily I'm on leave for some time, so I can try and figure something out."

"Sparks will break up the team."

Sloane gritted his teeth. "There's no way I'm going to let that happen." He'd use whatever resources he possessed, whatever sway he'd earned himself over the years. "I'm not letting them touch my team."

Dex materialized behind Ash, and Sloane relaxed. Where the hell had he come from? Glancing over by the pool tables, he saw Rosa and Letty trying to catch Calvin with Hobbs looking on helplessly. Turning back to his partner, he held back a smile when Dex put his hands on Ash's shoulders.

"You hurt my little brother, and I will spend the rest of my life annoying the ever-living fuck out of you."

Ash scoffed. "Too late."

"Oh no," Dex said with a hearty laugh. He came around and dropped himself into Cael's seat, his grin evil. "You haven't seen annoying. What you've experienced is your general grumpy displeasure toward my naturally charming and witty nature. Any attempts to purposefully annoy you were passing whims." He reached out and took a tiny sword toothpick from the container and stabbed it into a cheese cube before leaning in, his voice low. "By the time I'm done with you, you'll be asking for a transfer to Alaska, and even then it won't be far enough from me." He ate the cheese cube and waved the tiny sword at him. "I will become the thing your nightmares are made of." With that, he stood and headed over to Sloane to give him a kiss when Sloane discreetly pushed him to one side, whispering hoarsely.

"Fuck me. I think your dad's outside."

"Say what now?" Dex straightened and turned. He let out a groan. "Man, it's like he's got radar or something."

"Um..." Sloane's concerned gaze shifted to Maddock's hand. "Why's he carrying a baseball bat?"

Cael gasped from somewhere behind him. "Dex! It's Old Betsy!"

"Oh shit!" Dex's hands went to his head. "Shit! Shit! Shit!"

"What the fuck is Old Betsy?" Ash asked, looking from Dex to Cael.

Lou headed for the door, and Dex cried out. "No! Don't let him in—"

Dex's warning came too late, and Maddock thundered in, an old wooden baseball bat in his hand. Sloane and Ash stood. What the hell was going on?

"I can explain," Dex said, running in front of his dad, hands up.

"Dad—" Cael's concerned plea was quickly cut off.

"I don't want to hear a peep out of you or your brother."

Shit. Had Maddock found out about the unsanctioned mission? He knew Maddock wouldn't buy Cael getting hurt during a hockey game with the team. Shit, he'd somehow found out about the job. No wonder he looked so pissed off. If he knew Sloane had not only known about the job but allowed Dex to continue, he was dead. Didn't matter. Sloane had said he would take whatever came their way.

"Sarge, I know you're upset—"

Maddock pointed the bat at Sloane. "You don't know jack, boy. You and Keeler get your asses in the back. We have shit to discuss."

"About what?" Ash asked, looking puzzled.

"About where you two have decided to plant your dicks."

Sloane's slack-jawed expression mirrored Ash's. "Excuse me?"

Maddock moved Dex aside and stepped up close to them. "Now that the danger's over, you're going to be facing a whole new fear. Me. You think you can sleep with my boys and not face the consequences?"

"What?" The color drained from Ash's face.

"Dad!" Cael scolded. "Ash and I are not sleeping together."

Maddock ignored Cael, his hard gaze on Ash. "Keeler, you have so many issues, you could put the fucking *New York Times* out of business. Get your ass in there." He turned to Sloane. "You too. You pulled through, and I'm happy, don't get me wrong. You're recovering. Good. You're sleeping with my son. Let's discuss that."

"He's a grown man," Sloane said then immediately wished he could take it back when he saw Dex cringe behind Maddock.

Their sergeant blinked at him. "Oh, you're right. He is a grown man. Free to date whoever he chooses. Same for Cael. Except when they choose a couple of guys who've put them through emotional hell in the last year. Except when they put their careers on the line. Except when they're doing it under my nose. *Except* when my most trusted, senior agents who I have all but watched grow up on this team decide to keep it from me. Now I'm not gonna tell you what to do with your relationships, but I sure as hell am gonna tell you what *not* to do." He moved aside and pointed the bat toward the door leading to the back of house. "Now you two get your asses in there." Maddock called out to Bradley. "Son, I want three stiff drinks." He frowned thoughtfully. "And a Diet Coke. This is going to take a while."

"Dad," Dex sighed. "Come on."

Maddock pursed his lips before grabbing Dex by the ear and moving him out of the way. "I will deal with you two later."

Sloane reluctantly took his crutch and headed for the back with Ash beside him.

"Now what?" Ash whispered. "You don't think he's really going to use the bat?"

"Are you kidding? It's Maddock. The man chopped off my hair, remember?"

Ash was quiet for a moment. "We can take him."

"Shut up, Ash." Sloane stepped into the corridor and waited for Maddock to join them. On some level, he'd rather be facing a pissed-off Sparks than his boyfriend's pissed-off dad. He'd held his own against plenty of furious commanding officers, but dads? Uncharted territory for him, and he was pretty sure the same went for Ash.

"Fuck. What the hell do we do?"

Sloane's initial reaction was to run, but his leg and the fact he still needed crutches to get around made it a little too difficult right now. "It'll be fine. He's a rational man. We'll tell him how we feel. Promise we won't let it interfere with the job. Easy."

Maddock stormed in, nostrils flaring, dark eyes pinning them to the spot. Behind him the door opened, and Dex ran in. He dramatically threw himself in front of Sloane.

"But Daddy, I love him!"

Maddock rolled his eyes. "Yeah, all right there, Pocahontas. Get lost."

"Damn." Dex turned and patted Sloane's cheek. "I'm sorry, babe. You're on your own." He gave Sloane's lips a sweet kiss. "Love you." Then he bolted from the room like it was on fire.

"Coward!" Sloane called out.

"Did you just call my boy a coward?" Maddock asked.

Sloane held a hand up. "In the most loving way possible." He tried to give Maddock his most charming smile. Maddock's frown deepened, and Sloane leaned over to whisper at Ash.

"On second thought. Pray."

WHAT'S NEXT FOR DEX, Sloane, and the Destructive Delta crew? The adventure continues with Ash and Cael's story in *Against the Grain*, the fifth book in the THIRDS series. Available on Amazon and KindleUnlimited.

A NOTE FROM THE AUTHOR

Thank you so much for reading *Rise & Fall*, the fourth book in the THIRDS series. I hope you enjoyed Dex and crew's shenanigans, and if you did, please consider leaving a review on Amazon. Reviews can have a significant impact on a book's visibility, so any support you show these fellas would be amazing. The adventure continues in *Against the Grain*, available from Amazon and KindleUnlimited.

Want to stay up-to-date on my releases and receive exclusive content? Sign up for my newsletter.

Follow me on Amazon to be notified of a new releases, and connect with me on social media, including my fun Facebook group, Donuts, Dog Tags, and Day Dreams, where we chat books, post pictures, have giveaways, and more!

Looking for inspirational photos of my books? Visit my book boards on Pinterest.

Thank you again for joining the THIRDS crew on their adventures. We hope to see you soon!

CAST MEMBERS

You'll find these cast members throughout the whole THIRDS series. This list will continue to grow.

DESTRUCTIVE DELTA

Sloane Brodie—Defense agent. Team leader. Jaguar Therian.

Dexter J. Daley "Dex"—Defense agent. Former homicide detective for the Human Police Force. Older brother of Cael Maddock. Adopted by Anthony Maddock. Human.

Ash Keeler—Defense agent. Entry tactics and close-quarter combat expert. Lion Therian.

Julietta Guerrera "Letty"—Defense agent. Weapons expert. Human.

Calvin Summers—Defense agent. Sniper. Human.

Ethan Hobbs—Defense agent. Demolitions expert and public safety bomb technician. Has two older brothers: Rafe and Sebastian Hobbs. Tabby Tiger Therian.

Cael Maddock—Recon agent. Tech expert. Dex's

younger brother. Adopted by Anthony Maddock. Cheetah Therian.

Rosa Santiago—Recon agent. Crisis negotiator and medic. Human.

COMMANDING OFFICERS

Lieutenant Sonya Sparks—Lieutenant for Unit Alpha. Cougar Therian.

Sergeant Anthony Maddock "Tony"—Sergeant for Destructive Delta. Dex and Cael's adoptive father. Human.

MEDICAL EXAMINERS

Dr. Hudson Colbourn—Chief medical examiner for Destructive Delta. Wolf Therian.

Dr. Nina Bishop—Medical examiner for Destructive Delta. Human.

AGENTS FROM OTHER SQUADS

Ellis Taylor—Team leader for Beta Ambush

Levi Stone—Team leader for Beta Pride. Arrested for being a mole inside the THIRDS and part of the Ikelos Coalition. White tiger Therian.

Rafe Hobbs—Team leader for Alpha Ambush. The oldest Hobbs brother. Tiger Therian.

Sebastian Hobbs "Seb"—Newly promoted to team leader for Theta Destructive. Was once on Destructive Delta but was transferred after his relationship to Hudson ended in a breach of protocol and civilian loss. Middle Hobbs brother. Tiger Therian.

Osmond Zachary "Zach"—Defense agent for

Alpha Sleuth in Unit Beta. Has six brothers working for the THIRDS. Brown bear Therian.

OTHER IMPORTANT CAST MEMBERS

Gabe Pearce—Sloane's ex-partner and ex-lover on Destructive Delta. Killed on duty. Human.

Isaac Pearce—Gabe's older brother. Was a detective for the Human Police Force who became leader of the Order of Adrasteia. Was killed by Destructive Delta during a hostage situation. Human.

Louis Huerta "Lou"—Dex's ex-boyfriend. Human.

Bradley Darcy—Bartender and owner of Bar Dekatria. Jaguar Therian.

Austen Payne—Squadron Specialist agent (SSA) for Destructive Delta. Cheetah Therian.

Angel Reyes—Member of the Order. Former member of the gang Westward Creed.

Dr. Abraham Shultzon—Head doctor during the First Gen Recruitment Program who was personally responsible for the wellbeing of the THIRDS First Gen Recruits. He was also responsible for the tests that were run on the Therian children.

Arlo Keeler—Ash's twin brother killed during the riots in the 1980s.

Felipe Bautista—Drew Collins's boyfriend.

EXTREMIST GROUPS AND GANGS

The Order of Adrasteia—Group of Humans against Therians. Leader was killed by Destructive Delta. New leader is said to be rising through the ranks of remaining members, though most members have jumped ship.

The Ikelos Coalition—Vigilante group of Unregistered Therians fighting the Order. Leader is Beck Hogan. Beck's second-in-command Preston Merritt was killed by Destructive Delta during a hostage negotiation. Most of the members of the group were arrested, leaving only Hogan, his new second-in-command Drew Collins, and a small group of Therians.

Westward Creed—Gang of Human thugs who went around assaulting Therian citizens during the riots of 1985. Were arrested for causing the deaths of several Therians but released due to "missing" evidence. Eight members all together but only five became members of the Order: Angel Reyes, Alberto Cristo, Craig Martin, Toby Leith, Richard Esteban, Larry Berg, Ox Perry, Brick Jackson.

GLOSSARY

Therians—Shifters brought about through the mutation of Human DNA as a result of the Eppione.8 vaccine.

Post-shift Trauma Care (PSTC)—The effects of Therian post-shift trauma are similar to the aftereffects of an epileptic seizure, only on a smaller scale, including muscle soreness, bruising, brief disorientation, and hunger. Eating after a shift is extremely important as not eating could lead to the Therian collapsing and a host of other health issues. PSTC is the care given to Therians after they shift back to Human form.

THIRDS (Therian-Human Intelligence Recon Defense Squadron)—An elite, military funded agency comprised of an equal number of Human and Therian agents and intended to uphold the law for all its citizens without prejudice.

Themis—A powerful, multimillion-dollar government interface used by the THIRDS. It's linked to numerous intelligence agencies across the globe and runs a series of highly advanced algorithms to scan surveillance submitted by agents.

First Gen—First Generation of purebred Therians born with a perfected version of the mutation.

BearCat—THIRDS tactical vehicle.

Human Police Force (HPF)—A branch of law enforcement consisting of Humans officials dealing only with crimes committed by Humans.

ALSO BY CHARLIE COCHET

FOUR KINGS SECURITY

Love in Spades

Be Still My Heart

Join the Club

Diamond in the Rough

FOUR KINGS SECURITY UNIVERSE

Beware of Geeks Bearing Gifts

THE KINGS: WILD CARDS

Stacking the Deck

LOCKE AND KEYES AGENCY

Kept in the Dark

PARANORMAL PRINCES

The Prince and His Bedeviled Bodyguard

The Prince and His Captivating Carpenter

The King and His Vigilant Valet

THIRDS

Hell & High Water

Blood & Thunder

Rack & Ruin

Rise & Fall

Against the Grain

Catch a Tiger by the Tail

Smoke & Mirrors

Thick & Thin

Darkest Hour Before Dawn

Gummy Bears & Grenades

Tried & True

THIRDS BEYOND THE BOOKS

THIRDS Beyond the Books Volume 1

THIRDS Beyond the Books Volume 2

THIRDS UNIVERSE

Love and Payne

COMPROMISED

Center of Gravity

NORTH POLE CITY TALES

Mending Noel

The Heart of Frost

The Valor of Vixen

Loving Blitz

Disarming Donner

Courage and the King

North Pole City Tales Complete Series Paperback

SOLDATI HEARTS

The Soldati Prince

The Foxling Soldati

STANDALONE

Forgive and Forget

Love in Retrograde

AUDIOBOOKS

Check out the audio versions on Audible.

ABOUT THE AUTHOR

Charlie Cochet is the international bestselling author of the THIRDS series. Born in Cuba and raised in the US, Charlie enjoys the best of both worlds, from her daily Cuban latte to her passion for classic rock.

Currently residing in Central Florida, Charlie is at the beck and call of a rascally Doxiepoo bent on world domination. When she isn't writing, she can usually be found devouring a book, releasing her creativity through art, or binge watching a new TV series. She runs on coffee, thrives on music, and loves to hear from readers.

www.charliecochet.com

Sign up for Charlie's newsletter:
https://newsletter.charliecochet.com

facebook.com/charliecochet
twitter.com/charliecochet
instagram.com/charliecochet
bookbub.com/authors/charliecochet
goodreads.com/CharlieCochet
pinterest.com/charliecochet

Made in United States
North Haven, CT
29 July 2022